RESTITUTION

SPACE COLONY ONE BOOK 7

J.J. GREEN

INFINITEBOOK

1

Human civilization was laid waste. Where vast, busy metropolises had once thrived, only ruins remained. Decaying skyscrapers jutted up from streets choked with debris, like rotten teeth in diseased gums. Immense areas of urban landscape were burned to ashes or drowned in floods from burst dams and levees. Those relentless survivors, rats and cockroaches, had taken over, preyed upon by dogs turned feral.

Along the highways, vegetation thrust through cracks in asphalt or spread over it, infiltrating roots breaking up the hard surface. Abandoned vehicles rusted almost to oblivion formed desolate, motionless convoys. Once-mighty bridges had collapsed and shattered the roads below.

Explosions from processes run out of control had torn factories apart. Billions of hectares of agricultural land were lost to weeds and scrub. In harbors, sunken ships cluttered the water.

During the daytime, the world was silent save for bird song and noises of insects. At night, the sky was black and the stars glittered sharply.

Amongst it all, humanity clung to survival.

Groups of five or six up to several hundred roamed the lands, scavenging for food from the before-times, when people had bought groceries in shops or ordered it on the fabled 'net'. Sometimes, they hunted beasts, killing them inexpertly with blunt blades, hacking them to death slowly and painfully. Sometimes, they hunted each other.

No one wrote. No one painted. No one invented. The few who could read studied ancient books, poring over the brittle, yellow paper, trying to make sense of the unfamiliar words. On rare happy occasions, such as when a cache of aged cans of unspoiled food had been found, some would sing barely remembered songs—songs of love and longing and loss. But hunger always returned and the singers were silent.

How long life had been like this no one knew, only that it had not always been so. In the past, humankind had dominated the world. Yet the knowledge of how humans had risen to greatness was lost. Some said it was through magic, and a plague had wiped out the wizards and witches. Others said the wealthiest elites had gathered all the Earth's riches and departed hundreds of years ago. Less commonly, it was rumored the crumbling buildings had never housed people but had been the homes of another, superior species, now extinct.

So when the Scythians came, some believed they were returning to reclaim their world.

They announced their arrival by raining fire on the lands. Pulses from their starships blasted into the quiet cities. They attacked forests, starting wildfires that raged for months. They blew apart defunct factories and plants. A dying civilization was beaten into the dust.

So when the invaders' ships landed, no one and nothing stood against them. The crescent-shaped shuttles, hulls etched in the signature swirling, irregular Scythian patterning, set down, their hatches opened, and the aliens emerged, heads ensconced in breathing apparatus.

Aubriot jerked awake.

He sucked in a breath and stared at the ceiling, dim in the darkness, trying to remember where he was. Something— someone—lay beside him. He reached out and touched bare skin, turned his head and saw the back of a woman's head on a pillow.

Cherry.

He wasn't on Earth. He was on Concordia. He'd spent nearly two centuries in cryo, flying through space. He'd been revived and lived through... So much had happened. Yet his dream had been so vivid it was as if he'd never left Earth.

Cherry stirred. She moved onto her back and then onto her other side, curling onto his chest and draping her arm over him. He patted her shoulder awkwardly. If she weren't half-asleep she wouldn't be so affectionate. Neither of them was comfortable in a romantic relationship, but they were trying. The biggest problem was Cherry's attitude. She didn't seem to appreciate him as much as he deserved. He could have just about any woman in the colony and she knew it. Yet she never looked at him the way she used to look at Ethan when she thought no one was watching. That old sap had been dead years. Surely she should be over him by now?

"What's the time?" she asked.

"Don't know, Bandit." He lifted his head to peer out the window. The horizon shone pale gray. "It'll be dawn soon."

She groaned. "I better get up."

"What's the hurry? Go back to sleep."

"I have to get the harvester out. Going to be working all day today. It's supposed to rain tomorrow. Gotta get the wheat in."

"Ah, okay. I'll give you a hand."

She sat up and looked him in the eyes, her lips curved into a small smile. Her black, bed-head hair hung shaggy around her face. "Thanks, but there's no need. The harvester does most of the work. But I appreciate the offer." She bent and kissed him before climbing out of bed and padding toward the bathroom.

"Are you sure you can manage it one-handed?" he asked.

"I've done it before, remember?" She opened the bathroom door.

"What's the crop like?"

As she turned to answer, her expression was grim. "Not great, but a little better than last year, I think. We won't know for sure until it's in."

The bathroom door closed, and the sound of running water quickly followed.

Ever since the Scythians had destroyed most life on Concordia with their biocide, everything the colony tried to grow struggled to thrive. Kes had said it was because the soil was depleted of micro-organisms. A few bacteria and fungi had a natural immunity to the devastating virus and would multiply to fill the gap left by their dead counterparts, but the process would take years.

Plant life was similarly wrestling to recover. In many places, a single species proliferated out of control in the absence of competitors and predators. Between Annwn and the coast, a massive swathe of the rubbery Concordian groundcover plant shrouded the plain. Billions of sea jellies shaped like starfish filled the oceans. Life had survived but the planet's ecosystems had been whacked out of balance. When things would return to their former state, the scientists couldn't say.

Aubriot's ear comm chirruped. He picked it up from the nightstand and inserted it.

"Hello?"

"You're coming in to help today, right?"

It was Wilder. The fact that it was before dawn clearly didn't faze her when issuing her reminder. Day and night didn't seem to have any meaning for the young woman, except as an inconvenience when they got in the way of her work.

"Uh, yeah. I forgot."

The breath of a sigh came down the line. "Great. See you soon." She was gone.

He swung his legs over the side of the bed. The shower noises had stopped. A second later, the bathroom door opened and Cherry reappeared, wrapped in a towel. "You're getting up too? There's no need. I told you—"

"Got other things to do, and I wouldn't get back to sleep anyway." He held out a hand. "Come here."

She sat beside him on the bed. "Is everything okay?"

He put an arm around her shoulders. "I had a dream, a nightmare, really."

Her eyebrows rose in concern. "What was it about?"

"It's not important. I just wanted..." *to hold you for a minute.* He pulled her close. "What do you think Earth is like now?"

"How would I know? I was never there."

He snorted a laugh. "I was forgetting."

"You need to have this conversation with Kes."

"Yeah, you're right."

It would be awkward, though. They'd never been friendly, and Kes didn't seem to have gotten over the death of his wife. He was a shell of a man, mentally AWOL. The only time anyone ever saw him happy was when he was with his kids.

Cherry said, "Maybe a more important question is what it will be like when we get there. It'll take us years. Things change, and if the Scythians—"

"They won't have changed that much. I think the way things must be on Earth, they'll be the same for a long time. And we could be there sooner than you think."

"What makes you say that? Is there some news I haven't heard?"

"Well, nothing official..."

"Tell me. Go on, spill the beans." She tickled his ribs.

He swatted her hand away playfully. "It's not much, but..." he paused for effect "...Wilder thinks she can do it."

"You're kidding!" Cherry faced him. "Seriously?"

"Would I joke about something like that?"

"Yeah, you would."

He held up three fingers. "Scouts' honor."

"What the hell does that mean? Don't start using Earth English again. You know how I hate it."

"It means I'm telling you the truth."

"We'll be able to jump through space like the Fila?!"

"It's still early days, but probably."

"So she was right? Thank the stars we listened to her."

"Yep."

After the Guardian, Faina, had revealed the Scythians had obtained Earth's coordinates, it had become clear something had to be done to protect the home planet from the vengeful aliens. But with the Scythians' fast ships and head start, the Concordians didn't have a hope of arriving until after the damage had been done, not even with the aid of their friends in the Galactic Assembly.

That was until Wilder had come up with the idea of building a starship with jump capability, similar to their friends the Fila's but able to sustain human life. If they could use the faster method of space travel, they could arrive at Earth before the Scythians.

It was a huge challenge, even for Wilder, who had cracked the secret of anti-gravity, but, after two years' constant labor, she'd come up with the answer.

"How long will it take to build a ship?" Cherry asked.

"At least a year, and it has to be constructed in space, so you might not see much of me for a while."

"I'll cope." She stiffened, as if realizing the coldness of her words. "I mean, I'll miss you, but—"

"It's okay. I know what you mean."

She looked at him fixedly. "We're good, right?"

"Yeah, we're good."

"Okay, I'd better get that crop in."

2

C herry slipped open the lock on the shed and pulled out the two heavy wooden doors. Her breath puffed like smoke in the chill air. It was late in the season to be harvesting cereal crops, but the weather had been unusually wet. Damp grain rotted in storage, and the colony couldn't afford to lose any more food.

An empty ache settled in her stomach as she saw the looming form of the harvester, shadowy in the pre-dawn light. The sight of it always reminded her of Ethan. She recalled the first time they'd had a proper conversation, that day out by the lake, when she'd used the pretext of wanting to borrow a plow to talk to him. He'd saved her life that day, or rather, they'd thought her life had needed to be saved. The Fila had tried to grab her in order to take a closer look at this strange new species that had appeared on Concordia.

Later, he'd sat with her in the cab of a harvester when she'd brought in the colony's first crop. Perhaps it had been this very machine.

She blinked and drew her sleeve across her eyes. This was no time for tears.

After mounting the steps on the side of the machine, she opened the cab door and climbed in. It had taken her a while to figure out how to handle the machine with one hand, but a couple of adjustments had made it possible. She'd been glad. She didn't want to give up her role as a farmer. She continued to lead the military, but she was sick of fighting and death. Farming connected her with life and the land, her home.

She started up the engine. The welcome vibration coursed through her bones, and she drove the hulking machine out into the field just as the sun sent its first rays over the horizon.

An hour later, when a quarter of the wheat field was stubble, the engine suddenly quit. Inertia threw her forward, thrusting her midriff against the steering wheel.

She cursed and checked the dashboard screen. Nothing seemed wrong. The engine wasn't overheating, the battery held plenty of power. She pressed the ignition a few times, but the machine didn't respond. Turning off the music she'd been listening to on her comm, she hopped out of the cab. There were mechanics she could call out but fixing the problem herself would save time. Garwin had taught her how to deal with the most common problems with farm machinery.

The first thing to check was the cutters. If they hit something thicker than a twig the engine would automatically cut out. It was a fail-safe to prevent nasty accidents and animal bodies contaminating the harvest. Considering most wildlife had been wiped out, it was extremely unlikely anything was stuck between the blades, but it wouldn't hurt to check.

The cutters were clean and empty. Nothing was caught in the feeder house chains or belt either.

She walked around to the front of the machine to open the engine casing. The sun was now high enough to take a good look inside. What had Garwin said? She peered at the mechanical innards. Was the problem simply a connection come loose? She reached in and jiggled each one in turn.

The engine sparked to life and the harvester jumped forward. Realizing her mistake, she tried to snatch her arm out of the way but a protruding bolt, old and sharpened with rust, dug into her skin. Within a second the bolt cut a deep channel down her forearm to her wrist.

"*Aw shit! Damn!*"

The harvester died again as it sensed no one in the driver's seat, but the damage was done.

She swore some more as she inspected the damage. Blood coursed from her wound and dripped on her boots. Feeling like a fool, she comm'd her fellow farmers to take over for her but all were busy taking advantage of the dry weather. It couldn't be helped. She set off for the medical clinic.

The autocar dropped her at its doors just as the clinic was opening. She wordlessly held up her arm to the medic.

After a grimace, he led her through the empty waiting area to an examination room, sat her down, and inspected the wound. "Wait here while I get the irrigation equipment. Gotta clean that out before we close it."

When the door opened again, however, it wasn't the medic who appeared, but Kes.

"Hey," said Cherry. "What are you doing here?"

"I could ask you the same question," he replied, seeming equally surprised. "What's wr— Oh, I see," he added as his gaze alighted on her bloody arm and clothes. "That looks nasty. I hope it isn't serious."

"No, I was just giving myself a reminder not to be so damned stupid."

"I'm sorry?"

"It doesn't matter. Have you decided to switch professions and go into medicine?"

"No." He pulled up a chair. He was holding a small tray containing cotton bud sticks and clear tubes with stoppers. "I'm taking DNA samples from everyone who comes into the clinic. Would you mind opening your mouth?"

"Uh, sure."

He wiped a swab on her inner cheek and put it in a tube which he then sealed.

"Why are you sampling our DNA?"

The door opened. The medic was back.

Kes asked, "Do you have five minutes for a chat when you're done?"

She did, and he said he would wait for her outside. After her wound had been cleaned and closed with sticky healing gel, she found Kes in the street.

Annwn was waking up. The traffic had grown busier during her short time in the clinic. It was odd how quickly things had returned to normal after the destruction wreaked by the Scythians' biocide. Though many Concordians had been killed by the attack on Oceanside, most had survived the deadly virus. People had picked up their lives and carried on almost as if nothing had happened. But a current of dread underlay the daily routine. Shocked out of complacency, Cherry had a sense this latest generation of colonists finally understood the fragility of their existence.

"What's the big secret?" she asked jokingly. "Or did you only want some fresh air?"

He didn't smile. That didn't mean anything necessarily. Kes rarely smiled these days. Cherry inwardly winced. It was irrational, but she couldn't help feeling somehow responsible for his wife's death.

"This probably warrants a longer talk," he said. "The short version is, we're in deep trouble."

"Don't tell me the Scythians are coming back."

She was kidding, but if they were and Kes had somehow received the news before her, Concordia was sunk. Most of its defense capability had been expended in the most recent attack. They had begun to rebuild but it would take years to reach the original capacity.

"No," Kes replied. "Internal trouble. Where to begin? I suppose it started with the case of a young child who cut themselves. It wasn't a very bad cut but it required medical attention. The problem was—the cut wouldn't stop bleeding. The medics sealed it up, but the child continued to bleed internally."

Cherry wrinkled her nose.

"A doctor brought the case to my attention," he continued. "Not unreasonably, she thought a Concordian organism might be the problem. If something had infiltrated the wound..." He paused and shook his head. "The child has hemophilia."

"Right. And that is...?"

"An inherited genetic condition that stops blood from clotting. When I figured it out, I became curious. You see, Cariad screened out genetic disease carriers in the *Nova Fortuna* Project applicants. It should be impossible for hemophilia to appear in the colony except as a mutation. The child's case is due to a mutation, no question, but it prompted me to complete a survey to assess genetic diversity. I collected samples from schoolchildren first, then workers, and now patients at medical clinics, trying to vacuum up the few who slipped through the net. Cherry, the preliminary results aren't good. The colony's gene pool is too homogeneous. As time goes on more conditions will manifest. We could forestall the effect by enforcing restrictions on marriages, but it would only delay the inevitable."

She had kind of followed what he said, but not quite. "More people are going to get sick?"

"Yes, and, even more importantly, infertile. It's a common effect of inbreeding."

"I thought that was why Cariad created those extra babies —to prevent inbreeding?" Her memory of the influx of infants, saved by the Fila when the *Nova* was destroyed, was vivid.

Everyone at Sidhe had endured months of sleepless nights, regardless of whether they had personally volunteered to take on a child themselves.

"She tried, but it clearly hasn't worked. The Project was already skirting the edge of minimum numbers required for a healthy population according to genetic science at the time. This was always a possibility."

"Isn't there anything we can do?" Cherry had been feeling mildly optimistic since Aubriot's announcement about the jump engine. Kes's revelation had thrown a dampener on everything.

Before he could answer, she exclaimed, "Ow!" and slapped her neck. On her palm was a squashed, black insect about a centimeter long. Fresh blood stained her skin. Her own blood, she suspected. "Something bit me."

He inspected the mess on her hand. "We've been seeing a lot of those lately, though we haven't named them yet. They appear to be harmless—aside from the biting. We're developing a repellent."

Lifting one side of her upper lip, she wiped the dead insect on her pants. "So the colony's doomed?"

He tutted. "This is why I wanted to speak to you in private. You can't go around saying things like that, you understand?"

"I'm not a moron, Kes."

"I didn't say you were, only…"

"What?"

He sighed. "I don't know what we can do. When I think about the future, about the world I've brought Miki and Nina into, I…" He lapsed to silence.

She touched his arm. "No one knew this would happen."

"Maybe not, but we knew the Scythians would be back one day. I've been irresponsible. I imagined life here had turned out to be like it was on Earth—safe and secure. That couldn't have been further from the truth."

"Look, it sounds like all the colony needs is an injection of fresh blood, right? New genes to supplement our current ones."

"You say that as if it were the easiest thing in the world to achieve."

"Not easy, maybe, but possible. If we manage to get to Earth, we might be able to persuade some people to come back with us."

"*If* we get to Earth. How likely is that in reality?"

"According to what I heard this morning, it's likelier than you think. By the way, I've been meaning to ask you something. Aubriot sometimes calls me Bandit. Do you know why? What does it mean?"

The ghost of a smile flitted across Kes's lips. "Why are you asking me? Surely you should ask him?"

"He won't tell me. I thought it might be an Earth-English thing. Is it?"

"It's better you ask Aubriot," was all Kes would reply.

It started to rain.

"*Shit,*" Cherry muttered.

3

The problem with having your pick of alien technology, Wilder had discovered, was that a lot of the time you had no immediate use for it. She'd come to regret her decision to ask for one piece of top tech from each member of the Galactic Assembly in return for a working a-grav generator and specs. A new world for the Concordian colonists to inhabit would have been a better price tag to put on her invention. Planets hospitable to life were scarce, and planets that would sustain humans were probably even rarer, but if the friendly aliens had pooled their knowledge and resources, they might have found something suitable.

As it was, she had loads of tech she barely understood and mostly couldn't use, and the colony was stuck on a planet devastated by a viral biocide. Not only that, the prospect of the Scythians' return hadn't gone away. She'd thought she was being clever, like the person who, when the genie gives them three wishes, uses their first wish to ask for infinite wishes. But she hadn't been clever, she'd been dumb. The allure of new, fascinating, secret technology had seduced her, causing her to neglect the immediate needs of her fellow humans.

Yet it wasn't all bad. Before leaving Concordia, the Fila had explained how their starship jump engines worked, though it had taken months of work to figure out their translation, and now she knew how to stop the jumps from being dangerous for humans.

Or, rather, she *thought* she knew. She wouldn't be certain until they'd run a successful test. The test subject would have to be a human volunteer. No animals larger than a microbe now lived on Concordia except for people and Piddle and Puddle—and she was certainly never going to risk *their* lives. But perhaps a few creatures with natural immunity to the killer virus had survived out in the wild somewhere. Perhaps they could catch one and—

The lab door opened and Dragan entered, panting. He lived five klicks from the research center and ran to work every morning. Dragan was one of the original team who had been working on the a-grav drive, like Niall Cully. Dragan's pseudonym to maintain his anonymity had been The Artist, a much more grown-up and sensible alias than her own, Deadly After Midnight. She cringed when she thought about it. Still, Dragan was in his thirties and she'd been just a kid.

"Hi," he said after catching his breath. "Did you arrive early or have you been working all night?"

She yawned and stretched. She had to think for a minute before answering, "I got here a couple of hours ago. I woke up while it was still dark and couldn't get back to sleep, so I came in."

"Was it a blast of insight that woke you up?"

"Huh! No. Just anxiety, I guess."

The work to develop the jump drive had been painstaking. There had been no brilliant breakthroughs allowing them to leap forward, just slow, steady progress, detail by hard-won detail.

"Don't worry," said Dragan. "We'll get there." He stepped into the bathroom to shower and change.

The next person to arrive was Niall. He'd undergone a growth spurt in the two years since Wilder had first met him face to face, and he didn't show any signs of slowing down. His personality changed, too. She rarely glimpsed the eager young kid she'd met just before she'd gone with the Fila, Quinn, to the *Opportunity*. Niall become quiet and serious. She guessed seeing his mother killed by the biocide had something to do with it. That, and the time afterward he'd spent helping a group of vulnerable people survive while the deadly virus spread over the land.

He gave her his usual gruff greeting and immediately settled down at his interface to begin work.

She checked the time. She was expecting a new arrival today, now they were finally getting down to the nuts and bolts of constructing the starship that would take some colonists to Earth.

As if summoned by her thoughts, Aubriot walked in.

She stood up. "Welcome to the team."

"No problem. I'm looking forward to getting my teeth into this."

Niall's head jerked up. He stared at Wilder questioningly.

"He's going to help with the installation of the Parvus's weapon," she explained.

"I didn't know we were installing a weapon," said Niall. "Who made that decision?"

"Me, of course."

"Just like that? Unilaterally? I thought we were working together on this project."

"We are. I..." she hesitated "...I didn't think anyone would object."

"Sounds like you didn't *think* at all."

She blinked. Why was he being so rude?

"Let's see what Dragan has to say," said Niall. "Is he here yet?"

"Hey," said Aubriot. "Wilder's the one in charge around here, isn't she? What she says goes."

Niall replied without looking at him, "Thanks for your *input*."

An awkward pause stretched out. Niall continued to glare at Wilder, his lips set. She stared back helplessly, wondering what she'd done wrong. She wasn't very good at dealing with people. Machines and processes were far easier to understand.

"This is stupid," said Aubriot. "Tell me where to sit, and I'll get st—"

Dragan appeared, his hair still damp from his shower. He halted, taking in the scene, looking from Aubriot to Niall and Wilder. He said hi to Aubriot and then turned to Wilder. "I didn't know we were going to have a visi—"

"He isn't a visitor," Niall interrupted. "He's going to be working with us on the project. Installing an apparently *much-needed* weapon."

"Oh? This is the first I've heard of it."

"I thought so. It's the first I've heard of it too."

Wilder looked at Aubriot pleadingly, hoping he would be sensitive to the tension his arrival had caused, wishing he would leave so the three of them could discuss the problem she'd created. Niall was right. She should have consulted with him and Dragan, but she genuinely hadn't imagined they would mind. Should she gently ask Aubriot to give them time to talk it over?

"Look," said Aubriot, "you're going to need defensive weaponry on that starship. It's a no-brainer. Who knows what you'll find each time you complete a jump? What if you stumble into Scythian territory or encounter a different hostile species? If we can't defend ourselves, we're lambs to the slaughter. So let's forget about your stupid office politics and get started. Is this seat empty?" He gestured at Dragan's desk.

"Uh, no," said Wilder. "You can sit there."

He walked to the place she'd indicated, sat down, and turned on the interface. "I'm pretty familiar with the plans already, but I'll check them over and get up to speed."

"Wilder," said Niall between his teeth, "can I speak to you?"

Aubriot was either oblivious to the anger in Niall's tone or very good at ignoring it.

Feeling forlorn, Wilder followed her friend into the passageway.

"I'm sorry!" she exclaimed as soon as the door closed. "I really didn't—"

"So you already said. That doesn't change the fact that now we're stuck working with him."

"I don't understand what your problem is. Isn't he right? We do need some kind of space weapons, and the one the Parvus gave us in exchange for the a-grav device is perfect." Strictly speaking, it was the only weapon they had, and part of her reason for wanting it was her desire to make use of the alien tech she'd bargained for.

"*How* is it perfect?" Niall asked. "It might be incredibly powerful, but you have to be near a sun to use it."

"No, we don't," she replied excitedly, delighted at the opening to explain her reasoning and defuse his ire. "That's the beauty of what I had in mind. You see, as well as the Parvus's weapon, we can use the energy storage cell with a gigantic capacity I got us. We can gather energy for the weapon from the sun before we set off. If we end up in a battle, we'll be ready."

Niall's expression softened a fraction. He was, after all, a scientist at heart like her. As she'd predicted, the awesomeness of the tech and the utility of its deployment was appealing to him.

She continued, "I really am sorry I didn't ask you and

Dragan before inviting Aubriot onto the team to help with this. But he does know about this stuff, more than anyone else in the colony."

"Maybe, but he's also a complete prick. You know that, right?"

"I do know what he's like, yes." Her memories of traveling to and from the Galactic Assembly's space station were vivid. Aubriot had been almost unbearable to live with, and the long duration and boredom of the space flight hadn't helped. She hadn't been aware his notoriety had spread so far, however. "Can't you just try to get along with him for the next few months?"

Niall didn't answer. He narrowed his eyes at her and returned to the workroom.

4

———

Cherry dug her hand into the wheat she'd harvested prior to her accident, scooped up a portion, and allowed it to run through her fingers. The grains weren't the plumpest she'd ever seen, but they were dry. It was the rest of the crop she was worried about. Stepping out of the grain store, she surveyed her field. The downpour that had started while she was speaking with Kes had soaked the remaining three-quarters of the field. Other farmers were in a similar position. There were things they could do to mitigate the problem, but basically the harvest would be a disappointment again this year, and unless the weather turned dry again soon, it could be a disaster.

The destruction caused by the Scythians' biocide seemed to have even affected the climate. She'd never known the season to be so wet and humid. If they didn't get a break of a few days' sunshine, the cereals and other crops could become infested with mold. Mold spores were one of the few things to survive the deadly virus, naturally. They were not technically alive, Kes had explained, so the biocide hadn't affected them.

Something buzzed near her ear, and before she could react

a sharp pain lanced from her neck. She slapped the spot.
Another of those biting insects had attempted to feed on her.
She trotted to her autocar and climbed in. The insects had
followed her. They hung around outside, attracted to the
carbon dioxide in exhaled breath.

Oh, well. The fields were too wet to work today anyway.

A comm arrived. "Hello?"

"Cherry," said Kes, "can you come to the Annwn Town Hall
right away? The Leader wants to hold an emergency meeting."

"Sure. I'm not exactly busy. What's it about?"

"Just come." The comm went dead.

BARKER, the Leader elected shortly after the successful vaccination of the colony against the biocide was a short, tubby man in
late middle age. He was about as boring an individual as
Cherry had ever met. He was always so calm. He didn't seem to
experience strong emotions or hold any firm opinions. But
perhaps that was what the colonists needed right now—
someone who would listen and react rather than force his will
on everyone.

Barker's usually mild expression was full of worry. That, in
turn, worried her. Whatever the problem was, it had to be bad
if it was provoking a reaction in the unflappable man. Had Kes
told him about the inbreeding in the population? Was that
what this was about?

Wilder was also attending the meeting, along with the two
engineers she worked with, and Aubriot.

"Thank you for coming at such short notice," said Barker.
"I'd appreciate it if you were to keep to yourselves whatever is
said in this room today. No minutes will be taken, and if I am
challenged about what we're about to discuss, I will deny all
knowledge of it. So should you. When you hear the subject

matter, you will understand why. Kes, please go ahead and explain what you told me this morning."

Kes's face was grim. "As Cherry already knows, I've been conducting a survey of the human gene pool, and the results aren't good. I'll tell you more about that later. But first, I want to tell you about another survey I've been undertaking. I dispatched drones to collect soil samples from all over Lyonesse and Suddene to find out as much as I can about the pitiful remnants of life on this planet. It's taken many months, but the results are in. I'm sure we're all aware how bad the situation is. Well, it's worse than I thought, much worse. The lack of biodiversity extends to all parts of the ecosystem I've surveyed. In many areas the land is simply dead, entirely devoid of any life. In others, one microorganism has filled the niche and is reproducing exponentially. We've already seen the effects. Crops are struggling to grow. Single species dominate hundreds of square kilometers."

He rubbed his temples and then stared at each of them in turn. "I've never heard of or read about a situation exactly like this, but in similar examples in Earth history, where a non-native species was introduced to an ecosystem without its natural predators, the results were damned disasters. Plagues of mice, rabbits, toads..." He shook his head. "From what I can tell, the situation on Concordia is going to get a hell of a lot worse before it can get better. It will be thousands—possibly tens of thousands of years—before life reaches equilibrium and harmony once more."

"So what?" Aubriot challenged. "As long as we can grow enough food to survive, it doesn't really matter. Who cares if we never see another sluglimpet? I certainly don't."

"Of course it matters," said Niall. "Millions of species have become extinct. The planet is like a biological experiment gone wrong. It's a disaster."

"Still," Aubriot countered, "as long as we're okay, we

shouldn't sweat it. Species go extinct all the time. That's how evolution works."

"What happened here wasn't evolution!" Niall's face had turned pale. "It was a crime against nature."

Barker asked, "Can we put the philosophical discussion to one side for a moment? Kes hasn't finished."

"Thanks," said Kes. "I do have more to say. The fact is the state of the planet's ecosystem *does* matter to us. Cherry will vouch for the fact that the harvests since the biocide attack have been the worst in Concordian history. Right?"

She nodded, guessing what was coming next.

"Put simply," he went on, "the best we can expect is for yields to continue to diminish. That's if we're lucky. What's more likely is we'll see entire crops regularly wiped out by swarms of insects or pathogens."

"Bullshit," said Aubriot. "I know you've had a hard time, Kes, but don't drag us all down into your private hell. You're scaremongering. We can spray insecticides and pesticides or find other ways to protect the crops."

"Yes, we can, but it's a stopgap measure. Over the long term, that's only going to make things worse."

"I don't believe it."

"Well," said Kes, his jaw tightening, "go and get your PhD in bio sciences, then come and talk to me about it."

"The crops won't grow well in dead soil?" asked Niall.

Kes replied, "They won't thrive, but more importantly, this problem with single micro-organism species proliferating will spell disaster for them, and we'll see more and more cases as life re-establishes on Concordia."

"The colony will starve," said the other engineer.

"Exactly," said Kes heavily.

This new information put his earlier pronouncement about inbreeding in a distant second place. Cherry said, "There has to be something we can do. Otherwise, why are we having this meeting?" She addressed Barker. "You called us here for a reason, right?"

"I did. I especially wanted Wilder and her team to attend because Kes has proposed a solution."

For a man who apparently had the answer to their woes, Kes didn't look very happy about it. "The only answer I can think of is to seed the planet with as many other species as possible. It will result in environmental chaos for I don't know how long, but that's a better scenario than the one we currently face."

"Species from where?" asked Wilder.

"Earth," Aubriot answered. "He means Earth species. It's the only place humans co-inhabit with other species."

Kes nodded.

"So what's the problem?" Wilder asked. "We'll be going there in a year."

"We need to go there sooner," said Barker, "if the colony is going to stand a chance of survival. As I understand it, even if we began to seed Concordia tomorrow it would be touch and go."

Kes sighed and nodded again. "We desperately need other life forms, other food sources. The situation is more dire than I imagined, and the only possible solution is the last thing that was ever supposed to happen. The Mandate stated we were to preserve existing life on the colony planet wherever possible. We can't do that now. We have to turn Concordia into another Earth."

"The Mandate?" asked Niall.

A bittersweet sadness hit Cherry. How ironic it was that something Ethan, Garwin, and she had fought the Woken about so viciously in the early days of colonization was now entirely forgotten. How many Gens had lost their lives fighting for their freedom from Woken and Guardian tyranny? Their names were ancient history.

"It's just an old book," Aubriot explained. "It isn't important. And it wasn't *us* who killed Concordia, it was the Scythians, so let's forget the guilty tears. I say we go to Earth and bring back everything we can."

"We don't have a choice, unfortunately," said Kes. "Wilder, as well as the jump ship, we'll also need a vast storage container, somewhere to put everything we want to bring back. Soil, seeds, plants, insects, perhaps even larger life forms."

The young woman's brows furrowed. "We have enough to do already, just constructing the ship. And now you say we need the ship earlier, and on top of that, you also want us to build something that can support a huge range of life forms?"

"All the colony's resources will be at your disposal," said Barker. "Manpower, materials, you name it. This project is our absolute number one priority."

"What about the Scythians?" asked Niall. "I thought we were going to Earth to help protect the planet against them."

"We can do that too," Aubriot replied. "I don't see a problem."

"I'm glad you don't," Wilder commented, "because I see plenty." She asked Barker, "How much time do we have?"

"Can you do it in three months?"

"No," said Niall. "That's ridiculous."

"*Three months*?!" Wilder exclaimed. Then she said resignedly, "We'll do what we can."

5

"How's it going?" Wilder glided over to Niall, who was supervising the installation of the jump engine.

Even through the tinted visor of his EVA suit, she saw the look he gave her. If she hadn't seen it, she would have *felt* it. Niall had been giving her grief ever since the emergency meeting where she'd agreed to the three-month timescale for the construction of the starship.

"It's impossible!" he'd hissed at her as they'd left the town hall.

"He's right," Dragan had agreed as they descended the steps, though he'd sounded more disheartened than angry. "We've already been working all hours to get this thing done. How can we work any faster?"

"We'll draft more people onto the team," she'd replied. "We've done the hard work. We have the engine specs and the basic blueprint for the ship. Now it's only a matter of building everything, and the Leader promised us all the engineers, construction workers, and support staff we need. We also have Aubriot, don't forget."

Niall barked out a short laugh. "If you think *he's* going to make things easier for us, you really are deluded."

"He headed several massive corporations on Earth," Wilder retorted. "He must have been involved in hundreds of projects in his lifetime before he even got started on the *Nova Fortuna*."

"That was a long time ago," said Dragan.

They'd reached the autocar that would take them back to the lab. As they climbed inside, Wilder replied, "Not to him it isn't. He spent the journey to Concordia in cryosleep, and over a hundred years passed while he was traveling to and from the Galactic Assembly. By his reckoning, he only left Earth ten years or so ago."

"As recently as that?" asked Dragan. "I didn't realize."

"That makes it worse," Niall said. "He hasn't had time to adjust to being a normal person. He still thinks he's the boss of everyone. You can see it in the way he talks, acts, in everything he does."

Wilder sighed. "You hate him. I get it. But can you please try to get along with him? Just until we finish building the starship. For the colony's sake, okay?"

Niall hadn't replied, only stared out at the passing landscape.

His attitude toward Aubriot hadn't improved in the ten weeks that had passed since, but he hadn't entered into downright confrontations with the man. She guessed that was something to be grateful for.

"We should have it done before the end of the shift," he replied.

The jump drive took up more than a third of the starship, a far bigger proportion than the equivalent engines on Fila ships. The additional size was due to the alterations they had been forced to make so the ship's passengers weren't squashed like putty during a jump. Quinn had been correct in his guess that the human body wouldn't withstand traveling in a regular Fila ship. She'd thanked the stars they hadn't attempted it. Fila bodies were adapted to an aquatic existence and could withstand massive changes in pressure. In comparison, human bodies were extremely fragile. The drive she'd designed with Niall and Dragan's help created a slower, gentler jump, exerting less force on the organic entities it transported light years in one bound.

She gazed at the huge device, hanging within its casing, and the engineers in their suits hooking it up to its connections. "By the end of the shift? That's fantastic. You've done a great job, Niall. I appreciate it."

"Thanks, but I'm not doing it for you. All this taking everything too fast is for the colony's sake, remember?"

Ugh. Why do you have to be such an asshole? For all his complaints about Aubriot, he was turning out to be an awful lot like him.

"And as a member of the colony," she said, "I appreciate it."

"What's happening with the a-grav?"

"They're behind schedule, but they're making progress."

A-grav wasn't a priority. It wouldn't be needed until the ship departed, and during the construction phase it was actually an impediment. It was usually far easier to work when tools, equipment, and parts weighed practically nothing.

"Have you decided about joining the mission?" she asked.

"Not yet." He'd turned his attention back to the workers installing the drive.

She didn't understand his reluctance. She'd assumed he would want to go to Earth, if only for the sake of traveling aboard the ship he'd spent years working to design. It couldn't be fear putting him off. Assuming everything went to plan, they would arrive years before the Scythians and would have plenty of time to gather the material they needed to seed Concordia before setting off again. The second trip would focus on protecting Earth from invaders, and he didn't have to take part in that if he didn't want to. "Well, don't leave it too long. I want to complete the manifest by the end of the week. There are plenty of others ready to take your place if you don't want it."

Interest in the prospect of returning to the origin planet had been high among the colonists. Wilder had begun to avoid going out in public because people would come up to her in the street and make their argument as to why they should be included. Most of them didn't have a good reason. It was pure curiosity that drove them. She'd grown tired of pointing this out, and had taken to telling them to send her a written comm stating their formal request.

"I'll think about it," said Niall.

She clearly wasn't going to get any more conversation out of him today, so she pushed off from the scaffolding. Directing her movements with bursts of pressurized gas from nozzles in her suit, she headed for the airlock leading to the section of the ship already pressurized. This included the bridge, engine room, and living and leisure quarters. The shell of all these areas had been built but the interiors remained scenes of frenzied activity. As she stepped into the passageway, she nearly tripped over someone fixing metal sheeting over the deck struts.

The hand holds on the bulkhead had been the first items to be attached. After opening her visor, she pulled herself along them toward the bridge. She wanted to check in with Dragan. He was working on the conventional engine, needed to maneuver the ship short distances.

Before she reached the area, however, she was abruptly drawn toward the deck, landing on her side. Her EVA suit offered some protection, but the exposed struts still dug painfully into her hips and ribs.

Alarms blared, echoing along the unfinished passageway.

Dammit! Ship gravity had accidentally activated. That

would come as a surprise to everyone. She hoped no one had suffered a serious injury.

"Wilder?" It was Niall. "Are you okay?"

Before she could answer, he exclaimed, "Shit!"

"What's wrong?"

The alarms continued to blare. If he replied, she didn't hear it.

She was suddenly weightless again and drifting. Reaching out, she grabbed a hand hold and pulled herself over to the bulkhead. "What's wrong?" she asked Niall again, louder.

"The a-grav extended to the jump drive. It's...Oh no. Oh my god!"

The comm cut out.

After several attempts, she couldn't raise him. She sped down the passageway, returning to the drive section, comming Niall at the same time. He didn't answer. Giving up, she tried Aubriot. "Did the gravity field hit you? Do you know what's happening?"

He was on the ship's hull, involved in the installation of the Parvus's weapons.

His tone was grim as he answered, "The gravity field hit the jump dr—"

"I know! What's happened?"

"What do you think?" he asked harshly.

The answer was obvious, but she couldn't bring herself to admit it. She needed to be told. "I-I don't know."

"Some people got crushed between the drive and the casing. Rescue teams are trying to reach them now."

6

———

Thirteen people had died and six suffered permanent injuries from the disaster that occurred during the construction of the *Sirocco*. The event had thrown a pall over everything, and what had been an exciting rush toward the building of humanity's first jump-drive starship had turned into a somber, mournful effort to get the thing done. Now it was built, the Leader was attempting to inject some enthusiasm into his voice as he made the announcement, but his heart clearly wasn't in it.

Kes, who was watching Barker's speech at home, turned off his interface. He had observed the building of the ship from afar, through watching daily vidnews reports and via his sporadic contact with Wilder. They remained good friends, but she was incredibly busy and he wasn't into socializing these days. He preferred to spend the free time he had with Miki and Nina. They were his only source of happiness now.

He'd tried to move on from Isobel's death, but he'd found he couldn't, not in any meaningful way. He had taken Cariad's leaving him for Ethan on the chin. He'd pulled himself up, dusted himself off, and sought—and found—a new love, a new life in this colony light years from Earth. At the time, he hadn't thought he'd had any choice. How could he justify leaving his family and breaking all their hearts if he didn't make the best of whatever fate threw at him?

But so much had happened, so many unexpected, calamitous events. There had been so much death and suffering. Izzy dying in childbirth had been the nail in the coffin. He wasn't the same man anymore. He would do his job and continue to support the colonization in whatever ways he could, but he had to conserve his little remaining interest in life and focus it on his children.

What an amazing pair of little girls they were. Both reminded him strongly of his deceased wife in looks and personality. Smart, kind, gentle, and caring. He couldn't have asked for better offspring. All he wanted was to be the best father he could, especially considering how he'd neglected Miki in her early years. He didn't like to think about that time —the sense of shame was too great.

"What were you watching, Daddy?" asked Miki, throwing her arms around his shoulders.

"The Leader's announcement. The *Sirocco* is finished. She'll leave for Earth soon."

"Ms Marrak told us about that." She climbed onto his lap.

At five years old, she was getting a little big for it, but he didn't object. Ms Marrak was her teacher. "What did she tell you?"

"She said the ship's name is the name of a wind that blows from the south. They called the ship *Sirocco* because a ship that came to Concordia from Earth was called the *Mistral*, and the Mistral is a wind that blows from the north. So one wind blew a starship here..." she lifted her hands to represent the ship and puffed out her cheeks to blow them to her left "...and another wind will carry our ship back." She blew the ship to her right.

Her hands dropped to her lap and she gazed at him earnestly. "Is that right?"

"That's right. Well done for remembering. That's quite complicated."

Miki had a need to be certain about everything, often checking and re-checking any new facts she learned. Perhaps it was something to do with losing her mother so young. She remembered Isobel, but Kes wasn't sure how many real memories she had and how much she'd filled in from pictures, vids, and stories he'd told her.

She laid her head on his chest. "Is it true you come from Earth?"

He'd never told her where he was from. It wasn't a secret, he simply hadn't thought it was worth mentioning. "Yes, it's true. Who told you that?"

Her little body stiffened. "Some girls at school today."

He had a horrible feeling the conversation hadn't been friendly. "Were they teasing you?"

She nodded. "They said you're an alien because you weren't born here."

He gently lifted her upright. Her eyes were wet and her lips had turned down. "Do I look like an alien to you?"

"Your hair is a funny color."

Bad question. He was the only redhead in the entire colony. Blond hair and blue eyes still made infrequent appearances when people with the relevant genes happened to have children, but he'd never seen his brand of 'ginger' as Aubriot liked to put it.

"The girls said I'm half-alien because my hair's like yours."

In fact, her hair wasn't anything like his. It did have a reddish tinge, but that was it. He guessed that, to Concordians, it looked unusual.

"Sweetheart." He pulled her close. "Do I seem like an alien to you?"

She shook her head.

"Back on Earth," he said, "people had all different colors and types of hair, and there were many different skin shades too, from very pale to very dark. It's only because so few people came to Concordia that most colonists are black-haired and olive-skinned. Those colors predominated, and that was the way Earth's population was trending too. But a person's hair and skin color isn't important. It's what's in *here* that counts." He touched her chest. "What those girls said to you wasn't very nice. I'll speak to Ms Marrak tomorrow."

The Concordian curriculum probably didn't include any modules on the evils of racism, but it surely had something about discrimination and bullying. It was unfortunate, but wherever they went in the galaxy humans were apparently human.

"It must be nearly bedtime," he said. "Go and brush your teeth and get changed, then I'll read your story."

She hopped off his lap and skipped from the room. Nina was already asleep after a long, hard session in daycare.

His interface pinged. A vidcall request had arrived from Wilder. If it had been from anyone else, he would have ignored it, but he accepted it.

The young girl's face was framed by a halo of hair. Her hair was always messy because she rarely combed it, let alone had it cut, but in this case it meant she was in the *Sirocco* and the a-grav wasn't on.

"Hey," he said. "Congratulations."

"Thanks. We finally finished, and only two weeks after the deadline."

"The deadline was impossible to meet."

"I know, but it sure made us hurry up." Despite her upbeat words, her expression was pensive.

He knew what was on her mind. "Wilder, that accident, it wasn't—"

"I know what you're going to say. It's okay. I don't blame myself."

He wasn't sure she was telling the truth.

"Anyway," she continued with false brightness, "the reason I called is I wanted to know when you'll be joining us. We set out in three days, but you can come up anytime. It's probably better you get here early."

"But I... I'm not going to Earth."

"Of course you are! You have to. You're our chief biologist. How will we know what to bring back?"

"I've prepared a list, and you have plenty of people familiar with the typical range of living organisms. I know because I had to sign off on half of my staff going on the trip. It won't be hard to gather everything you need."

"No, no, no. You have to come too." She looked distraught. "You're the person who discovered the problems with the ecosystem, and you've lived on Earth. You know all the landscapes and seas. You know where to find all the organisms."

"I've given instructions on all that. And Aubriot is also from Earth. He can help you too. I take it he's going?"

"As if anyone could stop him. The way he acts, you'd think this is the *Nova Fortuna* Project and he's the boss again. Sometimes, it's like he's the only reason we're going to Earth. Kes, you *have* to come! How am I going to survive weeks aboard the *Sirocco* in his company without you? When we went to the Galactic Assembly, if it hadn't been for you and Cherry, I would have ended up strangling him."

He chuckled. "I'm sure you'll be fine. He isn't as bad as he was, and you'll have plenty more people around to keep him in check. How many are you taking?"

"Thirty-two."

"Is Cherry going?"

"Yes. I think part of her still believes this whole situation is her fault."

"She did make the decision to fight back against the Scythians, but if she hadn't we'd probably be living a worse reality now."

"And she would probably feel responsible for that," said Wilder. "It's hard to forgive yourself sometimes." She chewed her lip and appeared distracted.

"You can say that again. Look, I'm sorry, but I really can't go. My place is here with my children. I can't possibly leave them alone for... How long will you be gone?"

"Only six weeks. That's my estimate, anyway. Two weeks there, two weeks collecting what we need, and two weeks back. I thought you would bring Miki and Nina with you. I didn't expect you to leave them behind. They're only little so it won't matter if they miss time at school."

"The trip will be as short as that?"

"That's the beauty of a jump engine. We'll arrive years before the Scythians. We'll be able to gather the samples we need to seed Concordia, bring them back, and return to Earth in plenty of time to set up planetary defenses." She gave a short laugh. "I'd love to see the look on their faces when they arrive and our missile silos open."

When he hesitated, she went on, "Promise me you'll at least think about it."

"It isn't only the time involved. I don't want to risk Miki and Nina's safety. The jump drive is new technology. What if something goes wrong and there's another accident?"

Her face fell, and he winced. He hadn't meant to remind her about the gravity-field deaths.

"We've tested the drive prototype four times with human volunteers, and we'll be testing the *Sirocco*'s drive twice over the next couple of days. We don't have time for more tests, unfortunately, but I really doubt anything will go wrong. Please, will you at least think about it? You know you're the best person for the job. Wouldn't you like to see Earth again?"

Her last statement hit home. The idea of re-visiting the planet of his birth stirred something in him. But at the same time, the sound of Nina's wailing floated in. She'd woken up.

He had to be realistic. It was simply far too risky to take his children to Earth. Isobel would never have entertained the idea for a minute. And he couldn't leave them behind either. He couldn't bear to be parted from them.

7

I t was starting to rain again. Kes unfolded his umbrella and raised it. How long had people been using umbrellas? The simple technology had to be thousands of years old, and now here were Concordians, light years from Earth, still using them on an alien planet.

A few other parents were waiting to pick up their children outside the school gates. The line of moms and dads in autocars stretched down the road. Those men and women wouldn't be getting wet today, but he didn't mind a few raindrops. He liked the short walk home with Miki, listening to her chatter about her day.

The school bell rang and the postures of the waiting parents shifted. The children would be out soon.

Beyond the single-story building, vegetation covered the ground to the horizon, the Concordian equivalent to grass. Low-growing, it was wind-pollinated, like many plants on the planet. Flowering flora hadn't evolved yet, and probably wouldn't for tens or hundreds of thousands of years without human intervention.

The green blanket was a welcome sight in some ways. Up

until a few months ago the ground had been entirely bare and the wind had been gradually stripping it back to rock, blowing the unsecured soil into the ocean. But the domination of a single species was still concerning.

His conscience twinged as he recalled the mail he sent to Wilder last night, telling her he wasn't going to Earth and his decision was final. Everything she'd said was true. He wasn't one to blow his own trumpet, but he *was* the best person to collect the seeding material. He was also inured to space travel after his experience traveling to the Galactic Assembly. And he had a strong hankering to set eyes on the place of his birth again.

Yet his first duty was to his children. Others could do a perfectly adequate job of selecting the range of organisms required and ensuring their survival on the return trip. He wasn't indispensable.

The first children began to appear through the gates. Kes focused on looking for Miki, the red tint to her hair making her easy to identify.

The rain had stopped. He lowered his umbrella and closed it.

There she was!

She'd spotted him too. She ran to him through the bustling mob, her backpack bouncing.

"Daddy!"

He picked her up to hug her. "How was your day, sweetheart?"

He would gladly have carried her all the way home. In the past he had carried her everywhere. Isobel had warned him against spoiling her, but that had been before she'd lost her mother. He doubted Izzy would scold him now. But even he had to concede she was getting a little too big.

As he put her down, she asked, "What's that cloud, Daddy?"

She'd been looking over his shoulder, out across the sea of

green that formed the open countryside. He couldn't see what she meant at first. The sky was full of clouds. Then he spotted it. An indistinct, dark haze occupied a space between the ground and the sky. It wasn't a cloud. Its edges were undefined and they were moving too quickly to be any kind of precipitation.

"I'm not sure," he replied, though he had a sense of foreboding. "Let's go home."

He put her down.

Children continued to stream from the gates. He took Miki's hand and they went along the street. Their house was only five minutes' walk away, but he found himself speeding up. He glanced over his shoulder. Houses obscured his view of the hazy cloud.

"You're holding my hand too tight," Miki complained.

"Sorry." He halted. "Would you like a piggyback?"

"Yes, please!"

He took her backpack and swung it over his shoulder before squatting down. With Miki's arms around his neck and her legs tucked under his elbows, he set off, jogging.

Miki giggled as she bounced on his back. "This is fun."

Next she said, "Ow!"

Then he heard the buzzing.

They were all around them. A second ago the air had been clear. Now, it was full of small, flying black bodies. The insect species that had been growing in numbers, one of which had bitten Cherry outside the medical center, were swarming.

He felt a sharp sting on his face.

He ran.

"Ow! Ow!" yelled Miki. "Daddy, they're biting me!"

They were biting him too. Every area of exposed skin was being attacked.

Even running, they were still a minute or two from home. He squatted down again and told Miki to jump off his back. She sobbed and covered her face. The insects settled on her hands, sinking their proboscises into her skin.

He ripped off his jacket and wrapped it around her, batting the insects away. He scooped her up and ran again, thanking the stars she was wearing pants. His jacket wasn't large enough to cover her legs. He hoped the insects couldn't bite through cloth.

At last he was home. He sprinted up the path leading to his house and slammed his hand on the security panel. As the door began to open, he squeezed through the widening gap and then told it to close again. Then he gave the instruction to close all windows, not remembering if he'd left any open. Miki was still crying, but he was forced to put her down and leave her in the hallway while he raced around the house, checking all the windows were in fact closed and the house computer wasn't glitching. In many countries on Earth windows had been fitted with screens but there had never been any need on Concordia. Here, insect life didn't prey on human beings. Until now.

Satisfied nothing would be able to get in, he returned to Miki. She'd stopped crying, but red bumps were appearing on her face and hands. He hoped her reaction wouldn't be too severe.

She giggled. "Daddy, you look funny."

He felt his face. Bumps were rising on him too. But they were safe for the moment.

"How about you play in your room while I make you a snack?"

She trotted away, apparently already over the drama. He would have to find some soothing ointment for the bites, but he had more urgent matters to attend to first. He comm'd Nina's daycare center to warn them. Luckily, the swarm hadn't reached them yet. "You must bring all the children inside and close all the windows and doors."

"Yes, yes," replied the receptionist. "I understand. We'll get on it right away."

Next, he comm'd the Leader. His secretary tried to put him off, but he insisted on speaking to Barker immediately. She put the comm through. Kes explained the situation, and then continued, "I'm guessing it's all the rain we've had, or a plant that hosts the insect for part of its life cycle has spread widely. I don't know. But whatever fed on these insects isn't around anymore, and neither are the organisms they fed on, so they're turning to us."

"I seem to remember receiving a report about this just the other week," said Barker.

"You did. My department is in the early stages of developing a repellent."

"Only the early stages?"

"Yes." Kes paused as he chose his next words carefully. "Leader, I don't think you understand how serious this is. Some people could have a deadly allergic reaction to the bites. You need to put out an immediate alert and tell everyone to stay inside until further notice."

"But what will the further notice be? How the hell are we going to deal with these things?"

"I'm not sure yet, but—"

"Never mind. I get the message. I'll put out a general comm. Thanks for the update. Reception has just reported we're being swamped with calls. I appreciate you getting in touch." He cut the comm.

Kes's gaze remained on the blank screen, not seeing it, his mind elsewhere.

Miki skipped in from her bedroom. "Where's my snack, Daddy? I'm hungry."

The bumps on her hands and face had grown bigger and taken on a deeper crimson hue. He needed to get the ointment, but he had a question for her first.

"Come here, darling." Lifting her onto his lap, he wrapped his arms around her. "Would you like to go on a starship?"

She gasped and turned to face him, her mouth an O of surprise. "A real starship? In space?"

"Absolutely. What do you think?"

The colony was in even more of a crisis than he'd estimated. The next months and years were going to be miserable as the colonists eked out their existence on a planet in chaos. His department might develop a repellent to deter the biting insects, but another ecological emergency would loom, and then another, and the population would lurch from one to the next, clinging to survival.

Could he really trust the task of collecting the needed organisms from Earth to his colleagues? None of them had ever been there. Shouldn't he be doing all he could to safeguard his children's lives, even if it meant taking some risks?

He wouldn't—couldn't—leave them in another's care. Yet to ensure their future on Concordia, he had to take up Wilder's invitation.

Miki jiggled excitedly. "I would love to go on a starship! Can Nina come too?"

8

T he *Sirocco* hung like a jewel in space—a jewel with an ugly appendage. The appendage was the storage facility for the biological material and organisms to be brought back from Earth. It had inevitably been given the unofficial name, the Ark.

Aubriot's view of the two ships through the shuttle window was his first sight of them whole and complete. After years of preparation, years of dreaming of returning to Earth, his dreams were finally becoming reality. But what would he find there? His nightmare still loomed large in his mind.

Dragan was responsible for the main ship's design. The man clearly had an artistic flair, but the haste involved in the building of the Ark meant function had taken priority over form. The additional vessel lacked any beauty whatsoever.

The *Sirocco* was streamlined, though she would never travel through an atmosphere. Four sections widened out from a narrow tip, curved, and then flared at the tail to house the conventional engine. The jump drive was inside, its position not discernible on the silvery hull. According to Wilder, it needed no exhaust outlet. Dragan had managed to incorporate the Parvus's weapon into the design without affecting the overall shape. One of the hull sections—slightly dimmer than the rest—was the energy-capturing device, and the emitter formed the narrow tip.

The *Sirocco*'s shape was simple but elegant, and there was something about her proportionality that was easy on the eye.

Then there was the Ark.

An enclosed passageway protruded from the *Sirocco*'s side. The storage facility sat at the end, a square, plain box roughly as large as the parent ship. Even its hull wasn't pretty. It was dull, barely reflective. Though he wasn't close enough to see, Aubriot was confident even the rivets holding the thing together hadn't been covered. Strength against the vacuum of space had been the priority. That, and the range of refrigeration and freezing units. There had been no time for anything else.

The *Sirocco* grew rapidly larger until his view was swamped by the glistening hull. A round portal opened, revealing bright lights in the interior. The next second, the shuttle swept through it and he was looking at the bay. The shuttle landed and her engine's vibration cut out.

He and Kes were the last mission members to arrive. Kes's kids had been chattering annoyingly when the shuttle had taken off, but then they'd both fallen asleep, thankfully. While Aubriot walked down the aisle, Kes put the younger kid over one shoulder and was trying to wake up the older one.

He considered giving the man a hand but decided against it. It wouldn't be wise to set a precedent of helping with his kids. Kes might turn to him when it was inconvenient and kids were pains in the backside at the best of times, especially the little ones. Bringing them along was insanity but it was the only way the scientist would agree to come. He had to admit, when it came to biological stuff, Kes knew what he was talking about.

Of course, if they were his own kids, his feelings would be different. But he couldn't have any, so that was that.

As he descended the steps, an odd feeling hit him. Excitement? Nostalgia? When he'd entered cryo on the *Nova Fortuna*, he'd never imagined he would be returning to Earth one day. Yet here he was. He'd known about and been involved in the preparations for two years—hell, it had all been his idea—but it hadn't felt real until now.

The pilot was also disembarking the shuttle. His name was Zapata, and he would be the *Sirocco*'s main pilot. He was Cherry's choice, so Aubriot assumed he was the best Concordia had to offer.

He headed for his cabin. Leaving the bay, one of Kes's kids began wailing. He hurried away, hoping the scientist wasn't his neighbor.

He had half an hour before the first general meeting, when everyone would be introduced. Should he skip it? He already knew all the important people and had no desire to meet any of the others. But if he didn't turn up Cherry would give him grief later.

She wasn't in their cabin, so he wandered along to the meeting early and took a seat at the back to watch as the other participants arrived. The chairs were arranged in a horseshoe around an open area where a holo could display for presentations. A couple of the women caught his gaze as they walked in, holding it a fraction too long. He returned their looks, smiling to himself. All his adult life he'd attracted female attention. He'd never really tired of it, apart from a short time when he'd been depressed.

"Pleased we're finally setting off?" asked Cherry, taking a seat.

He'd been lounging with his arms out. As she sat down he straightened up and pulled his arms down. "Uh, yeah. Where were you? I thought you said we'd meet in our cabin."

"I was giving Wilder a pep talk. She's nervous as anything."

"What about? Does she think the ship isn't ready?"

"No, this meeting, idiot. She's nervous about addressing everyone. It's the first time she's done anything like this."

"Why? What's there to be scared of?"

"Talking to a lot of people can be nerve-wracking."

"Can it? Does she want me to do it? I don't mind." He began to get up.

"Sit down!" She tugged on his elbow. "Stars, you're not slow to take the lead, are you?"

He put an arm around her, grinning. "I can't help it. I've been genetically programmed to dominate."

"Seriously?"

He shrugged. "Don't know, but it wouldn't surprise me."

While they were talking, Wilder had walked to the front of the briefing room. She looked a mess as usual. She seemed to have adopted the never-brushed-hair-and-unmatching-clothes look as a style. No one else was paying any attention to her, and her eyes searched the faces, as if hoping everyone would magically shut up and listen.

He coughed loudly, so loudly everyone looked at him. When he had their attention, he folded his arms over his chest and stared at Wilder. Like pinballs bouncing from one deflector to another, their gazes traveled from him to her.

She gave him a grateful glance before saying, "Thanks for coming, all of you. We know why we're here, so hopefully this won't take too long. I thought, as there aren't very many of us and we'll be living in close quarters over the next six weeks, it would be worth taking the time to introduce ourselves before I go over the mission."

Aubriot quietly groaned. Cherry elbowed him.

Wilder continued, "We'll go around the room. If you wouldn't mind stating your name, your role on the ship, and anything else you'd like to say, like maybe your thoughts or feelings about the trip."

"Jesus," Aubriot whispered. "She'll be having us singing Kumbaya next. Was this your idea?"

"Just the introduction part," Cherry whispered back. "She added the bit about feelings herself. It isn't so bad, is it?"

"Who cares about *feelings*?" he sneered. "We're here to do a job."

"Cut her some slack, can't you? She's trying her best. She's still a teenager."

"Yeah, exactly. I don't know why the Leader thought it was a good idea to put *her* in charge when there are others with decades of leadership experience. She might be a brilliant engineer, but she isn't a people person."

"And *you* are?"

The first two attendees had spoken. A third person rose to her feet. After giving her name and role—she was a botanist—she started on a spiel about how excited she was to see the birthplace of humankind in a way that promised to go on for some time.

"Fuck this," Aubriot muttered. Not only was he absolutely uninterested in hearing about other people's motivations and desires, he had zero intention of sharing his own.

He got to his feet.

"Hey, where are you going?" Cherry quietly admonished.

"Out of here."

He edged along the row, bumping knees and eliciting annoyed murmurs and glances, before he reached the freedom of the passageway.

The first jump was planned to take place in two and a half hours. Then there would be a period of recovery when the docs would check everyone for effects, and the jump drive would build power for the next jump. It would take five jumps to reach Earth. The passengers and crew would sit in jump capsules designed to protect against the crushing and distending forces of the process. The *Sirocco* was reinforced to withstand the unusual pressure, but the human body was not.

It was too early to go to the jump room, so Aubriot wandered around the ship. He was already familiar with the layout but this was his first sight of her since her construction was complete. He stuck his head in the little refectory with its empty, white tables and benches bolted down in case of a-grav failure. He gave the gym a cursory inspection. It was poky and only had five basic pieces of equipment, but it would do. The next place he reached was the bridge. Only two people occupied it: Zapata and the captain, Vessey.

Vessey was about the only person who he would have been interested in listening to at Wilder's stupid meeting. He had no idea why she'd been picked as captain over the obvious choice: him. She was Vice-Leader, but apart from that he didn't know what else qualified her for the role.

"Aubriot," she said as he walked in. "Is the meeting over already?"

"Doubt it. It's going to take them at least another hour to get through everyone's life story."

He sauntered to the screen displaying the view outside the ship. Concordia spun lazily in its axis He hadn't seen the planet from afar since he'd been aboard the *Mistral*, battling the Scythians. It was hard to believe that in a couple of weeks he would be looking at a similar view of Earth.

"Uh, can I help you with something?" asked Vessey.

She and Zapata were watching him as if wondering why he was here. Why shouldn't he be here? If it weren't for him, they wouldn't even exist. There would have been no deep space colonization project, no generational starship, and no Gens.

"Nah," he replied. "Just taking a look around."

He left and went to his cabin, where he idly watched entertainment to pass the time.

9

The long, oblong capsules reminded Cherry of the vessel she and Ethan had traveled in to visit the Fila's ocean-bed metropolis. Perhaps that was where Wilder had got the idea for the design. She'd had many long discussions with Quinn about jump tech before he'd left Concordia with the rest of his kind. The aquatic aliens couldn't risk coming into contact with any remaining biocide, and the chances of encountering it were higher for them than land-based life forms.

It made sense, but Cherry had wondered if they were also leaving because associating with humans had brought them so much trouble and loss of life. That made a lot of sense too. Until the arrival of the *Nova Fortuna*, the Fila had lived on Concordia in safety and peace for many years, not attracting attention from the Scythians.

Others were getting into their capsules. Aubriot was already in his and looking impatient.

He could be such an asshole sometimes. Poor Wilder's face had fallen when he'd walked out of her meeting. Not that it was worth telling him about it. He wouldn't care. He would say he'd helped Wilder by getting everyone to be quiet. He had, but...

"Are you getting in or not?" he snapped.

She glared at him and stepped into the open capsule. "You know we might not ever see each other again? Do you really want that to be the last thing you said to me?"

"Wind your neck in. It's been tested. It's safe."

He wasn't usually this mean and nasty. This was Aubriot at his worst. She knew what was bothering him. He just couldn't stand it when he wasn't in charge. He'd hated the fact that she'd led Concordia's military and he'd been second-in-command. If it hadn't been for their close relationship, he would have given her a far harder time of it.

Soon, all the capsules in the jump room were full. Everyone, including the pilot and captain as well as the doctor and medics, would be ensconced for the duration of the jump.

Cherry had completed two trial runs in a capsule and each time had been awful. The experience was much worse than it had been when she'd gone to the Joining Ceremony with the Fila.

It was one minute until the jump. Her capsule's lid descended and sealed with a hiss. A heartbeat later, a circle of nozzles below the seal squirted gel into the chamber. At the same time, a mask extended to cover her nose and mouth. Within seconds, the gel rose over her legs and torso and crept rapidly up her chest. When it hit her shoulders, she couldn't help but gasp, even though she knew she was already breathing the special oxygen-nitrogen mix that would protect her lungs from the jump effects.

The gel surged up her neck. Her pulse was loud in her ears, drowning out the countdown.

How much time was left?

What had it said? Fifteen or fifty? She couldn't remember.

Her chest labored, forcing the oxygen mix in and out of her lungs.

Wet stickiness crawled up her cheeks.

She closed her eyes.

The gel covered her lids.

She couldn't breathe!

She *could* breathe. She *could*.

Forcing her hands to remain still, not to tear the mask from her face, not to beat against the capsule while she screamed, begging to be let out, she willed herself to inhale and exhale steadily.

The jump would take ten seconds. She only had to endure ten seconds, then the gel would be sucked away, the mask would be lifted, and the capsule would open. Just ten seconds. She could do this for ten seconds.

Had it started?

Ten.

Nine.

She couldn't feel anything different. What did it feel like to go through a jump? What had the test volunteers reported? She couldn't recall.

Four.

Three.

Two.

One.

That was it. It had to be over now. She waited for the gel to be removed. Why wasn't the gel leaving the capsule? She couldn't stand it. She groped for the emergency release.

Then reality twisted.

There was no other way to describe it. Her sense of her position in space warped. A split second later a heavy shock shook her, almost bouncing her from her seat. At the same time, an explosive *bang!* reverberated.

Shit!

She opened her eyes. All she could see was the fuzzy lines of the crosspiece in the transparent lid.

Waa, waa, waa!

The alarm had started up. The lighting pulsed.

What had happened?

The jump must have failed. Had the jump drive exploded?

There was no point in waiting for the gel to be sucked away. The mission had to be over, for now. The important thing was to get out of the capsule and off the ship now her safety was compromised.

She reached for release and pressed it.

Nothing.

She pressed again, harder.

Still nothing.

Panic rushed up her throat. Fear crushed her chest.

The threads of self-control she'd clung to for the last minute dissolved.

She screamed.

Pummeling her fists on the capsule lid, she heard her cries as if they were from another person. She kicked and writhed. She had to get out. What if the ship was on fire? What if her air supply was cut?

Why wasn't anyone helping her get out?

Was everyone dead?

A cracking, splintering sound came from her right. Instantly, the gel slopped away. A hand reached in and wiped her face clean, then pulled off her mask.

Aubriot was peering in through a shattered hole. "You okay?"

She took a breath and gasped, "Yes."

He was gone.

The capsule lid was broken. She grasped the edges of the hole and pushed. The flexible material bent outward but didn't break. She had to ease herself through it to climb out.

The jump room was in chaos. While the alarm continued to sound and the lights flashed, people were wandering aimlessly or standing still as if confused, coated in gel. Others were smashing fire extinguishers into the capsule lids to free trapped occupants. Wilder stood in the corner, her face pale and her eyes wide.

Cherry couldn't help with the rescue effort. She would never lift an extinguisher one-handed. She stepped through the remains of destroyed capsules and gloopy gel to Wilder.

The girl was trembling.

"It'll be okay," Cherry said.

Only one capsule remained unopened and Aubriot was attacking it. He broke through, dropped the extinguisher. and reached inside. The person moved and turned over.

"Is the ship on fire?" Cherry asked. Wilder would be in comm contact with the *Sirocco*'s computer. "Has she depressurized? Are we in danger?"

Wilder shook her head.

Even if the air supply to the capsules had been severed, so little time had passed it was unlikely anyone had died.

"Don't worry," Cherry continued. "We can figure out what went wrong. You can rebuild the drive and try again. We'll still reach Earth years before the Scythians."

Wilder shook her head again, more vehemently. She seemed to want to say something but couldn't.

"I know it must seem like the end of the world, but it isn't. No one's going to blame you or the other designers for what's happened. Everyone knows you were under tremendous time pressure. The Leader shouldn't have pushed for such a tight deadline."

Wilder croaked, "You don't understand. It's over. It's all over."

"What's over? The mission?"

Aubriot arrived, covered in sweat and gel. He wiped his

forehead with his forearm. "Christ, what a disaster! What a mess. We were lucky only a few of the capsules were affected. We could have all died."

"Is everyone all right?" Cherry asked.

"Think so. The docs and medics are doing the rounds. I reckon it was the bump that jammed the releases. It was a helluva kick. Was that the jump drive conking out?" He addressed the question to Wilder.

She nodded, drawing her lips to a thin line.

"Don't take it too hard," said Aubriot, patting her shoulder. "Everyone makes mistakes."

He seemed a little pleased. Cherry predicted that tonight she would be hearing all about how nothing would have gone wrong if *he'd* been in charge.

The alarm cut out and the lights returned to normal. The crisis had apparently come to an end.

"That's it," said Aubriot. "It looks like it's back to the drawing board for you."

"No!" Wilder exclaimed. "You don't get it!" Tears overflowed her eyes and her hands were fists. "We're done for. Screwed. It's hopeless." She wept and covered her face.

"What's wrong?" asked Cherry. "You said a minute ago it's all over. But everyone's all okay, and you can fix the jump drive. Once you find out what went wr—"

"The jump drive worked!" Wilder choked out between sobs. "It malfunctioned, but it worked. We've jumped...somewhere different from where we were supposed to be. The computer's still figuring it out. We must be light years off track. And now the drive's not working and we have no way of getting home or to Earth!"

10

A somber mood hung over the briefing room, far different from the excited, eager atmosphere of just a few hours ago.

No one had been killed in the accident, but that seemed the only upside. Cherry's heart went out to Wilder as she stood at the front giving the preliminary report. The girl's face was pale and she regularly had to pause and swallow before continuing, as if she were trying to avoid bursting into tears.

She was talking about the jump drive and what had gone wrong. Cherry didn't understand a word of what she was saying and she suspected she was far from alone.

Her guess was confirmed when a man blurted out, "Get to the point. No one gives a shit about why we're in this predicament. What we want to know is, where the hell are we and how long will it take us to get back to Concordia?"

Murmurs and grumbles of agreement came from the audience.

Wilder blinked. "I was getting to that. I'll bring up the holo to show you." She gave the command and instructed the lights to dim. In the near darkness, pinpricks of light shone in the open central area. A red line ran across the center of the holo display, from one side the other. Four yellow dots were roughly evenly spaced along it.

Wilder's figure was shadowy in the corner. "So what you're looking at is our planned route. Concordia is to the left and Earth is to the right of the line. The yellow dot nearest Concordia is where we should have appeared after the first jump. There were four more jumps, the final one bringing us out in Earth's star—"

"Get on with it," growled the man who had interrupted before.

"As we know," Wilder continued in a trembling tone, "the jump drive malfunctioned, throwing us off course. The computer figured out our new location with the help of the star map the Fila gave us before they left. The position we actually arrived at is..." She stated a set of coordinates for the holo generator.

The stars winked out and the red line vanished. An entirely new starscape appeared.

Gasps and exclamations of dismay resounded. Cherry was shocked too. She was no astrophysicist, but even she understood the implication of the changed display. They were far, far off course. Wilder's intuition about the result of the accident had been correct. The *Sirocco* was light years from Earth and Concordia, the only two planets they knew of where humans could survive.

A single star shone out brighter than the rest.

"I've highlighted the nearest sun," said Wilder weakly.

"Are we closer to Earth or Concordia?" Aubriot asked abruptly.

Cherry jumped. She'd almost forgotten he was sitting beside her. He'd been unusually quiet throughout the meeting.

"Earth," Wilder replied.

"How far away are we? Not in distance, in time."

"Without a working jump drive, it's hard to say."

"Bullshit," said Aubriot. "It's not hard for someone like you to figure it out. How long will it take us to reach Earth using the conventional engine?"

Cherry wondered how wise he was being to push for an answer. The news had to be bad, or Wilder wouldn't be reluctant to give it, and the panic and rage in the room was already nearly palpable.

"A-assuming we can get the energy to power it..." Her voice trailed into silence.

There was a rustle as someone stood up and gave the command to raise the lights. Cherry knew the young man vaguely. His name was Niall, and he was one of the team who had created the jump drive.

"To reach Earth from here," he said, "it's going to take us nineteen years, give or t..."

The remainder of his sentence was lost in a roar of shock and outrage.

"Nineteen years!" a voice yelled. "My parents will be dead by the time I get back."

"No way!" another shouted. "I left my children behind. I'll never see them grow up. Will they even remember me?"

"Everyone on Concordia's going to think we're dead," a third person called out. "And how are they going to survive without the seeding material from Earth?"

Cherry was in shock too. She'd guessed the situation had to be dire, but even she had underestimated *how* dire. What was worse, she knew how it felt to be gone from home for decades. When she'd returned from the Galactic Assembly to a Concordia over a hundred years further on in time, the sense of displacement, of loss and not belonging had been devastating. And the third person who had spoke had been correct: without the organisms from Earth, would there even be a Concordia to return to?

Kes, who was sitting on the other side of the room, met her gaze as he hugged his little girls. He hadn't been at the first meeting, and Cherry hadn't had time to speak to him before they set out. He also knew how terrible it felt to be moved on in time and severed from the people you loved. But, perhaps more importantly, he had to be thinking of his kids. They would grow up aboard a starship, not having the freedom to run and play, not feeling the rain or the wind, not seeing a sunset.

She caught a snatch of loud conversation: "Can we even do it? We don't have nineteen years of supplies. This was only supposed to be a six-week trip!"

The protests and angry reactions were growing louder. People were getting up from their seats and moving toward Wilder, who was backing into a corner. The young woman looked frightened. Cherry flashed back to the day she'd met her outside an entrance to Sidhe, being set upon by two bullies. If someone didn't do something, she was going to get hurt.

"Oy!" Aubriot yelled, rising to his feet. "Simmer the fuck down!"

His large frame and booming voice drew the attention from Wilder. The volume in the room dropped several notches.

"I said shut up!" he roared.

Silence and stillness reigned.

"You!" He pointed at the people nearest Wilder. "Back off! Leave the kid alone, unless you want me to crack your bloody skulls together." He glared at them until they did as they'd been told.

"Right, sit down." He waited until everyone had complied. "Listen to me. We're screwed. That's clear. I just wanted Wilder to get that fact out of the way. Now we all know where we stand. No one wants it and no one predicted it, but here we are. Get over it."

He rested his hands on the back of the seat in front of him. "I'm assuming control of this mission. And before you say it, no, it's not because of my massive ego, though I'm not denying it. It's because what we need most right now isn't scientists and engineers, it's someone who can take charge and give orders. And that's me. Anyone who wants to argue about it can talk to me outside, now. Any takers?"

His stare traveled the length and breadth of the room. None met it.

"Good. First, no one touches a hair of Wilder's head or they'll answer to me about it. She tried her best, so I don't want to hear a word of blame against her or the other engineers. They're in the same predicament as us, don't forget. Second, you all need to calm the fuck down. Hysterics isn't going to help anyone. Third, we need to figure out a survival plan that'll keep us alive until we reach Earth. That means food, water, and energy, but also a rota and distractions so we don't go crazy. Luckily, you're some of the most intelligent and capable people on Concordia. Act like it. Organize yourselves. Check the supplies and fuel. Plan ahead."

He turned to Cherry. "Cherry Lindstrom is Chief Survival Coordinator. Send all your reports and suggestions to her."

She muttered, "Thanks, dear."

11

A s Wilder's cabin door opened, she deeply colored. Rising from her chair, she said, "Kes, I'm so s—"

"Shh! There's nothing to apologize for. You didn't mean for any of this to happen."

"Hi Wilder," said Miki, skipping through the door. She immediately climbed onto Wilder's bunk and started bouncing. Nina ran over and also tried to climb up, but she was too small.

"Hey, girls," Kes admonished. "Remember what I said? You have to behave yourselves. How about you play with the toys you brought?"

"It's okay," said Wilder. "They can bounce if they want. They don't exactly have a lot of space to run around." As she'd spoken, her tone had grown higher and by the time she finished she was choking on her words. She covered her face and her shoulders shook as she wept.

Miki, immediately concerned, hopped down from the bed and patted Wilder's back. "It's okay. It's okay," she soothed. "Don't be sad."

Nina sat on her bottom and began wailing too, in sympathy.

Kes wondered if this had been the best idea.

In the days following the jump drive disaster, he had wavered between despair and anger. He knew the latter was irrational. It had been his decision to join the mission and his decision to bring Miki and Nina. Wilder had pressured him, but he couldn't blame her for that. What she'd said had made perfect sense—he *was* the best person to supervise gathering the seeding material from Earth. Only it looked like he might never see Earth at all, and he might have condemned his children to a lingering death.

Yet he knew Wilder had to be hurting too. So when he'd calmed down somewhat, he comm'd her, asking to see her.

"Miki, that's very kind of you. Wilder and I would like to talk now. Can you play with Nina?"

This did the trick. In another minute, his daughters were in a corner playing a make-believe game and he was comforting his friend.

How could he ever have been angry about the situation? It was just another terrible event similar to all the others that had dogged the colony since Arrival Day. No one was to blame.

Wilder's tears seemed to be lessening. He waited patiently, his arm around her shoulders. Should he say something? He decided it was better to let her cry it out. It might be the first time she'd given vent to her feelings since the accident.

Eventually, she murmured, "I keep going over everything I did, everything *we* did, trying to figure out the mistake, but I can't find it. I still don't have any idea what we did wrong. The prototype worked fine. The tests were all successful. I can't figure it out."

"You've checked the drive?"

She took her hands away from her tear-stained, blotchy face and nodded. "We've all taken a close look at it. It's damaged, though it's hard to see how it happened."

He asked softly, "So there's absolutely no way you'll be able to get it working again?"

"None that we can think of. Not unless you know of a jump drive repair shop within a few light years?" She smiled wanly.

"Sorry, I can't help you with that."

Fresh tears ran from her eyes. "Oh, Kes, I'm so—"

He held up a finger. "I won't hear it. Not a word. You understand?"

She hung her head. Quietly, she said, "There's more. Things are worse than you think."

A heavy feeling settled on his chest. He guessed what was probably coming. "Is this about the supplies?" At the meeting when they'd learned the desperation of their situation, he'd known it was impossible they had enough food and water to last them until they reached Earth.

"We only have six months' worth," said Wilder. "We thought we were probably overdoing things loading so much for what was supposed to be a six-week trip, but..."

He stopped listening. Six months. They had only six months before everyone would begin to starve. A lump rose in his throat. In six months Miki and Nina would begin to feel hungry all the time and ask him for food, and he would have nothing to give them. What would he do then? Would he be able to do the kindest thing and put them out of their misery? The sick bay had to have strong sedatives.

He cleared his throat. "What about power?" he interrupted aimlessly, his mind shying from horror.

"I just told you," said Wilder, looking at him strangely. "Didn't you hear me? Energy shouldn't be a problem. We can use the energy-gathering capability of the Parvus's weapon system to supply the regular engine. We'll have to work out how to safely divert the stored energy to the engine, but I'm confident it can be done."

"That's something at least." His words belied the image in his mind's eye: a starship of rotten corpses arriving at Earth nineteen years from now, everything in her working perfectly, every system functioning—except the life she'd once supported.

"What about our friends in the Galactic Assembly? Do any of them live in these parts?"

"Not that we're aware of. We're broadcasting a general distress comm—Aubriot argued against it, saying we shouldn't announce our vulnerability to the entire galaxy—but the distances between intelligent civilizations are immense. You remember how long it took us to get to the Assembly's space station? And Concordia is in a section buzzing with life. But comparison, we're in the middle of a barren desert. If our message does happen to reach a friend, we'll have died of old age before they find us."

A bolt struck him. He gasped. Perhaps there was a way... Then his shoulders sagged as another realization hit.

"What?" Wilder asked. "Did you think of something?"

"I did, but it won't work."

"What was it? Maybe I can help."

He replied heavily, "Theoretically, if we have energy, we can have food. All the food we eat is primarily formed from light and carbon dioxide."

"CO_2's no problem. We breathe it out." Wilder's features brightened. "And we can re-purpose the ship's lights."

"Plants also need macro- and micro-nutrients, but maybe we could get those from planets."

"We could convert the Ark to *grow* things rather than simply store them, using planetary dust as the growing medium. That's brilliant, Kes."

"Except..." He paused.

"What?"

"Think harder."

Her face fell. "We don't have any plants."

"No, we haven't. We don't have anything fresh in the supplies, do we?" He already knew the answer. Concordians had been surviving on stored food since the Scythian Plague. Everything to eat on the *Sirocco* would be dried, canned, frozen, or pasteurized, all potential for regrowth destroyed.

Wilder shook her head sadly. "I'm pretty sure you're right, but I'll ask Cherry to double check to be sure."

"It's definitely worth double checking. If we only had potatoes, they could keep us going a long time before malnutrition set in."

Eating nothing but potatoes for years would be a miserable existence, and he was pretty sure there was nothing else that *would* sustain them for nineteen years, yet perhaps some form of life was better than none.

"I'll look into it," said Wilder.

"How have you been?" he asked gently, worried that his question would start up her tears again.

She did blink several times before answering, "Awful. Just awful. I'm grateful to Aubriot for protecting me against revenge attacks, but most people have made it clear through their looks what they'd like to do to me."

His guilt over his anger twinged. "That's very unfair."

"Is it? If it hadn't been for me, Concordians would have left for Earth years ago. They would be right on the Scythians' tail. Now, help probably won't arrive at all. And without the seeding material, the colony is sunk. Humankind will sink back into barbarism. And it's all my fault." Her lower lip trembled.

Despite the situation, he chuckled. "Humanity brought to its knees by the actions of one young woman. That's quite the charge to lay at your own feet. Aubriot would like a word with you about who has the largest ego on the ship."

She smiled. "I guess it isn't *all* my fault."

"Not quite *all* of it."

After a pause, she said, "Thank you."

"For what?"

"For trying to make me feel better."

"What else are friends for?"

12

C herry stared at the man. She was reminded of a time, decades ago, when she'd been in his place. She'd been the angry, bitter one, and Cariad had been the interviewer. How she'd hated Cariad at that moment. She'd hated all Woken but especially the woman Ethan loved. Their relationship had improved later, when she'd accepted Ethan was as principled and sincere in his feelings as he was in everything else, and the lines between Gens and Woken had blurred.

Time changed things.

Except maybe in this case.

"What if I refuse to tell you?" the man repeated, snapping at her. "What then?!"

She slammed the interface on the desk. "What do you expect me to say, huh? What *exactly* am I supposed to say? I'm in the same situation as you. We all are. We're just trying to make things a little more bearable. Is that a crime?"

All she wanted to know was his professional background. The ship's database didn't contain detailed information on the mission members, and Aubriot had asked her to create a profile for each of them. He wanted to know the types and range of skill sets they had aboard.

"Why?"

"Why what?" she asked irritably. She glanced down at the interface. She'd forgotten the man's name.

Bernard Garcia.

"Why bother making things more bearable?" he asked. "What's the point? We're all going to die anyway. We might as well blow up the ship and get it over with."

There it was.

She put a check next to his name. Garcia wasn't the first person to express suicidal thoughts in their interview. It was something else Aubriot had asked her to note.

"Everyone dies," she said. "It's just a matter of when. We're going to keep going as long as we can."

"And what if I don't want to?" His voice had softened and he broke eye contact. This was why he was being obstructive: desperation and dread.

"Then..." She paused.

What Aubriot hadn't told her was how to handle the people who wanted to end it all right now. She was no psychiatrist. Hell, she wasn't even a good listener. She was the last person people came to with their problems, needing a sympathetic ear.

"You know who I am, right?" she asked.

He nodded.

"Then you know I arrived on the *Nova*. I was there at the beginning. A lot's happened since then. Terrible disasters. So many people died trying to make the colony a success. But we kept going. Looking back, I'm not even sure why. It seemed impossible we would survive." An image appeared in her mind: Ethan in Sidhe as they awaited the Scythian's return, going from section to section, bolstering confidence, focusing minds and hearts in the face of almost certain annihilation. If it hadn't been for him they would never have made it.

If only he were here now.

"I don't know what's going to happen," she continued. "Maybe this really is finally it. It's over and we're done. But we're not giving up. It's been decided. You're one of us, and we need you. So hang in there, okay?" Her words sounded hollow. She winced but tried not to show it.

Garcia appeared unmoved. "I guess so."

"Good. Now, you're a horticulturist, right? Can you explain what it is you do in your job? In detail, please." She started up the voice-to-text on the interface.

His face twisting with unspoken emotions, he said, "I propagate plants from cuttings. My role on the mission was to..."

She zoned out and let the recorder do the work. It had been a long day, and she'd spent most of it dealing with others' anxieties and fears about what was going to happen. She'd tried to help, but she had no answers. She didn't even know what to tell herself.

GARCIA HAD FINISHED and left and she sat alone in the small room, the barely discernible hum of the ship's engine her only company. All her strength seemed drained from her though she hadn't moved for hours. The thirty-odd faces she'd seen today passed through her mind. Would she see them change over the next nineteen years? Would they have the opportunity to grow older? Or had her day's work been a futile exercise, a distraction? Did Aubriot really think they had a chance or was he only enjoying himself playing the big boss in the finale of his life? So much for his potential immortality.

She dragged energy from somewhere in the depths of her being and collated all the files she'd created before sending them to the database. Leaving the interface where it was, she walked out.

Aubriot wasn't in their cabin, and he hadn't left a message letting her know where he'd gone.

The man was so annoying. His lack of consideration was getting worse. Here she was, being his freaking *secretary* while he swanned around the ship acting like he was the Leader, and he didn't even have the decency to wait for her before he went... where? It wasn't like there were many places to go. He must have gone to dinner without her.

She comm'd him.

As soon as he answered, she barked, "You could at least have waited for me!"

"Eh? What are you talking about? I was wondering where you were."

"Where I was? I've just spent the last eight hours doing the freaking interviews you asked for. Did all my hard work slip your mind?"

"Oh, yeah. I forgot about that. Uh, thanks. Come to the Ark."

He cut the comm.

Her jaw dropped in disbelief. The arrogance of the man. Just when she thought she was used to his ways, he got worse. Maybe he was doing it on purpose, gradually loosening the restraints on his awful personality traits, turning up the heat under the pot he'd put her in, until she would finally be cooked.

Come to the Ark.

Why? What could he possibly be doing there?

She marched through the passageways, thinking up angry accusations to throw. She would let him know exactly what she thought of him, tell him all his faults, all the reasons he was unbearable to live with, and then she would tell him she was done. The *Sirocco* wasn't big, but there had to be a spare cabin somewhere. If there wasn't, she would sleep in the briefing room or the refectory. Any place that Aubriot wasn't would be just fine.

And yet here she was still doing what he'd told her.

Dammit.

She carried on walking.

The Ark was 125,000 cubic meters of refrigerators, freezers, and dry rooms. There was nothing aesthetically pleasing about it. The decks, bulkheads, and overheads were unpainted metal, and the layout was basic: passageways ran from one side to the other of the five levels, dividing the chambers, and an elevator stood at each end.

As she crossed the short linking bridge, Cherry realized Aubriot hadn't told her where he was in the Ark. Exasperated, she was about to comm him when she spotted his tall figure at the end of the bridge. Kes and Wilder were with him.

"Huh," he said as she arrived. "It's us four together again. Weird, right?"

"Hi Cherry," she replied sarcastically. "Thanks for coming. How was your day?"

Kes and Wilder threw each other a look.

"Uhh..." Aubriot looked nonplussed. "So, Wilder had this idea—"

"It was Kes who thought of it," Wilder interrupted.

"Whatever. We might have found a solution to the food problem."

"You're kidding," Cherry said, all her anger and frustration dissolving. "What?"

"We grow our own," Wilder replied excitedly. "Here in the Ark. We've come to take a look at it and see how we can convert it."

"Convert it into a greenhouse?" Cherry asked. "Put in lights and irrigation and so on? That's brilliant!"

It seemed so obvious. Why hadn't she thought of it? Out of all the mission members, she was the only farmer. As she knew well after interviewing everyone, she was the only person experienced in growing crops. She'd been an idiot.

"Wait," she said, "do we have enough energy for lighting? And where would we get the extra water from?"

"Energy isn't a problem," said Kes, "thanks to the Parvus's weapon."

"Which *I* argued we needed to install," Aubriot added smugly.

Cherry caught Wilder's brief eye roll before she said, "We'll have to use some of the ship's lighting. Things will be a little darker over there. We didn't make lights a priority here."

Kes explained, "We wanted to keep the biological material as inert as possible for the return trip, and light stimulates growth."

"Right," Cherry said. "But it can be done?"

"We think so," Wilder replied. "We really think so. Water shouldn't be a problem either. It's pretty common in space and I'm sure we can figure out a way to harvest it."

"That's fantastic!" Cherry gazed up and down the gray, dim passageway, imagining an open, bright, humid, green space, lush and rich with nutritious calories to keep everyone alive.

Something niggled at her. It wasn't a complete answer to their predicament. They would still need to spend nearly two decades in space, Concordia wouldn't receive the seeding material as soon as needed, and who knew what they would find on Earth when they finally reached it, but at least they weren't sentenced to death by starvation.

None of those wrinkles in the plan were what was bothering her. Then it came. "But where are the crops going to come from? We were supposed to be picking up the seeds. We aren't bringing them with us."

"Ah," said Wilder, her eyes twinkling, "that's what Kes and I wondered too. But then I remembered the galactic map Quinn gave us. The Fila have been roaming the galaxy for eons, finding watery planets for their ever-growing populations. Their jump drive has probably made them the most widely traveled species in existence, in our galaxy anyway. They keep records of every planet they encounter that harbors life, regardless of whether it's habitable for them."

Aubriot said, "We're going to collect plants from other planets. Anything we can eat, we'll grow here. Simple. I knew there was a solution. We just needed time to think about it."

Cherry didn't see how he'd contributed anything to the answer, but she let it go. He *had* kept them together when everyone was about to lose their minds. She asked Kes, "Are you sure we'll find something safe for us to eat? You guys didn't find much on Concordia that wasn't poisonous to humans."

"It might be a challenge, but we can try. It's certainly worth trying."

13

'Auntie' Cherry's face as he left Miki and Nina with her was a picture Kes would never forget. Despite the severity and danger of the situation, he smiled to himself as the *Sirocco*'s shuttle made its way through the alien planet's atmosphere. Cherry's features had been a mixture of discomfort, confusion, and plain fear. He knew she would do a good job caring for the girls nevertheless, or he would never have entrusted them to her. She'd helped bring Nina into the world. She would protect those girls with her life. He wasn't happy about being parted from them but it was a better alternative than bringing them on the expedition.

Was it a fool's errand to try to find plants to grow as crops? Most likely.

He hadn't wanted to throw a dampener on the hopeful, excited discussions about turning the Ark into a massive greenhouse, but their chances of success were tiny. What people like Aubriot, Cherry, and Wilder didn't know was that humanity's food crops had been selectively bred over millennia. Wild plants from the planet he was about to visit weren't only unlikely to be edible, they would also be low in calories, taste terrible, and have unknown growing requirements, making them difficult to cultivate.

But it was the only chance they had. At the very least, making the attempt would give the mission members hope for a little while longer.

Additional weight had been settling on his shoulders as the shuttle descended. At 1.5 g, the planet's gravity would make for a tiring trip, though its atmosphere's 30 percent oxygen would alleviate the effects somewhat.

The vessel suddenly dipped, sending his stomach somewhere above his head. He gripped the armrests.

"Sorry about that," said the pilot, Zapata, over the intercom. "We've hit turbulence. It's gonna be a rocky ride for about twenty minutes."

He wasn't kidding. The shuttle rose and fell like a boat tossed in a storm. Kes gripped his armrests tighter as bile rose in his throat. He swallowed and focused on not being sick. Just when he thought he couldn't hold out any longer, the disordered motion stopped.

He relaxed and wiped sweat from his forehead.

Aubriot, who was seated in front of him, leaned around his seat back and winked. "The fairground ride is complementary. No need to thank me."

Kes didn't even attempt to react to the weak joke.

Aubriot raised his eyebrows before facing front again.

Zapata was the best pilot in the colony, as Kes understood. He hated to think what might have happened if they'd been in less-skilled hands.

The planet's surface was rising rapidly toward them. A sea of green spread out to the encircling horizon. The scant information the Fila had gathered on the alien world before concluding it wouldn't suit their species was that, while there was plenty of the water they needed, it was spread out in lakes and marshes and dispersed through massive archipelagos and shallow reefs. There were no deep, wide oceans to support their large metropolises.

From a human perspective the information was mostly useless. They needed to know about the planet's land masses, which were irrelevant to the Fila. From what Kes could see, there was plenty of plant life. What fauna might lurk among the vegetation, they had no idea. Again, the Fila hadn't bothered to investigate, apart from commenting the planet appeared to host no intelligent life forms. The lack of built structures seemed to confirm the deduction.

Zapata requested his and Aubriot's presence in his cabin.

Kes unfastened his seat belt and followed Aubriot down the narrow aisle. As well as the pilot, seven people were accompanying them on the trip: three men and two women Kes had picked for their skills with plants, one of whom was an old work colleague, Trish, and two burly men Aubriot had wanted to bring along in case of difficulties. Everyone was armed.

When Kes and Aubriot entered the cramped cabin, Zapata told them to close the door before saying, "I don't know where to land. Take a look."

Kes peered at the bird's eye view through the shuttle window. It was the same green expanse he'd seen earlier.

"Just find a bit of solid ground," said Aubriot. "What are you expecting? A spaceport?"

"That's the problem," Zapata replied evenly, "there isn't any solid ground. The scanners haven't picked up any dense rock since we entered the atmosphere. Nothing except marshland for hundreds of kilometers. So unless you're planning on finding these plants five meters under the surface, we need an alternative plan."

"Shit," Aubriot muttered.

"What about nearer the poles?" Kes suggested. "Does the planet have an equivalent of the Earth's tundra? If we can't find rock, maybe we can find permafrost."

"Nice idea," Zapata replied, "but the shuttle's thrusters will melt any ice we land on."

Kes frowned. "You said the scanners haven't identified solid rock, but what about sand? The Fila reported lots of shallow oceans. Perhaps we could land on a seashore."

"Ah, yeah," Zapata said. "Didn't think of that. Let me take another look at the map."

The Fila's record of the planet's topography was like a negative of a regular map. The river and lake beds and oceans floor were represented in detail, but the land masses were empty and featureless, only their outlines showing. Nevertheless, the three men were able to locate where the nearest beach appeared to be. Kes and Aubriot returned to their seats, and then the shuttle banked and turned.

Time passed, and turquoise watery expanse came into view. As they flew nearer, a thin black line demarcating it from the vegetation became visible. It was a beach of a kind, though not the color Kes was expecting. Perhaps the sand was volcanic in origin. The flatness of the planet implied it was young, though the Fila hadn't mentioned an estimate of its age. A youthful planet was a good thing—hopefully no large predatory life forms had evolved. Kes still remembered the days of the sluglimpets, before his team had developed a repellent.

The black line grew wider until the shuttle was directly above it and began to descend. The vertical takeoff and descent capability she'd been given in preparation for predicted conditions on Earth had certainly come in useful.

White-capped waves rode a blue-green sea on his right, and green branches reached toward the sky beyond the window on the left-hand side of the aisle. The branches were interesting. They lacked any stems or large leaves. Perhaps the plants were a kind of gigantic moss.

Inedible, no doubt.

He moved in his seat uncomfortably. Carrying half his body weight again was already becoming a drain.

With a small bump, the shuttle settled on the sand. Zapata asked the passengers to remain in their seats. He stepped out of his cabin and opened the hatch. Warm, humid air gusted in, carrying a strange, earthy scent.

"Seems safe enough," Zapata said. "Hot, though. It's forty C out there, but the sun's going down in a couple of hours."

Aubriot's men checked the immediate area and gave the all clear. Next came the grueling process of unloading the equipment and setting up camp on the beach. The task would have been arduous in normal circumstances, but at 50 percent extra gravity it was taxing in the extreme. Sweat soon bathed Kes's brow and soaked through his clothes.

Aubriot, however, seemed to be in his element. He strode over the loose, powdery, black sand, carrying item after item from the hold and dumping them in the open spot chosen for the camp, leaving the unpacking and constructing to others. He was naturally muscular and strong and appeared unaffected by the additional mass.

While Kes was trying to extract a pop-up tent from a bag, Aubriot arrived, reached down, and hauled the tent out one-handed. Telling Kes to step back, he released the catch, and the tent sprang into shape.

Aubriot put his hands on his hips. "Not bad eh?"

"What?" Kes asked irritably. "What isn't bad? The tent? The planet? The whole twenty years from human civilization thing?"

"What's got *your* goat? Hey, do you remember that night we met in the bar before the Third Scythian Attack?"

"No, I don't." He actually did, but he was too hot, tired, and worried to admit it. He recalled the night too well, not only because of the attack but also because it was directly after Izzy had left him for being a terrible husband and father. He knew exactly what Aubriot was going to say and he hated him for it, because he was right.

"'Course you do. We were saying how we hadn't expected things on Concordia to turn out so normal. You had your office job, working for the government. I was pissing my life away, bored out of my mind. We'd come all that way to a new world, spent nearly a couple of centuries in cryo, only to end up living in suburbia and doing the same old same old."

He turned to survey the landscape. "I don't know about you, but I'd imagined deep space colonization would be something like this. Adventure. Living on the edge. Fun."

Kes squinted at him. "A – we didn't 'meet' in the bar, you cornered me. B – I thought you were too drunk to recall anything we said, and C – how you can call this fun is beyond me. *Some* of us have people we care about whose lives have been irrevocably affected by these circumstances we find ourselves in. Maybe that's the difference."

All Aubriot replied was, "Huh. I knew you remembered."

Kes watched the man march back to the shuttle's open hold, stepping over the electric guard wire someone had just finished setting up.

He looked over the sea, taking a deep breath. Each lungful of oxygen-rich air renewed his vigor but the effect was short-lived. A bone-weary ache had invaded his back, neck, and all his limbs, reminding him of anxiety dreams where he would feel as though he was walking through treacle.

The sun was going down. The camp would be set up just in time in the failing light. Stars twinkled to life In the darkening sky. Slow, lazy waves dragged themselves up the shore before collapsing and disappearing into ebony sand. The strange forest whispered.

14

While waiting for Aubriot and his goons—as Kes had come to think of them—to put the finishing touches to the rafts, he decided to give his team a few final tips about what they were looking for.

"Obviously," he said, "anything edible is better than nothing, but ideally we want plants that yield a high amount of calories preferably without taking up a lot of space. Plants that produce grains, tubers, nuts...that kind of thing. Potential food that's dense in starches or oils."

"But surely we'll need leafy plants too?" asked a horticulturalist called Garcia. Cherry had warned against bringing him, saying their dire situation had made him mentally unstable, but the man had the exact skills required for the trip. "I mean, we'll need the range of nutrients over the long term, not only calories."

"Honestly," Kes replied, his gaze roaming the landscape, "we don't have a clue what approximations to the vitamins and minerals humans need we might find here. On Concordia, our digestive systems absorbed some of the local nutritional chemicals and not others. We'll certainly turn our attention to leaves

—or what passes for leaves—but for now it's best to focus on calories. We need energy to keep us going. Without it we'll quickly become weak and stop thinking straight. It'll take a while for malnutrition from lack of micro-nutrients to set in."

His comment sparked another idea, but he filed it away to bring up with Cherry, Wilder, and Aubriot later. "You have your field testing devices to check for known poisonous compounds. If a sample passes the test, log the exact location you found it, take plenty of pictures, and bring a piece back."

"How much do you want us to collect?" Trish asked.

"A sample about as big as your finger is fine for starters. After we've carried out more checks we can take seeds, roots, whatever makes sense."

"What about the local fauna?" asked Trish. "Should we collect insects too?"

"I'm more worried about the fauna *attacking* us," Garcia muttered.

"That's why we'll be working in threes," said Kes. "You're with me, by the way," he added.

Garcia snapped his mouth shut and nodded.

To Trish, he said, "Good question. Well done for thinking outside the box." Concordians ate very little animal protein, only a sea creature similar to Earth shrimps. Some people wouldn't even eat those. The *Nova Fortuna* generational colonists had eaten locusts bred aboard the ship but that was ancient history to these people. "I'm certainly open to the proposal of growing insects as well as plants in the Ark. However, we have to bear in mind that we'll also have to grow the plants to feed them. I would need to do some calculations about whether devoting the required space would be worth it."

"The rafts are ready for boarding," called Aubriot, standing on one of the two structures and holding a long pole sticking up from the water. "Please show your ticket on entry."

They had decided to build rafts because traveling on foot

through the marshy jungle would be laborious, hot, and dangerous. A short scouting mission at daybreak had revealed that, once under the odd, skeletal canopy, the ground was treacherously boggy and visibility extended only as far as the thick stems of the next 'tree'. If something wanted to attack them it could get close before they spotted it, and then they would have a hard time running away or killing it without risking shooting each other.

Faced with the prospect of a challenging, risky trek, Zapata had come to their rescue by suggesting this wide estuary farther up the beach after studying the Fila map. The slack movement of the water indicated the current was slow. It seemed feasible to move upstream to conduct their investigations.

Carrying their equipment bags, Kes and Garcia waded out the short distance to Aubriot's raft accompanied by Trish and her partner, a man called Ryan. Aubriot's men were to take turns poling the other raft, with two more of the scientific team as passengers. Zapata remained at the camp.

Aubriot drove his pole into the water, and, bobbing and wobbling, the raft eased away from the shore.

It had taken all morning to construct the vessels from dead 'wood' that had washed up from the ocean. It was fortunate they had suitable tools for the task, originally intended for use on Earth. The sun was high overhead and Kes had unbuttoned his shirt in an attempt to cool down. As they moved out onto the water, a soft breeze lifted it, drying his sweat.

"That's better," Garcia commented, wiping his neck with a cloth.

Kes pulled his hat low over his brow. He would burn to a crisp in the brilliant sunlight.

Aubriot had stripped to the waist while building the rafts. He gazed ahead as he guided his vessel inland, looking pleased with himself. It was clear he was seeing himself in his mind's eye: tall, well-muscled, good-looking, performing his manly task in a manly manner. He was loving this whole experience.

Kes rolled his eyes, sighed, and wondered how Cherry was getting along looking after Miki and Nina.

The darkness of the sand on the estuary bed made it hard to see anything in the water, but he looked into it nevertheless while they went along. He vaguely remembered some aquatic plants on Earth that produced edible, nutritious corms. Growing crops in water wasn't the most obvious solution to their problems, and if the a-grav went out it would be a disaster, but he was worried that air-breathing plants might not thrive in the comparatively lower oxygen levels on the ship.

He spotted some trailing, dark green fronds but nothing promising. Holes in the sand indicated creatures living beneath the surface, but that was to be expected. Every ecological niche would be filled. The question was, were they filled by anything not poisonous to humans?

Thick vegetation grew along the banks and overhung the water, seemingly impenetrable. Whenever he looked up, everything was unchanged except the banks drew in more closely.

After an hour and a half of slow progress, conversation on both rafts had dried to silence and Aubriot had mentioned a couple of times that the current was growing stronger and hard to move against. Kes was about to suggest attempting to get ashore by pushing through the greenery. But before he could speak, one of Aubriot's men called out, "There's some dry ground."

The piece of land wasn't easily visible because it was covered in very low-growing plants curling into the water, but it seemed solid.

Without waiting for a discussion, Aubriot propelled his raft toward it. The edge bumped against a firm surface within the vegetation, and he leapt out, calling to Kes to toss him the rope. In another couple of minutes, he'd tied up around the thick, tough stem of one of the tree-like plants. The second raft came to shore.

They split into three parties of three. Aubriot accompanied Kes and Garcia. Their group was to explore inland while the other two parties would head up and down respectively of the banks of what had become a wide, shallow, slow river. Each team would move forward for two hours, searching, and then return to the rafts. There was no chance of getting lost. With the *Sirocco* in geostationary orbit, she would track them via their ear comms and relay the information to hand-sized interfaces everyone carried. The planet's rotation was slower than Concordia's. At this latitude and longitude the days currently lasted twenty hours and the nights seventeen, but at 1.5 g four hours of locomotion would be about all most of them could manage.

Aubriot strode ahead, leaving Kes and Garcia lagging. The ground was drier here than near the coast, and it had risen marginally higher as they'd journeyed, the vegetation growing less thickly. They were able to walk more or less in a straight line.

"Slow down," Kes called out to Aubriot. "It's not a race." He stopped to examine the base of a plant composed of long, soft leaves sprouting in clump directly from the black soil. He pushed his trowel into the ground and levered the plant up. Its roots were thin and straggly, not tuberous as he'd hoped.

"This looks promising," said Garcia. He was pointing at dry, brown pods hanging from the branches of a shrub.

"Break one open," said Kes.

Aubriot had walked back to join them. "I'll do it. Could be dangerous."

Kes bit his lip as he stifled a laugh. Aubriot was taking his he-man role very seriously.

He grabbed one of the pods. There was a loud report, and

suddenly the air was filled with flying beans and pieces of pod casing. Several hit Kes in the face.

"Wow," Garcia remarked. "Excellent seed-spreading strategy."

"Yes," said Kes. "Impressive."

Aubriot stood as if stupefied, holding the remains of one of the pods in his hand.

"See if you can find one of the beans to test," Kes told Garcia. "I'll continue looking."

"What *was* that?" asked Aubriot. "Is it safe?"

Kes replied, "Just a plant trying to give its babies the best start in life. Nothing to worry about."

"Oh, right."

A few meters away a vine coiled up a tree. Its tendrils appeared particularly thick and fleshy. Were they nutritious?

As Kes walked toward it, Aubriot said, "Going to answer a call of nature. I'll be back in a bit."

Kes heard but didn't reply, his interest taken by the vine.

He cut off a small piece and popped it into his analyzer. While he was waiting for the results, Garcia came over to him. "Those beans are full of toxic alkaloids."

"Damn. Never mind. It's early days. We have an entire planet to search."

"Are we going to carry on looking until we find something edible?" Garcia asked. "That could take years."

"We don't have a lot of choice. We don't have enough food to last us until we reach Earth." The reason they were searching for plants to grow as crops wasn't any secret but, aware he was straying into dangerous territory in terms of the man's mental health, Kes didn't say any more.

"What if we don't find anything?"

Kes patted Garcia's back. "We're bound to find something. We did on Concordia. You found those beans within twenty minutes of—"

"*Arghhh! Shit! Fuck!*"

It was Aubriot.

Kes and Garcia sped in the direction of his voice.

They found him on the ground, curled up on his side, his pants pulled up but open at the front.

"I-I wiped my-my..." He let out a groan.

Kes and Garcia shared a look of dismay and disgust. It was clear no one had warned Aubriot to never trust any unknown leaf for toilet purposes.

"He's *your* friend," said Garcia.

'Friend' implied a far more amicable relationship than was the case, but Kes had to admit he had been Aubriot's acquaintance for many long years. "All right. I'll do it."

Garcia left the scene.

Kes fished in his bag for a soothing ointment.

15

Aubriot's demeanor was different during the return journey from the river. The bravado and pride were gone, replaced by a subdued, reflective air. The trip had also been unsuccessful in research terms. None of the three teams had discovered any vegetative material that passed the initial poisons check. The only sample they brought back was the thick, starchy stem of a plant that did contain poisons but they were all soluble. The stems could be made edible, though the process would require lots of water.

The sun had sunk below the forest canopy, and the shadows of the thin, contorted branches stretched out over the water like a crone's grasping fingers. Everyone was hot and tired after their hours of searching but as they were now traveling downstream, poling the rafts was easy and everyone took turns.

Kes removed his hat and lay down, putting it over his face. It was too dark to see the surrounding vegetation properly anymore and his eyes ached from hours of constant searching. The movement of the water was so gentle it was barely perceptible. He could have been at home in bed or floating in space.

He began to drift off.

"What's that?" someone said.

The voice had come from another raft but it was loud with excitement.

He grabbed his hat and sat up.

Trish was standing, raft pole in one hand, pointing at something in the water. Following her gaze, he saw small, dark brown lumps breaking the surface. The more he looked, the more of them he saw. A field of the things spread out far and wide. They must have risen up since the rafts had passed this area earlier. There were so many, they were unmissable.

"We'll check them out," said Trish eagerly, driving the pole down. Her raft moved toward the nearest lumps.

Kes was excited too. Maybe this was the aquatic plant he'd been hoping to find. But something made him uneasy. The brown lumps seemed tempting somehow, and if they were tempting to humans...

Trish's raft had stopped. She held it steady against the trivial current while another one of her team reached out with a knife.

Kes said, "Wait a min—"

The water erupted.

The torrent hit Kes's raft and upended it, dumping all the passengers in the water. He was swept away by the force, pushed toward the bank. Then it tugged him under.

Stirred-up sediment had turned everything murky and dark. Which way was up? Flailing, he tried to reach a firm surface. He needed to find where the riverbed lay and so how to reach air.

Something hit his back. He extended an arm behind him, wondering if he'd bumped against someone. His hand brushed some hard, thin things.

Claws?!

He tried to get away, but water pressure pushed him into them. Soon, he was right in among them. The claws gripped his clothes, his legs, neck, hair, dragging at him. A scream tried to force itself from his aching lungs. He grappled with them, fighting against them, writhing and turning to free himself.

Then the force that had pushed him underwater and into the grasp of the clawed creature turned. Now he was being pulled in the opposite direction. Bubbles and muted murmurs of sound were all he could hear. He could see nothing in the opaque water.

The water's movement hauled him from the creature's hold. The claws opened, releasing him. His head broke the surface. He whooped in air, filling his lungs. In the dim light, he spotted gray, tangled roots rising up to plant stems. *That's* what had held him? Not claws. Not a predator, wanting to eat him.

He swiveled, treading water, toe tips brushing the muddy bottom. What had happened to everyone else?

Two rafts bobbed nearby, empty. Where was the third? And what had happened to Trish and her companions, who had been closest to the eruption?

What had happened to everyone else?

The rafts were moving, slipping toward the center of the river. He was moving in that direction too. He kicked against the drag, beat his arms like wings, craning to see the cause.

His heart froze.

The water idly turning, spinning. As he watched, the spin grew faster.

Whatever the plant—or animal—Trish had spotted was, it had a strategy: entice the prey with tasty pods and, when the quarry got close enough, explode the water with such fury the victims were forced under and drowned. Then, to mop up any survivors, create a whirlpool to drag them in.

He kicked harder.

He turned onto his front and drove his arms powerfully through the water. The roots he'd become entangled in were about five meters away. He swam like crazy toward them. Soon, he was gasping, his muscles protesting. But the river bank wasn't getting any closer. He wasn't making any headway. If anything, the back was moving farther away.

He tried to redouble his efforts but he was already exhausted. The long, hard day in 1.5 g, the oxygen deprivation of long submersion, the horror that his companions were probably dead, all took their toll. No matter how hard he tried he couldn't extract any more power from his arms and legs.

The roots edged away from him, darkening in the dusk. The whirlpool pulled him in inexorably. The sound of rushing water became louder.

A cry of despair blurted from his lips.

What would Miki and Nina do without him? They'd already lost their mother. If he died they would be orphans. Cherry, Wilder, and the other mission members would be kind, but they needed their parents. No one would love them like he did. No one else would take the same care of them. And they were stuck on a starship in a galactic wilderness. Would they even survive?

His thoughts on his children, he slipped under the water.

16

W ilder's comm chirruped.

"Hi, Ch—"

"Get here, now," Cherry said.

"Sure, but where are you?"

"Kes's cabin. I need help." There was the sound of wailing in the background and an out-of-tune song.

It had to be the kids. Kes had asked Cherry to look after them while he was gone. Wilder wasn't sure why. Cherry didn't have the first idea how to handle children. Wilder knew *that* too well from personal experience. Her intentions were good but her execution was terrible.

Kes's cabin door opened on a chaotic scene. Miki was bouncing on the bed where Cherry was sitting, bashing her on the head and singing to the beat of a song. Nina sat on the floor, legs splayed, screaming.

Cherry looked at her pleadingly. "I've tried doing everything they asked but it isn't working. Nothing I do pleases them. They won't shut up."

"Well, Miki seems to be having a good time," Wilder commented as she picked Nina up.

She cuddled the little girl and soothed her, rubbing her back. Nina's sobs quietened.

"Why didn't I think of that?" Cherry asked.

"To be fair, it isn't easy to do with one arm. I think she's just tired."

"I thought she might be. I asked her if she wanted to sleep but she said no."

"Hm," said Wilder. "I don't know much about kids but I think they always say that." She'd spent some time with Tycho and Stephie and their grandchildren and picked up some second-hand knowledge. A twinge of sadness hit her. Tycho had died not long after he'd heroically offered himself as a test subject for the Scythian Plague vaccine. He'd been a good friend and yet she'd rarely made time to visit him. "The trick is not to ask them, just go by the clues they give out and decide when it's bedtime yourself."

"Oh, really?" Cherry asked, frowning. "If they're tired, why don't they just go to sleep?"

"I don't think they know tiredness is what's making them feel grumpy."

Cherry's frown deepened. "That doesn't make a lot of sense."

"They aren't logical like adults."

"Adults aren't very logical either, but at least they know to go to bed when they're tired."

Nina's head flopped onto Wilder's chest and her eyelids drooped.

"Miki," Wilder said, "could you draw me a picture of your house? I don't remember what it looks like."

"Okay," she replied happily, leaping from the bed and landing with a thump. She skipped to the table interface and turned it on.

"I asked her if she wanted to do some drawing!" Cherry protested, her eyes round. "She said she wanted to sing instead. She didn't mention anything about the bouncing."

"Most kids like to feel useful, valued. Miki likes helping people out, don't you?"

The little girl nodded, her gaze intent on the interface.

Cherry sighed heavily. "I'm not cut out for this. I hope the expedition to the surface returns soon. I don't know how much more I can take, or how much longer the girls can put up with my terrible babysitting skills."

Nina's little body had gone limp and her breathing was regular and heavy. Wilder placed her carefully in the small cot in the corner and put her stuffed Fila toy under her arm before covering her with a blanket.

"You'll be fine."

Cherry looked skeptical.

"I can help out a little if you want," said Wilder, somewhat reluctantly. She had plenty to do already. Though she didn't want to tell anyone and raise false hopes, she hadn't entirely given up on fixing the jump drive. And work had already begun on transforming the Ark.

Cherry's expression brightened. "You wouldn't mind? It would be great if I could get a break every now and then."

"No problem. You know, it isn't fair that this job's been left only to you. We have a ship full of people who could help."

"Kes wouldn't like just anybody looking after his kids, but I know he trusts you."

"Okay." She sat next to Miki. "They might like to play with Piddle and Puddle. I wonder how Kes and the others are getting on."

"Will Daddy be back soon?" asked Miki, naturally fully aware of the conversation.

"Probably not for another few days," Wilder replied, "but Auntie Cherry and I have lots of fun things for you to do while you're waiting."

"We do?" Cherry asked.

NINA HAD WOKEN from her nap. Wilder balanced her on one hip and held Miki's hand as she walked into the Ark to see how Niall was getting on with the remodeling. He was bent over, looking into a conduit. His eyebrows lifted and he stood up as she arrived.

"I've taken over from Cherry for a few hours," she explained, "so she can get some sleep."

"Right." He squatted down again. "Good luck with that."

"What's been happening? Have you made much progress?"

"I think it can be done," he replied into the opening. "We'll have to strip circuitry from the *Sirocco* and remove every other light from the passageways, but I think we can do it. Dragan's figuring out what isn't essential on the main ship."

Miki released Wilder's hand and ran to the conduit.

"Hey!" Niall exclaimed, pushing her away. "Stay back. It's dangerous."

"Come here," said Wilder. She took Miki's hand. "Sorry," she said to Niall.

"You shouldn't have brought them in here," he remonstrated. "You know that."

"You're right. Come on, girls, let's leave Niall to—"

"But that's typical of you, isn't it?"

Wilder had half-turned away. She turned back. "Huh?"

"You're so irresponsible. Everything you do is slapdash."

She could only stare at him.

"The first time you made a-grav you nearly killed yourself. That's why you needed me to give you the parts, remember? Before you went to the *Opportunity*."

"Of course I remember."

Niall had been a scrawny little kid when she'd met him

face-to-face for the first time. He'd changed, and not only physically.

"You always rush ahead. Everything has to be done yesterday. And look at where that attitude has got us."

"That isn't fair! You're blaming me for what happened to the jump drive?" She only recently been able to convince herself it wasn't all her fault. Niall's words were blowing all her hard work away. "The Leader said, at the meeting, we had to..." She swallowed as tears flooded her eyes.

"We should have waited. We should have done things properly. Completed all the tests."

"You think I don't know that?" Wilder asked. "You were on the team too, don't forget. You could have spoken up. Why are you making this all about me?"

Nina wriggled uncomfortably. Miki had been staring, open-mouthed, at each speaker for the duration of the spat.

"I did say we needed to slow down," Niall argued. "Dragan and I both argued we should delay the launch."

"You did?"

"We did, but you didn't listen."

"I don't remember." It was the truth. The weeks leading up to the departure of the *Sirocco* were a blur of exhaustion. Many things had been said. She'd thought that, reservations aside, they'd been in agreement to push forward regardless. She wasn't sure how much Niall's memory had been influenced by the catastrophe and perhaps his own feelings of regret and self-blame.

"We can talk about this later," she said. "When we have some free time." It wasn't an appropriate conversation to be having in front of Miki, who seemed to absorb everything going on around her whether or not she appeared to be paying attention.

"Fine," Niall said bitterly. "Enjoy your time with the kids, considering it'll be the only chance you'll have."

"What?!"

What was he on about now?

He returned his attention to the interior of the conduit. "Figure it out. By the time we reach Earth your child-bearing days will be nearly over. Factor in the time we spend there, the journey back—assuming *can* ever go back—you'll be old when we get home. I don't know if you ever wanted to have kids, but unless you think it's a good idea to bring new life into our hopeless situation here, you can forget it."

17

As he was going under, Kes heard something slap the water. The noise came from near his head. Reflexively, he reached up and grabbed. A line or rope of some kind lay in his fist. The line moved. Either it was alive or someone or something was on the end of it. Was it part of the predatory creature's ensnaring tactic? Whatever it was, it was his last chance. He held on.

The line dragged him through the water, just under the surface. He seemed to be moving in the direction of the bank. He began to struggle for air again. His legs aching, he kicked, propelling himself upward a few centimeters until his head was no longer submerged. A blurry scene greeted his tired eyes: a dusky sky, a shadowy river bank, the line in his hand black and stretching out toward...Aubriot.

The man was hauling him in, hand over hand, like a fisherman lifting an exhausted marlin from the ocean after hours of battle.

He hit vegetation. His face was full of wet leaves and stems. Roots like the ones he'd mistaken for claws earlier—only a few minutes ago—were entangling his clothes.

But he was saved, for now.

The rafts were gone. Remnants of one were scattered on the bank, shattered to pieces by the explosion. The other two had disappeared into the whirlpool.

Trish was gone too, along with the two men with her. Aubriot, Kes, and Garcia had possibly survived because their vessel had been farthest from the plant/creature when the water erupted. Aubriot's man had survived too, and the woman accompanying him, but the third passenger on their raft must have drowned.

The way Aubriot told it, he'd swum to shore after the torrent hit, avoiding the whirlpool pulling everyone else back to the center of the river. Then he'd pulled a vine down from a tree to use as a rope to rescue people.

He *had* saved them. Kes had to give him that. But he didn't have to be so smug about it. Four members of their party had died. Trish had been a work colleague and long acquaintance.

It was well after dark by the time they reached the beach where they'd set off. Where the forest was impassable, they'd been forced to wade along the river margins, despite the danger. In some places the water was deep and they'd had to swim.

Kes waded through the shallows to the shore, last of the party to reach it, weariness dragging at every step. By some miracle Aubriot's ear comm hadn't been washed out in the disaster. He'd comm'd the pilot about their situation and Zapata had offered to fly them the rest of the way to the camp. Zapata was waiting, as he'd promised. Before climbing aboard the shuttle, Kes took a final look at the dark, silent expanse of water.

∽

HE WAS SHARING a tent with Garcia. He would have preferred to sleep alone, especially after the ordeal they'd endured, but it was a part of his strategy to keep an eye on the man following Cherry's warning. The way he felt at the moment, he sympathized with Garcia's feelings. If it weren't for Miki and Nina, he might also be tempted to simply give up. The trip was a disaster and their chances for survival were so slim it hardly seemed worth going to the effort. The seeding material wouldn't reach Concordia in time even if they did survive and make it to Earth. And what would they find there? The Scythians would have reached it before them the planet would be under their control.

What was the point?

He'd eaten and washed and settled down in his sleeping bag when Garcia arrived. The man uttered a brief greeting and climbed into his own bag.

"Is it okay if I turn out the light?" asked Kes.

"Sure. I'm dead beat after today."

Kes reached out and pressed the button. "We'll have a rest day tomorrow. I think it would be nice to hold a ceremony for the people we lost."

"We're continuing with the mission?" Garcia asked.

"Of course. Did you think we'd be returning to the ship?"

"But four people died today! It's far too dangerous to continue."

There was a shuffling sound, as if Garcia was turning on his side to stare at Kes, though the tent's interior was pitch black.

"We have to find food we can grow on th—"

"I *know* why we're here!"

Kes didn't know how to answer him. He was too tired and heartsore to think up something to ease the man's fears. He'd known Trish years. She'd been instrumental in creating the Scythian Plague vaccine.

Garcia was right. The deaths had shown how dangerous the

mission was. Only the mad or desperate would carry on. He wasn't sure which of the two they were.

"How many more of us have to die before we give up?" Garcia asked.

"We'll take every precaution we can, but the day after tomorrow we have to set out again. We don't have a choice about it."

"Why not? Didn't you guys find this planet on the Fila map? Can't you find another one? Maybe there's somewhere safer than this."

In fact, there wasn't. Planets harboring life were rare in the galaxy. They had been extremely lucky this one was only a couple of months' flight from the spot where the faulty jump drive had flung them. The next world where they might find crop plants was years distant, and it was 2.3 g, a gravity Fila anatomy could tolerate but humans would struggle to move in.

Kes replied, "We don't have sufficient information to know we'll find better or safer conditions somewhere else. We have to thoroughly explore this place. It could be our best option and we won't be coming back."

Another rustle issued from Garcia's side of the tent. Perhaps he was turning onto his back. "Maybe we should try to settle here," he muttered, "rather than continuing on." He continued, louder, "What about it? The gravity isn't too bad once you get used to it. We could bring down the supplies from the ship, and there's plenty of water. If we had a permanent base we could take our time about finding local food we can eat. We wouldn't have to rush and take risks. We could at least live out the rest of our lives in the sun and fresh air, not stuck in an artificial environment, breathing each other's stinky breath and drinking recycled piss."

"There aren't enough of us to build a sustainable colony," Kes replied. "You know that."

"I suppose so. Just thinking aloud."

He sounded sad and wistful. Kes wished he could think of something to say to make the man feel better, but Garcia's words had conjured a dreadful vision in his mind: Miki and Nina, fully grown, everyone else long dead, the only surviving humans on an entire planet, utterly alone. And then, one day, one of them would die…

"It's out of the question," he reiterated. "We're going to continue to Earth."

Garcia didn't say anything for a long while. Kes thought he'd fallen asleep and he was drifting off himself when he heard, "Have you ever wondered if we're being punished?"

He opened his eyes. "What?"

"I learned all about what happened in the early days of the colony when I was at school. About the Guardians, the Natural Movement saboteurs, and the first Scythian attacks. I learned a bit about Earth too, how humans had ruined their own civilization. It's like someone is telling us we destroyed one civilization so we shouldn't be allowed to have another. Every attempt we make to build ourselves up, something comes along to beat us down again."

He had a point.

Kes said, "It's true that, when we were working on the *Nova Fortuna* Project, the worst challenges we imagined were things like engine problems and crop failures. No one ever thought the destination planet might be claimed by another species, or the Natural Movement had infiltrated our ranks. So much was unknowable. We couldn't ever have predicted what happened. But I don't think we need to look to the supernatural for an explanation of the disasters that have dogged us. The range of variables is so wide, the experiment is bound to throw up highly unpredictable outcomes."

After a pause, he went on, "Besides, you're only looking at

the bad things that happened, not the good. Humankind has befriended other intelligent species, and for many years the Concordia Colony was very successful. It kept the flame of human civilization burning when it had gone out on Earth, in spite of the enormous odds against us, or, if you like, the terrible hardships fate has thrown at us. That says something, don't you think? Something about our endurance, adaptability, and sheer determination. This time will pass. Things will get better. I'm sure of it."

His words had lifted his own mood, though he didn't know if they'd had the same effect on his companion. Garcia only grunted "Good night" and was silent.

As Kes fell asleep, he was calm and hopeful. Losing Trish and the others was awful, but what he'd said was correct. Concordia had clung to existence for decades. He was confident that, somehow, it would continue to do so.

When he woke in the morning, Garcia's sleeping bag was empty and the tent flap was open. Kes climbed out and stood up, sucking in lungfuls of the heady air. Though he'd slept many hours, the sun was only just coming up and the camp was quiet.

After climbing out of the tent. he looked around for Garcia but the man was nowhere to be seen. Guessing he must have gone to freshen up or get something to eat or drink, Kes returned to his sleeping bag. But he was fully rested and didn't need any more sleep. After fifteen minutes or so, he exited the tent again. There was still no sign of Garcia.

Concerned, he woke up Aubriot.

They searched everywhere, all the tents, even the supply ones, the shuttle, the forest fringes, and up and down the beach, calling the man's name. Soon, everyone joined in the search. It was hours before Kes spotted the footprints of bare feet in the few meters of untrammeled wet sand leading down to the water's edge. The sand's dark color made them hard to see.

The footprints led into the ocean, but none could be found emerging from it.

18

The Fila map showed an island a couple of kilometers off shore. They hadn't spotted it due to its being so low-lying and nearly the same color as the ocean. Aubriot felt confident he could swim out to it but, considering the incident on the river, he wasn't willing to risk it. Plus, he needed the scientists to go too. He didn't have a clue what an edible plant might look like and he didn't want to know. Plants were boring, when they weren't trying to kill you. Though, he had to concede, they were necessary for survival.

Zapata said, "I'm willing to give it a try. It won't hurt to take a look."

The map was, predictably, free of any information relating to the ground above the waterline and the island was small. If there was a beach, it was likely to be narrow, perhaps too narrow to land the shuttle.

"Let's do it," said Aubriot.

Kes seemed hesitant but he didn't say anything. Aubriot would have overridden any objection anyway. The expedition needed a strong leader and sense of purpose more than ever now. That idiot walking into the ocean and offing himself had thrown even more of a downer over everything. Some people were so selfish.

The others standing around the interface in the supply tent hadn't moved.

"Come on," he said, snapping his fingers. "Wakey wakey. Let's go."

Like mannequins slowly coming to life, his companions moved away.

"Get your equipment," Kes said to them tonelessly. "We'll meet at the shuttle in ten minutes."

As he was about to leave the tent, Aubriot grabbed his shoulder. "Can I have a word?"

They waited until the tent was empty.

"You need to smile more," Aubriot told him.

"I need to..." Kes narrowed his eyes. "We've lost five people, one of whom killed himself, and you're telling me I need to *smile*?"

"Yeah, because, for better or worse, you're a de facto leader on this expedition too. The rest of them aren't only taking their cue from me, they're taking it from you. And if you go around like your mum's died, it affects everyone. So get your nose out of your navel and put on a brave face. Get it?"

Kes slowly nodded. "You're right. It's hard though. When I think about what I've brought Miki and Nina into, it's difficult to be upbeat."

"Your kids are probably better off on the *Sirocco* than on Concordia right now."

"Maybe. I feel bad about Garcia too. Cherry warned me about him. If I'd woken up when he left the tent, or if I hadn't brought him along in the first place, he would still be alive."

"Bah, he would have walked out an airlock instead. There's no stopping some people. We've got a job to do, so let's do it, all right?"

"Okay." Kes inhaled deeply before stepping out into the sunshine.

ZAPATA LANDED on a tiny strip of beach not much wider than the shuttle. As his passengers disembarked, waves slapped against the landing pads nearest the ocean.

"I'm taking her back to the mainland," he comm'd Aubriot.

"You don't want to wait?"

"I'm not taking any chances. I know there are no moons and supposedly no tides, but this bird is our only way of getting back to the ship. She'll be safer at the original landing site."

"Fair enough," Aubriot replied. "I'll comm you when we want to be picked up."

"Copy. If we lose contact I'll be back at sunset. Tell everyone to move away from the shuttle, at least thirty meters. I'll wait for your all clear."

Aubriot chivied the others, telling them to hurry up with collecting their equipment from the hold. When everyone was at a safe distance, he comm'd Zapata. The little party watched as the shuttle engines fired and the vessel flew the short distance to the farther shore.

"Right," Aubriot said when the small flare from the shuttle's engine vanished. "Time to start work. This island's pretty small. I reckon we should split into pairs and search half each. We can cover it all in one day."

"Agreed," said Kes. "I'll take Marcus with me, and Goslin, you go with Aubriot."

Goslin didn't look too pleased with the proposal but if that was the case she was too polite to say anything about it. Splitting up the scientists made sense so Aubriot also didn't voice any objection. Most of the ear comms had been lost in yesterday's disaster. They were down to two. Kes wore one and Aubriot had the other.

"We'll take this side," he said, pointing left. "Meet you back here when we're done. Ah, wait a minute." He'd spotted a largish rock near the water's edge. He dragged it up to the center of the beach. "This marks our starting spot. You ready?" he asked Goslin.

When she nodded, he said to Kes and Marcus, "See you later, you two."

"Good luck," Kes replied, turning away.

Goslin was medium height and black-haired like most of the Gens. Not bad-looking in his estimation. She hadn't said much so far. Like most of the cerebral type, she was quiet. That didn't matter. Most people didn't have anything interesting to say.

That was one good thing about Kes. If he was in the mood, he could hold a conversation. And his red hair made him easy to spot. If that ginger mop hadn't been so visible disappearing under the river water, they might be six people down, not five.

Goslin had wandered closer to the shallow waves.

"Hey!" he called out. "Maybe you shouldn't go there. Remember what happened at the river?"

She threw him an annoyed glance. "As if I could forget! I want to look for seaweed. There isn't any near the campsite but there might be some here."

"What's the point?" he asked her retreating back. "Who wants to eat seaweed?"

Her shoulders lifted and sank and turned fully to face him. "All the seaweed on Concordia is edible, and it's highly nutritious. It's just that people aren't used to eating it. It would also be easy to grow on the ship. Now if I can *please* do my work? You stick to fighting off ravening beasts and whatever else it is you're good for."

"All right, don't get your..." He was about to say *knickers in a twist,* but Cherry had told him off too many times for using Earth English.

"Don't get my what?" Goslin asked irritably.

"Never mind." He folded his arms. "I'll keep an eye out for ravening beasts."

"Aubriot," Kes comm'd, "where are you?"

"What do you mean, where am I? I'm on the flipping island, the same as you. Do you want latitude and longitude?"

"Get over here. Hurry, please."

Shit.

He checked Kes and Marcus's position on his small interface. Goslin was in among a clump of trees, scraping at something growing on their trunks. "We're leaving," he called out. "Gotta help the other two. They're in some kind of trouble."

It took twenty-five minutes to reach Kes. They'd decided to return to the beach and run around the coastline rather than attempt to take a direct route across land. There was no telling what might stand in their way in the island's interior. Some areas had proven impenetrable.

In all the time it took, Kes never answered his comm again.

Aubriot hoped it had only fallen out.

He spotted Kes's back first. For some reason, he was coated in black dirt, head to toe, though his signature hair color was still visible. He was squatting down and his back was curved as he appeared to be pulling at something.

He was.

Aubriot sprinted to reach him.

Kes was pulling on a vine, in the same way Aubriot had hauled the man from the river yesterday. Only Marcus wasn't in water, he was up to his shoulders in mud.

"Can't...get...him..." Kes gasped.

His ear comm *had* popped out. The small, white device lay on the ground next to him. Kes looked to be at the end of his strength. He must have been pulling on the vine the entire time it had taken them to reach him.

Aubriot took it, and Kes collapsed onto his side. "Don't move," he shouted to Marcus. "Don't struggle. It'll only suck you in more."

"We already figured that out," Marcus replied dryly.

"Goslin?" Aubriot looked behind him. He'd gone ahead of the scientist in his rush to get to Kes. She had just caught up. "Come and grab this vine. Give me a hand."

They pulled.

Together, they slowly managed to reverse what must have been Marcus's gradual descent into the quicksand. Following Aubriot's instructions, he went limp except for his grasp on the vine, and Aubriot and Goslin's combined strength gradually eased him out to his waist. When Kes had recovered, he joined them. Eventually, when everyone was near exhaustion, Marcus crawled from the mire and collapsed on solid ground.

"See?" Aubriot said to Kes as he rubbed his tired arms. "It isn't all bad. Just need to be on our toes."

"You're right," he agreed. "In fact, it's better than you think." He pulled a plastic bag from his pocket. A piece of white root about the size of a finger lay inside. "I'd asked Marcus to dig up a plant similar to the one I took this from. That was how he got into trouble. This tuber passed all the toxicity screens. I think I may have found one of our future crops."

19

FIVE YEARS AFTER LEAVING CONCORDIA

The Ark was a restful place to go when things got heated on the ship, and things had been more and more heated lately. Wilder liked to sit in one of the growing rooms, where brilliant lights overhung the lush beds, lighting the rest of the space in a soft glow. The atmosphere was warm, humid, and enriched with additional oxygen to meet the needs of the plants. Most importantly, the growing rooms were quiet.

In the *Sirocco*, it was hard to escape other people and their noise. There was always someone shouting down a passageway, playing their music too loud, or arguing with a neighbor. The conditions reminded her of Sidhe and its surfeit of screaming babies as the colony struggled to rebuild its numbers. Only then she'd been able to escape by building her own hamlet among the trees and inviting her friends to live with her.

It seemed like another life. She'd spent so much time aboard the ship, sometimes it was hard to remember living another way. More than one-fifth of her years had been spent traveling in space and yet she was only one-quarter into the journey to Earth. She would be in her late thirties when they arrived, assuming they arrived at all.

The door opened.

"I thought I would find you here," Kes said.

If it had been anyone else, with the possible exception of Cherry, she would have been annoyed at being disturbed, but her dejection lifted a little at his appearance.

"Is it okay if I come in?" he asked.

"Sure."

"Is everything okay? I heard about the argument."

She sniffed. "Puddle died this morning."

"I'm so sorry. I didn't know."

"It's okay. He was lonely after Piddle died. Only lasted a few weeks."

Kes sat next to her but didn't say anything. The sad but comfortable silence stretched out.

"I like to come here too sometimes," he eventually said, "to hide from Miki and Nina."

She chuckled. "You hide from your kids? I thought it was supposed to be the other way around."

"As you know, they're inquisitive and lively. There are only so many questions I can answer and only so much squealing and giggling a man can tolerate." He sighed. "Izzy would have had more patience, or she would have known how to quieten them down."

"Don't feel bad. You're a great parent."

"Thanks. I don't think I am, but thanks anyway."

It suddenly struck her: this was why he was here. He was parenting *her* too, as he had all her life, right from the time he'd brought her the sluglimpet repellent spray for her settlement. Or maybe he wasn't being a parent exactly, more like a big brother.

"I had to get away," she blurted.

"I know, and, for what its worth, I think you did the right thing."

The argument with Niall had been getting out of hand. She couldn't even remember what it had been about. Their yelling must have been heard all over the ship. Everyone was in everyone's business as always. It was suffocating. She'd had to get away. "You mean walking out of there?"

"Sometimes, arguments aren't about what they seem to be about, and they can't be resolved by settling the issue at hand. Sometimes, it's better if both parties take time to cool down and think about what's really bothering them."

"That's the problem. Nothing *is* bothering me, except sadness about Puddle, and the usual anxiety about this position we're in. It's Niall. He's the problem. He's hated me for years, from even before we set out. I don't know why. We used to be friends. He was one of the team working on the a-grav machine."

"He *hates* you?"

"From what I can tell, yes." Her vision became blurry and she struggled to keep her voice steady. "He's been cold toward me for years. Then, after we left, for the first few months he would verbally attack me, blaming me for the jump drive failure. Then after that he took to ignoring me, like I didn't exist to him. Lately, he's started up with the verbal attacks again."

"I've noticed."

"You have?" It felt good to know it wasn't her imagination. "Could I be doing something to annoy him?"

Kes smiled. "You aren't annoying. It isn't that."

"Is he... Is he losing it, do you think?"

Since the expedition that had succeeded in discovering seven plants they could grow to survive, two mission members had nevertheless given up hope. They had spaced themselves, one in a dramatic fashion involving an armed fight at the airlock, the other quietly when no one was looking. Their deaths made three suicides so far, including Garcia's. If Niall was about to give up too, it would devastate the already fragile ship's morale, and break her heart. Though sometimes he seemed to hate her, she couldn't help feeling close to him after their years of working together.

Kes replied, "If, as you say, this has been going on since before we left Concordia, his feelings are only tangentially related to our circumstances. I would say it's something to do with his relationship with you."

"We don't have a relationship, unless you would call constant arguing a relationship."

"It can be, yes."

"I try to avoid him as much as I can, but it's hard."

Kes was silent, looking down as he seemed to think over her problem.

She turned her attention to the rows of plants in their beds. *How much easier life would be if all you had to do was grow.*

"You know," Kes said, "when Izzy left me, it wasn't because she didn't love me. It was because she couldn't stand to be around me anymore. She couldn't take the constant disappointment and frustration my behavior caused."

"I'm sorr—"

"It was a long time ago," he said dismissively, though his expression told another tale. "My point is, she *could* get away. She went to stay with one of her sisters, the one who had always disliked me. Here on the ship, there's no real getting away from anyone. We're forced to live cheek by jowl whether we like it or not."

"Isn't it horrible?" She would have to return to the *Sirocco* to sleep, and then she would see Niall at meal times or pass him in the passageways. "But I don't understand. You and Isobel were married. Niall and I only know each other because we're colleagues."

"I remember him from the time of the plague. He'd taken

charge of a group of vulnerable people and kept them safe until the vaccination reached them. He was and is an intelligent and caring young man. I find that hard to square with his attitude to you."

"Me too." She wondered what his point was.

"What happened to him when the biocide hit?"

"Uh..." She frowned as she thought back. "His home was destroyed in the Oceanside attack and a biocide capsule landed nearby. He and his mother ran from it, but he ran faster. It caught up to his mom and she died. He said he looked back and she was gone. It must have been terrible."

"What about his father?"

"I can't remember exactly. I don't think he knew him."

Another silence commenced. She relaxed into it. There didn't seem to be any explanation for Niall's baffling dislike of her, but it felt good to talk to someone with a sympathetic ear.

"Wilder," Kes said, "is it possible your friend has deeper feelings for you than you think?"

"Deep feelings of hatred, you mean?" she asked sarcastically.

"No, I don't mean that. You know what I mean."

"You think he actually *likes* me, and that's why he's so mean to me?"

"Listen. Imagine you lost the closest person in the world to you when you were just a child, that you saw her die an awful death. How would you feel about being close to someone else in a similarly dangerous situation? Imagine how scared you would be of having that person taken from you. And you have absolutely no control over what happens. You can't help how you feel, and you can't get away from the person. You have to see them day after day, feeling how you feel, knowing they could be torn from you any minute."

"But isn't that how it is with you and your kids?" she asked quietly. "Yet you aren't nasty to them."

His face tightened in pain. "We're talking about you, remember? Anyway, it's different for me. I'm older and, dare I say, somewhat wiser than Niall. I've learned to cherish and be grateful for every moment I have with the people I love."

She recalled something Niall had said to her once when she'd been babysitting Miki and Nina. He'd cruelly pointed out that having her own children was now off the table. Had that been because he'd been mourning the life they could have had if disaster hadn't struck?

Kes's explanation of his behavior seemed far-fetched, but it was *an* explanation and Kes was a man too, so maybe he would know.

She hugged him.

"This is nice," he said, hugging her back, "though I'm not sure what I've done to deserve it."

20

Spending time on the planet surface was mandatory for all mission members for mental health purposes. Cherry would have done it anyway, as would, she guessed, absolutely everyone else on the *Sirocco*. She hadn't set foot on soil in years, not since visiting the world where Kes and the other scientist, Goslin, had discovered the crop plants. That had been a hot, high-g place. The *Sirocco*'s scanners told them this planet was cooler and its gravity was also closer to Concordia's. As well as hopefully improving their mental health status, they would also take the opportunity to boost their vitamin D levels, supplementing the mandated sessions under a UVB lamp. Kes had been the instigator of that requirement. To avoid being cold when they stripped off and gave their skins a chance to harness the sunlight, the shuttle was to drop them near the equator.

"Got your bikini?" Aubriot asked, lifting his eyebrows suggestively in the neighboring shuttle seat.

She rolled her eyes. "You know I don't have a bikini. Why would I have packed a bikini for a mission to Earth?"

"I know. I just like thinking about it." He grinned.

"What are you? Fifteen?"

"I'm young at heart, that's all."

He was young in body too. Aubriot hadn't aged in all the time she'd known him, whereas she was becoming painfully conscious of her fine wrinkles and gray hairs. Kes was aging too, and Wilder was now a woman in her early twenties. Yet they weren't even halfway to Earth.

"What are we going to do when I'm an old woman and you're still in your prime?" she asked.

His playful expression faded and he looked into the middle distance. "Hadn't really thought about it." His tone implied the opposite. He clearly had thought about it. A lot.

She winced. She hadn't guessed he was already one step ahead of her. But of course he was. That was Aubriot all over— calculating, planning, thinking about how the future looked *for him.*

"Has anyone noticed, do you think?" she asked quietly, diverting the subject from their relationship.

"I've had a few funny looks from time to time," he replied, grimacing.

"It's going to come out eventually. People aren't stupid, especially not the people on this trip. Maybe you should just tell them and get it out in the open."

"Make an announcement? *By the way, everyone. I could be immortal. In other news...*" He shook his head. "I'd be lynched."

"Lynched? What does that mean?"

He tugged at an imaginary rope around his neck.

"You think you'd be murdered?! Why would anyone want to kill you?"

"Think about it. You said yourself you're worried about growing old before we reach Earth. How do you think people are going to feel when they realize I won't? I'm not exactly Mr Popular already. That's not my style. They would hate me even more."

She tutted. "They don't hate you."

Aubriot wasn't far wrong when he said he wasn't popular, but would the rest of the mission members really turn on him?

"You don't feel it, do you?" he asked.

"Feel what?"

"The tension. The pressure everyone's been under ever since we knew we wouldn't die of starvation. It's been building for years. All it needs is a trigger to set it off. Something like hearing one person has it better than them. People hate a tall poppy. They'll cut me down."

"You're being paranoid."

"I hope so."

She kissed his cheek. "Don't worry. If they come for you, I'll protect you."

He put an arm around her. "I know you will, Bandit."

She rested her head on his shoulder. "Why do you call me that?"

"Too hard to explain, and you don't like Earth English. Do you know what Cherry means?"

"Isn't it just a name?"

"It's a fruit. Small, sweet, and beautiful."

A CRYSTALLINE SURFACE spread out as far as the eye could see, white and glinting in the sunlight. Zapata had set them down on a dried-up salt lake bed. They unloaded the equipment and then the shuttle left. The pilot's next task was to collect fresh water ice from a colder region of the planet.

They began to set up tents for shade and to store the supplies for their stay. The plan was to expose themselves to the sunlight for short periods only at first, to avoid burning. Even the darkest-skinned Concordian was pasty after the years aboard ship, and pale-skinned Kes wouldn't be able to tolerate more than a few minutes' exposure at a time.

"It would have been nice to have a break like this on our trip to the Galactic Assembly," he commented to Cherry as they worked.

"Stars, yes," she replied, recalling the months of utter boredom. "But then it would have taken us even longer to get home." *And I would have missed Ethan's last moments.*

She drove a peg into the crusty soil and straightened up. Miki and Nina were playing a chasing game that involved a lot of screaming. She marveled at their adaptability. Neither of them had been off the starship for five years, yet here they were acting like playing outside in the fresh air was the most natural thing in the world.

It was so good to feel the sun on her back again, even if it wasn't Concordia's sun. "Kes, I've never asked you—which do you miss most, Concordia or Earth?"

"Ah, that's a hard one. Hm." He frowned. "I'm afraid I would have to say Earth. I grew up there, you see. It's hard to let go of the place you grew up."

"Well, I grew up on the *Nova*. I don't get homesick for her."

"I suppose a starship doesn't inspire as much of an attachment as a landscape. We tried our best to make her a nice place to live, and to prepare you all for the reality of living on a planet surface. But, when I think about it, we were clueless. It's a miracle you survived and established a successful colony."

Cherry still sometimes had to remind herself Kes was a Woken, one of the people who had worked on the project, the reason behind her existence. So was Aubriot, but he had always seemed different from everyone, neither a Woken nor a Gen.

"You did your best," she said. "Are you ready for some sunbathing?"

"Actually, I'm going to sit in the shade here. The reflected light will be enough for my skin."

"Just the reflected light? You must be a vit D-generating machine."

He smiled. "One of my many talents."

That was the last of the tents set up. She joined Aubriot, who was already lying in the sun wearing nothing but shorts. The rest of the group was doing the same. She began to strip. "What do I do with this?" she asked, taking out her sidearm.

"I put mine with my clothes," he replied. "I mean, what are the chances of something attacking us here?" He gestured at the surrounding emptiness.

The place did appear entirely devoid of life. Dragan had found the old, dried-up skull of a three-eyed animal when they'd first arrived, but there were no tracks or other signs of habitation or activity.

Following Aubriot's lead, she put the gun on her piled garments after stripping down to her shortest shorts and a halter top. She lay down on her front and pulled her hair to one side to expose her back.

"Cook yourself fifteen minutes on one side," said Aubriot. "Then turn over and cook the other side. That's enough for today, according to the doc."

"Only half an hour?" she asked, basking in the warm rays. "I could get used to this."

"Gotta build up tolerance, and we're collecting salt today too, don't forget. That'll give us more exposure."

She *had* forgotten. While they were on the surface, she and Aubriot were tasked with replenishing the ship's supply of sodium chloride. They had to dig up quantities of the salty soil, rinse water through it, collect and filter the water, and then leave it to evaporate.

"Ugh," she said. "Never a day of rest."

Aubriot softly chuckled. Their days aboard the *Sirocco* were mostly filled with nothing but rest.

Miki and Nina, in their sundresses, had finally given up

chasing each other and were building a den out of odds and ends they'd scrounged from the equipment stores. Cherry's heart twinged a little as she watched them. She'd never thought of herself as a mother. Yet sometimes, such as when she watched Kes braiding their hair, she could see the appeal. Not that it would have been a possibility with Aubriot anyway.

She sighed and turned onto her back. Her feelings were undoubtedly an effect of the long years spent in unstimulating, claustrophobic conditions. The two little girls had become a focus for everyone, not just her. They were doted on, though it hadn't seemed to make them spoiled.

The strains of an argument drifted from the nearest tent, the one she and Kes had put up.

She lifted her head to peer over Aubriot's torso. Kes was sitting in a chair under the tent's awning, alone. He wasn't the source of the argument. He'd turned and was gazing into the interior through the open tent flap.

Aubriot sat up, blocking her view.

The voices grew louder.

She sat up too and leaned forward to look around him.

"I knew it!" a man shouted. "You bitch! I knew you'd been screwing someone else."

Aubriot met her gaze. Her eyes widened.

Miki and Nina had stopped what they were doing and were looking at the tent.

Kes rose to his feet and moved to the tent entrance.

"It isn't how it looks," came a woman's voice. "Let me explain. Oh!"

The sound of a hard slap accompanied the exclamation.

"Hey!" Kes yelled, running inside

Cherry stood up. "Girls," she said to Miki and Nina "come with me."

Their gazes flicked to her and back to the tent.

"And you," the man continued, "you're as bad as her! You knew she was with me."

There was the sound of a scuffle. Kes ran into the tent.

"Come on," Cherry repeated, but the children were transfixed. "Girls! Go in your house!" They finally listened and crawled into their flimsy construction. Cherry parked herself in front of it. "Don't come out until I say so."

"I'd better sort this out," said Aubriot.

But before he could move closer, a woman was pushed out, stumbling into the light. She was clutching her face. It was Maddox, one of the soil specialists.

"No!" Kes hollered. "Stop!"

A man emerged, followed by another who was wrestling with Kes. The second man was armed and trying to aim at Maddox. The sun-bathers began to get up and move away.

"Cut it out!" yelled Aubriot, dodging from the line of fire.

A pulse round hissed out.

Maddox screamed, but the shot had missed.

Kes got the armed man on the ground and they tussled. "NO!" There was a second hiss.

"Shit! *Shit.*"

He rolled back on his heels. The man he'd been fighting with lay motionless, smoke drifting up from his head.

21

All was still, the only sound stunned silence, every person frozen. The entire event had taken only moments. From the beginning of the argument until the man's suicide, only a handful of seconds had passed.

Then the spell broke. Maddox ran to the dead man's side and collapsed, sobbing, onto his chest.

"I'm sorry," she cried out. "I didn't mean for this to happen. I'm sorry. I'm so sorry."

The onlookers regarded the scene uncomfortably.

Maddox lifted her head and said to Kes, "I didn't know he would... I really didn't mean..."

Kes ran a hand through his hair, his features stricken with sadness and horror.

Cherry was also at a total loss as to what to say or do. The only saving grace in the situation was Nina and Miki hadn't witnessed the murder. She peeked into their den. "Are you okay playing in here for a little while? We're having some problems and Daddy's busy."

"Sure, Auntie Cherry," Miki replied.

"Good girls. I'll sit out here."

"Is there something we can cover the body with?" Aubriot asked Kes. "Can't have everyone looking at it."

He nodded and disappeared into the tent.

Aubriot's words seemed to ease the tension. People began to move and talk.

"This is your fault," someone muttered, addressing the man who had run out of the tent, Clarkson, one of the two doctors on the mission.

Clarkson looked at his feet.

Maddox got to her knees, her face a red and shiny mess of tears and mucus. She croaked, "We were only having a fling. Just a bit of fun. Brian was never supposed to find out. If he hadn't caught us kissing... Oh, stars!" She thrust her face in her hands and began sobbing again. "What have I done?"

Cherry expected Clarkson to comfort her but he didn't. Maybe he feared the judgment of the crowd.

Kes reappeared with a couple of towels and Aubriot helped him cover up the body.

Another suicide. At this rate, would anyone make it to Earth or would the *Sirocco* arrive at her destination empty?

Clarkson finally responded, growling through his teeth, "It isn't my fault. It's that damned engineer, Wilder. She's the one who built the jump drive. *She's* the one who got us in this mess."

"That's right," said Maddox, stepping out from under the awning and wiping her eyes. "We're all bored out of our minds. I was just looking for a bit of excitement. Something different to do. Something to look forward to. Can anyone really blame us for trying to have some fun?"

"Hold on," said Cherry. "You're seriously blaming Wilder for your affair?"

"She's right though," someone said. "If it wasn't for those stupid engineers, none of us would be here. The four people who've killed themselves would still be alive. Those people who drowned, they would be alive too. Wilder's the head of the team. The buck has to stop somewhere."

Dragan studied the skull he'd picked up. Did the speaker even know he was here?

Cherry retorted, "A lot of things would be different if the jump drive hadn't failed. That doesn't make any of this Wilder's fault." She looked to Kes and Aubriot for support, but they'd apparently decided to move the body out of sight. She couldn't see either of them and the body was gone.

Wilder and Niall weren't here to defend themselves. They were in the group who would be coming to the surface next week.

"Who *is* to blame, then?" asked Clarkson angrily.

"No one's to blame," Cherry retorted. "It was an accident. They happen."

"Especially around incompetent people," Maddox spat.

What she and Clarkson were doing was clear. Everyone present was witness to the fact that her infidelity had driven her partner to suicide. The conditions they were all living under had contributed to the act, no doubt, but the two were at high risk of being censured and ostracized. Trapped aboard a star-ship for many years to come, their lives could become even more miserable than they already were. They were trying to shift the focus away from them and onto someone else. Wilder was an easy scapegoat.

"Wilder is not incompetent," said Cherry, "and neither are the other engineers. She's the smartest person you'll ever meet. They were under time pressure. You know that. You know we had to try to get the seeding material from Earth as fast as we could."

"And look how that turned out," Clarkson responded. "It isn't only *us* down the drain, it's the entire colony. Is anyone even still alive back home? Or have they all starved to death, waiting and wondering what happened to us?"

"Don't bring Concordia into it!" Cherry exclaimed. "This is unbelievable. A man has killed himself because *you* couldn't keep it in your pants!"

"What's going on?" Aubriot was back. "What's all the shouting about? A man's dead for stars' sake. Have some fucking respect."

Chagrined quiet fell. Maddox went to Clarkson's side but he turned away from her. He was smart. The two couldn't be seen together now or everyone would associate them with her partner's tragic death. Her shoulders slumped and she dropped listlessly to the ground, softly weeping.

"Kes is making a report for the ship's log," Aubriot said to Cherry. "Then we'll bury the body. Best to get it over with quickly."

"Can I talk to you?" She took his arm and led him out of earshot of the others before filling him in on the guilty couple's tactical response.

"Damn," he said. "Bad news for Wilder."

"I know. I thought we'd seen the last of the recriminations and complaints against the engineering team. And why are they singling her out? She wasn't the only one involved in building the jump drive."

"No, but it was her invention. And she's young, female, and not good at sticking up for herself. She's vulnerable, someone to pick on. It's like I said on the shuttle, there's a lot of fear, anger, and resentment simmering under the surface. What's happened today has turned up the heat."

22

The first sign that something was wrong was the water shutting off as Wilder was brushing her teeth. She pressed the faucet again to rinse her mouth but nothing came out. They'd run out of toothpaste years ago, so it was no big deal in that sense—she just spat into the washbasin regardless—but in every other sense the sputtering pipe was worrying.

She comm'd Dragan.

"Your water's out too?" was the first thing he said.

"Uh huh. Has someone else contacted you about it?"

Was the problem localized or shipwide?

"Not yet. I wanted a drink, but, nothing."

"Okay, can you tell Niall? I'll see if I can find out what's wrong."

It was better to leave informing Niall to Dragan. Maybe Kes was right that his animosity came from a deep-seated affection for her, but it was animosity, nonetheless.

She quickly pulled on a shirt and pants and opened her cabin's interface, from which she could access all the ship's data. If they had a blockage or a leak, internal sensors should have picked it up and activated an alert.

Nothing showed up.

Ugh.

Something was wrong. There was no doubt about it. The fact that the ship wasn't telling them the problem meant the relevant sensors were malfunctioning too. She, Dragan, Niall, and whoever else they could rope in would have to search for the leak or blockage manually, going over the plumbing system inch by inch.

She wrinkled her nose, hoping the issue was in the clean, not dirty, water pipes. People thought building starships was exciting and glamorous. But in fact, in many ways you were just constructing a giant house that happened to be flying through space. The passengers had the same bodily needs and functions as they had everywhere else. They pooped, peed, shed skin, and sweated just the same, and it was the engineers' job to deal with it all.

Maintaining the *Sirocco* was becoming more and more challenging over the years. The ship was aging. Her structure and systems were wearing out. Every month, it seemed, they had to dip into the small stock of spare parts. One day, the stock would be used up, and then what would they do? There were no handy suppliers to contact for replenishment. Neither would there be any on Earth.

They had begun to resort to greater levels of ingenuity to fix things. Nothing was ever thrown away. Where they could repurpose materials they did, and they avoided replacing a worn-out or broken part whenever they could, choosing rather to mend it or rejig the system to function without it. In the beginning, she'd relished the challenge. It broke the endless days of monotony. Now, every time she was reminded that the *Sirocco*'s working life was playing out, it only added to her stress level.

The complaints about the lack of water began to come in. First, the cook comm'd her, saying breakfast wouldn't arrive until the water in the galley did. Next came a flurry of personal messages, asking why the bathrooms weren't working.

Her comm chirruped again. "I know, I know!" she exclaimed in answer. "We're doing everything we can. Please be patient."

"Uh, I guess you already know about the problem with the water," said Cherry.

She closed her eyes. "Yes, sorry. I didn't mean to snap. You're about the twentieth person to tell me."

"Okay, as long as you know. I guess I should just mop it up as best I can until you get here."

"Huh? You have a leak? Why didn't you say?"

"I just did. I said—"

"Never mind. Where are you?"

"The Ark. Deck Two. I wanted to check the water potatoes."

"I'm on my way." She rushed out of her cabin. "What's it like? How bad is it?"

"Bad. I wish I was taller. I'm in danger of being...*Whoa!*"

The comm cut out. Wilder tried to raise Cherry several times but she didn't answer.

After telling Dragan and Niall where to meet her, she sped toward the Ark.

She got there first.

The lowest deck was awash and water was flooding from the elevator shaft.

"Holy shit!"

The ceiling lights were shining down on the mess.

Why was the power still on?

She ran back into the bridging passageway, gingerly stepping on the dry deck between tongues of water. Where had they put the isolator?

Niall and Dragan appeared at the farther end of the bridge.

"Don't come down here," she called out. "It isn't safe."

Where was it?

Thin lines marked the edges of a square panel shoulder height in the bulkhead. She slammed it with a fist, popping it open. Inside was a lever. As she pulled it down, the lights shining from the Ark side of the passage went dark.

"Cherry? Cherry?" she comm'd desperately. "Are you okay?"

Niall approached. "Is it that bad you had to cut off the entire section? Without heat, the plants will begin to die."

"Yes, it's that bad," she hissed. "Look!" She pointed at the water snaking out of the Ark.

Niall's eyebrows popped up. "Holy shit."

"That's what *I* said. Cherry? Are you there? Can you hear me?"

No answer came.

She bit her lip as a lump swelled in her throat.

"Cherry's in there?" Niall asked.

"Are you competing in the stupid question of the day contest?!"

Dragan arrived. "It must be the supply to the flooded beds."

"Yes," said Wilder. "Cherry said she was in the water potatoes room."

Niall commented, "I said we should have put them on Deck One."

"Stars," Wilder exclaimed, "if you don't have anything useful to say, can you please shut up? I need to think."

Meanwhile, Dragan was running back into the main ship.

"Where are you going?" she called.

"To get flashlights."

THEY SHUT off the water supply to the Ark and then climbed the service shaft to Deck Two. The water was ankle-deep. As they waded through it, ripples and splashes hit the walls, their noise echoing around the metal-walled chambers. The air was moist and rich with the scent of wet soil.

"Which way is the water potatoes section?" Dragan asked.

"I can't remember," Wilder replied, annoyed. The question was reasonable, but she'd been fielding numerous complaints and questions from personnel on the *Sirocco*, demanding to know when the water supply would be reinstated. She'd taken her comm device out of her ear, turned it off, and put it in her pocket. Dragan had comm'd Captain Vessey, to let her know the situation was being investigated and things would return to normal soon.

"You're sure that's where Cherry said she was?" Niall asked.

She rolled her eyes and didn't reply.

"I'll start looking for the leak," said Dragan. He sloshed away.

Wilder and Niall continued in silence. The light from their flashlights danced on the water, sending shimmering reflections over the bulkheads and overhead.

Though her duties didn't include any agricultural tasks, she came to the Ark often. It had become a sanctuary to her, an escape. She knew the place well. Yet the darkness was disorienting. Everything looked different. Which way were the flooded beds?

"I think..." She turned in a circle, running her flashlight's beam over the surfaces. The conversion of the Ark to growing beds had involved removing many of the inner walls, opening out the rooms. The result was a mixture of large sections for main crops and smaller nooks for seed germination and propagation of cuttings.

"I think the water potatoes area is over there." She moved forward. "Cherry! Cherry! Can you hear me?"

Her friend hadn't responded to a single comm since she'd

reported the leak. There were so many electrics around. Lights, heating, sensors. Wilder's grip on her flashlight tightened.

"We should never have run the two supplies together," said Niall. "We should have kept the main ship's water entirely separate from the Ark's. If the bridge was ever severed, that would be it. We would lose every drop we have into space."

"If we get cut off from the Ark we'll have a helluva lot more to worry about than not having any water. Any more helpful comments? I mean, this is really helping us find Cherry."

A beat later, her light brushed the tops of water potato plants. In truth, the foliage was nothing like an actual potato plant's, but the white, starchy corms the plant produced vaguely resembled the vegetable when cut open. They would only grow when their roots were submerged in about half a meter of slowly circulating water.

The tank was empty, the leaves collapsed and soggy at the bottom.

"She has to be somewhere around here," Wilder said. She ran around the edge of the tank.

"Take it easy," Niall warned, "or you'll—"

She slipped and fell heavily, landing on her backside. Her pants were soaked through. But it didn't matter. As she'd fallen, the beam from her flashlight had skimmed something she recognized. "She's here! Cherry's here."

She crawled forward, shining the light in the right direction.

There was the familiar sight again: the soles of a pair of boots.

Cherry was on her back, motionless with her eyes closed.

23

———

An unfamiliar ceiling appeared in Cherry's vision. She moved to sit up, but a thousand hammers pounded in her head. She gave up and lay down.

"Ah, you're awake at last," said a voice.

She turned and squinted in the speaker's direction.

*Clarkson. **Doctor** Clarkson.*

She was in sick bay.

"Try not to move around too much," he said.

"Don't worry. I wasn't planning on it."

He approached, smiling. "Glad to see you still have a sense of humor. That's a good sign."

If she could have shrunk away from him, she would have. The man's presence evoked feelings of disgust. It wasn't that he'd been having an affair—she was in no position to criticize in that regard—but the way he'd turned the spotlight onto Wilder to save himself made her sick.

"You have a severe concussion," he went on. "Gave yourself a real good whack on the head when you slipped."

Ah, yes. Her memory of what had happened to land her in sick bay was returning. She'd gone to check on the water potatoes. They were nearly ready for harvesting. But then water had spurted from a bulkhead and begun to flood the deck. She'd comm'd Wilder, and...that was the last thing she remembered.

"How long until I'm better?" she asked.

"Two weeks, minimum, until your symptoms resolve, and you could be suffering from long term effects for months, I'm afraid. Like I said, your fall did a number on your brain. If it's any consolation, it could have been a lot worse. People have died in similar accidents."

"I have to lie here for two weeks?"

"I doubt you'll have a lot of choice. Watch my finger."

He held his forefinger over her face and moved it to the left and right. "Not bad. How's your vision? Any ringing in your ears?"

He *did* appear out of focus, and she realized she'd been hearing a high-pitched background noise ever since she'd woken up. She gave him her answers.

"You see?" he said. "It's going to take a while for your brain to recover. The best thing you can do to speed up healing is to take it easy, remain as still as you can, and rest."

"Okay, I get it. Could you tell Aubriot I'm awake?"

"Will do. Anything else you need?"

"What happened in the Ark? Did they find the leak?"

"It's fixed. They're recovering the lost water now. They'll filter and clean it and return it to the system."

That was a relief. She'd been worried they would have to return to the last planet they'd visited to restock with water. Not only would the trip delay them even more, it would remind everyone of the altercation and suicide, and perhaps of Clarkson's blame-casting.

It was better for morale to move on, literally and figuratively.

∽

"Hey." Aubriot leaned down and kissed her forehead. "Thank fuck you're all right. I was worried about you."

"How long was I out? I forgot to ask Clarkson."

"A couple of hours. Have you seen the lump on your head?"

She reached up and her fingers touched a large bump under a cold poultice. "I'm only just beginning to remember what happened. My foot caught on something floating in the water, maybe a lead or hose? I recall falling, but I couldn't save myself. The nearest thing I could grab was a growing tank on my left, and..." She lifted her left shoulder and small stump, all that remained of her arm.

"Ah well. You're okay now. That's all that matters."

Over the course of the day, Wilder visited her too, and Kes. But Clarkson only allowed each visitor to stay for ten minutes before asking them to leave and let her rest. She was secretly grateful. She couldn't concentrate on a conversation for much longer than that, and she kept dozing off.

The next day, however, she began to get bored. She hated inactivity. It was one of the reasons she enjoyed farming. There was always something to do. Yet she didn't want to risk further injury to her brain so she followed doctor's orders, staying put for fifteen days. On the sixteen day, Clarkson finally discharged her with a list of dos and don'ts to aid her long-term recovery.

The doctor hadn't given her any notice she was nearly ready to leave. He waited until the day itself, perhaps not wanting to get her hopes up, so the news came as a pleasant surprise. She packed her small bag of belongings and stepped out into the passageway. She hadn't set eyes on anything outside sick bay in over two weeks. The experience was disorienting, as if she was seeing the ship for the first time. She was thrown back to the moment she'd boarded the *Sirocco* longer than five years ago.

Had so much time really passed?

Yet her life on Concordia seemed a distant memory. Arrival Day, the sluglimpets, the Scythian Attacks, the shuttle explosion, the Guardians, Ethan, Cariad, Garwin...the events of her past melded together in her mind.

Extreme dizziness and nausea were assaulting her. She reached for the bulkhead to steady herself, swallowing the saliva that had poured into her mouth. Should she return to sick bay? Clarkson would want to know about her symptoms.

No.

She'd lingered in that tedious place long enough. If she could just make it to her and Aubriot's cabin, she could rest. She would probably be fine if she lay down for half an hour. All she could do to recover was rest, the doctor had said. She could do that in her 'home' as well as she could anywhere else.

The cabin was a few minutes' walk away. She made her way slowly along the strangely unfamiliar passageways, taking care to stay near a bulkhead in case the dizziness hit again. She managed to reach the cabin without collapsing. Relieved, she put her hand on the security panel.

She'd made it.

The door slid open.

Aubriot was lying on his back in bed, naked, the sheets crumpled around his feet.

Maddox, also naked, sat astride him.

24

Maddox turned to face Cherry, her face a picture of surprise and embarrassment. Then her expression shifted to a smirk.

Aubriot grinned sheepishly. "Well, this is awkward."

Cherry took a step backward in shock.

The door slid closed.

She staggered away down the passageway, numb and confused, not sure where she was going.

She didn't know what to think. She'd always known about Aubriot's womanizing. There had been a time when he was at a low ebb that she'd wondered if he was planning on sleeping with every available woman in the colony.

But she'd thought those days were over. They'd never discussed it, but she'd thought they were exclusive, a couple.

She shook her head. She hadn't imagined it. They *were* partners. He knew that.

"Cherry!"

Footsteps sounded behind her.

"Cherry, stop. Wait a minute."

She couldn't get away from him. After her long bed-rest she was too weak, and the dizziness had returned.

His hand fell on her shoulder. He was barefoot and bare-chested, wearing only shorts.

"Leave me alone!"

"Come back to the cabin. Maddox has left. We can talk."

"I don't want to talk. Don't touch me."

She pulled his hand off her and continued down the passageway, leaning on the bulkhead to steady herself.

"Cherry, don't be stupid. You aren't well. Let me help you."

She ignored him. The shock was wearing off. Tears over-filled her eyes. She kept her head turned away from him so he wouldn't see them. She wouldn't allow him to see her weakness, how much she was hurting, what he'd done to her.

He kept pace with her. "Where are you going? Back to the sick bay? Is your concussion bad?"

She had no strength to answer him. It was all she could do not to drop to her knees and let her rage and sorrow over-whelm her.

"Where are you going?" he repeated. "I'll carry you. I don't mind if you don't want to be in our place for a while. You need time to think. I understand."

Something between a sob and gasp of outrage at his conde-scension escaped her lips. She halted momentarily. "Fuck off," she hissed. "*Fuck...off!*"

"All right, all right!" He backed away, hands raised. "What-ever you say."

But he didn't leave her alone. He stayed by her side until she reached the place she'd been unconsciously heading for: Kes's cabin.

She thumped the door with her fist. It would have made more sense to press the buzzer, but she badly needed to hit something.

"Why have you come here?" Aubriot demanded. "Why him?"

Kes's immediate look of concern when the door opened cut to her soul. It was the look Aubriot should have been wearing when he'd seen her a moment ago—concern, or happiness that she was finally discharged from sick bay. Not that abashed smile, like a little boy caught stealing cake. His expression would be burned into her memory forever.

"What's wrong?" Kes asked. "Are you okay?"

Her chest heaving with the effort to not cry, she could only look at him.

He asked Aubriot, "What's happening?"

"Nothing," he replied sullenly. "Cherry, come with me. This is stupid."

Kes seemed to guess something was off. "I'm pretty sure she doesn't want to go with you. That's right, isn't it?" he asked her.

She looked down and shook her head.

"Come inside," he said, moving out of her way.

"No," said Aubriot. "She needs to come with me." He reached for her shoulder again.

Kes stepped between them. "Cherry's made it clear she doesn't want to speak to you right now. Respect that and leave."

"She isn't in her right mind. She's had a shock, that's all."

"Hmpf. I think I know exactly what kind of shock you mean. In which case, she's *completely* in her right mind. Go away."

"I'm not going without her. I know what you'll do. You're going to turn her against me. Poison her mind."

"From what I've heard you've already done a fantastic job of that yourself. Now piss off."

Kes moved into his cabin, but Aubriot followed him.

"I said" Kes raised his tone "leave!"

He put his hands on the larger man's chest and pushed him into the passageway.

Aubriot swung for him. Kes swerved but not quite in time. Aubriot's fist grazed his jaw. Kes attempted to punch him back but his opponent brought up his forearm to block the blow. Aubriot hit him again, and this time his fist landed squarely on Kes's cheek, flooring him.

"Stop it!" Cherry screamed. "If you hit him one more time I will never, ever forgive you and I will never speak to you again!"

With a thunderous look, Aubriot unfolded his clenched hand and his arm dropped to his side. He stomped off without another word.

She helped Kes to his feet. "Are you hurt? He's such an asshole."

"I'm fine." A reddish-purple bruise was already forming on Kes's cheekbone and around his eye.

"Do you want to go to sick bay?"

"No, I'll just put some cold water on it. Not much of a knight in shining armor, am I? Falling at the first blow."

"Oh Kes, don't say that." She didn't know what a knight was but she knew what he meant.

She was glad to see Miki and Nina weren't home. She would have felt terrible if they'd witnessed the fight.

Kes sat on his bed as she wet a cloth with cold water.

"Thanks, I can do it," he said, taking the cloth from her. "You sit down too. You look in a worse state than me. Were you discharged today?"

She nodded. "About ten minutes ago. I didn't tell Aubriot, just went straight to our cabin, and I found him..." That awful knot of pain fastened around her chest and throat again and she couldn't go on.

Kes put his hand over hers. "You don't have to tell me. You know what things are like around here. It's impossible to keep a secret."

"So everyone knew except me? How long has he been seeing her? Do you know?"

"I'm afraid it's been going on at least a week."

Aubriot had visited her in sick bay every day ever since her accident. She wondered if he'd hooked up with Maddox before or afterward. Or was it both?

The emotions she'd been battening down rose up. She turned her head onto Kes's shoulder and wept. Huge, wracking sobs consumed her. Kes hugged her tight. She hadn't cried her so much since Ethan died, and that time it had been Aubriot who had comforted her. How ironic.

"I don't even know what I'm so torn up about," she said when her feelings were a little more under her control. "I've always known what he's like. This shouldn't have been a big surprise."

"You're making it sound like this is your fault. It isn't. His behavior is inexcusable. You don't deserve any of this."

"Don't I?" She sniffed and wiped her sleeve over her eyes.

"Of course not."

"I'm not so sure. I was in Maddox's shoes once. Maybe you don't know, but I was one of Garwin's affair partners, a long time ago. Is this payback, I wonder? It sure hurts to be on the receiving end."

"I didn't know that," said Kes. "But I do know it was rumored Twyla was aware of her husband's habits and didn't have a problem with them. And you were much younger then."

She smiled sadly. "I think I was only doing it to make Ethan jealous. Or I was screwed up."

Kes put the cloth against his face again. "Did you ever read the colony records from the decades we missed?"

"No, I didn't. Too depressing."

"There were a lot of problems with family relationships. Lots of divorces, poor parenting. The colonists really struggled with living in nuclear families and raising children. You remember Wilder building her forest settlement?"

"How could I forget?"

"The couple she was assigned to in Sidhe never gelled with her. From what I can tell, she was basically neglected."

"Maybe she was, but she didn't go around having affairs, if that's what you're getting at."

"No, but she couldn't get used to living with two 'parents' and the parents couldn't get used to being responsible for a child's upbringing. They didn't know what to do. The *Nova Fortuna* Project creators made a huge error in assuming that the Gens would simply pick up relationship skills that hadn't been practiced on the ship for six generations."

"That was dumb of them," said Cherry, "but it doesn't excuse Aubriot, does it? He wasn't a Gen."

"No, it doesn't. Aubriot's a prick. Always has been and always will be. And I say that as someone whose life he saved. I was thinking more in terms of what it did to you. So, please don't blame yourself for your choices in life. You were dealt a shitty hand."

She heaved a heavy sigh and rested her head on his shoulder again. "Thanks for saying that. I'm not sure I completely believe you, but it's a kind thing to say."

"Something else to bear in mind is what Aubriot told me once. In a rare moment of camaraderie, he said he, you, Wilder, and me were all screwed up. He and I in particular."

"Huh? Why?"

"We were the ones who went to the Galactic Assembly. We missed decades on Concordia, and he and I had also missed nearly two centuries while in cryosleep. He said we were out of our natural time and therefore fundamentally broken. Not in those words, of course."

"No." She gave a short laugh. "He said something like..." she put on his accent *"We're fucked in the head."*

Kes chuckled. "Actually, I think that's exactly what he said."

She closed her eyes.

Since she'd surprised Aubriot in bed with Maddox, while he'd followed her to Kes's cabin, and during the argument when he'd tried to get her to go back with him, he'd never once said he was sorry.

25

TEN YEARS AFTER LEAVING CONCORDIA

People would often say, as if sympathizing, it must be hard growing up on a starship, but it was the only life Miki knew. She vaguely remembered the place she'd been born, and she had even fainter memories of Mom—she wasn't sure how real they were, or if her mind had only created them from what Dad had told her—but nearly all her childhood had been spent on the *Sirocco*. The ship was her home and the people aboard were her family even though they weren't related to each other.

Her favorite people, after Dad, were Auntie Cherry and Auntie Wilder. That was what she used to call them. These days, she called them just Cherry and Wilder. It was more grown up. Nina had copied her, like she always did.

Miki sighed and rolled her eyes.

"What's wrong?" asked Nina.

They were in the middle of their homework assignment: an essay on how to manage a starship, what roles were involved and how it contributed to the successful running of the ship.

It was a tedious task. Miki suspected Dad hadn't thought very hard to come up with it. He seemed to be in a dreamworld a lot of the time.

"Nothing," she replied to her sister. Then she said, "This is boring. Let's write something else."

"No, we have to do this one."

"I bet if we wrote something different, Dad wouldn't even notice. He would think whatever we gave him was the work he'd set us. Especially if we back each other up."

"But that would be lying!"

"I suppose so, but it wouldn't be a serious lie. It would be fun, and if he finds out, we can pretend it was a joke. Yes! That's it. Let's do it as a joke."

Nina looked uncertain.

"Dad won't mind. You know he never gets mad."

"Hm, okay. What should we write about?"

Miki drummed her fingertips on the table. Her eyes widened. "I know. We could write about the Final Day Five."

"What?" Nina's mouth had opened wide in horror. "No! We're not supposed to know about them."

"That's what makes them the perfect thing to write about. We can show Dad he doesn't need to sneak around anymore trying to 'protect' us." She made quote marks in the air with her fingers and rolled her eyes. "It'll tell him we already know all about it and that we're grown up enough to handle the truth."

Nina folded her arms over her chest. "But then he would *definitely* know we haven't written the assignment he set."

"It doesn't matter. This is a much better idea."

When her sister didn't answer, Miki continued, "You do what you like. *I'm* writing about the Final Day Five."

Shaking her head, Nina said, "You're going to get in So Much Trouble."

"I don't care." Miki wasn't sure where her determination

was coming from, but it felt exciting and good to write about the rumored group and to show her father she wasn't a little girl anymore. She deleted what she'd written so far and started again.

What is the Final Day Five?

THE FINAL DAY *Five is a mysterious organization said to exist aboard the starship* Sirocco. *When exactly the group came into being, no one knows for sure, except its members, naturally. Some say it began soon after the disaster that took place among plant-hunters on an expedition to an alien planet, when four souls were lost to a fresh-water predatory organism.*

She paused and re-read her words, nodding approvingly to herself. For an opening paragraph it wasn't bad, clearly introducing the subject and hinting at the information to come. She particularly liked the fact she'd used 'souls' rather than 'lives'. Her choice was more interesting and poetic.

Another person died on the trip, a man named Bernard Garcia. One of the last things he said before his disappearance and presumed death by drowning, was he believed the Concordia colony was being punished by some sort of higher power. Garcia proposed the idea that everything bad that had happened to the colonists was a result of humanity's destruction of its home planet. He suggested there was something supernatural preventing humans from ever succeeding in re-creating a thriving civilization because it did not deserve the reward.

She frowned, unsure she was expressing exactly what she wanted to say. Reminding herself she had plenty of time for edits, she plowed on.

It is rumored that Garcia was not alone in thinking this way, and a small subset of the Sirocco's *personnel have continued to hold this opinion or belief. These people are known as the Final Day Five. Their title is self-explanatory...*

Miki mentally patted herself on the back at the neatness of 'self-explanatory', which captured so much meaning in one word.

... but for the purposes of this essay it is best to be clear: the group is supposed to consist of five people who think an apocalypse approaches. They've concluded that Concordia has followed Earth in its demise and our starship is the last remnant of human civilization. The Five say a cataclysm will strike before the Sirocco reaches her destination, destroying everyone aboard and putting out the flame of humanity forever.

Who are the people with this...

She couldn't think of exactly the right word. She switched from her assignment to a thesaurus and looked it up.

...nihilistic conviction?

That is the great mystery. On the one hand, no one has ever proclaimed the belief aloud (to the writer's knowledge). On the other hand, whispers about the group continue. The only conclusion to be drawn is that one or more members of the Five began the rumors themselves, hoping to draw others to their cause while at the same time not showing their hand.

What is the purpose of the Final Day Five?

The most chilling aspect of the existence of the group isn't what they think, but what they might do. Without hope for the future, why should they continue with tasks essential to the ship's mainte-nance and passenger survival? And if their predicted apocalypse doesn't arrive, will they create their own?

The implication of what she was writing hit her. She shivered. Maybe the change of assignment subject wasn't such a good idea after all.

"How are you getting on?" Nina asked, peering at her interface. Her eyes moved from side to side as she scanned the text. She looked at her sister. "Are you sure—"

The cabin door opened.

"How are you getting on, girls?" asked Dad. "Nearly finished? The assignment was a bit mediocre, wasn't it? I'll try to think of something more interesting for your next one."

"I'm done," said Nina, proudly giving him her interface.

"Excellent. How about you, Miki?"

"Um..."

Her fingertip rested on the Delete icon. But if she wiped her essay, she wouldn't have anything to show for all the time she'd spent.

"Miki didn't do the work you set," said Nina innocently.

"Nina!"

Nina kept her attention on Dad, refusing to look at her. She could be a real bitch sometimes.

"Really?" Dad asked. "Is that right? That isn't like you, Miki."

"I did write *something*, only..."

"Oh well, that isn't too bad. Can I read what you've written so far?" He handed Nina's interface back to her, saying, "This looks good. I'll take a closer look later."

Tendrils of apprehension creeping over Miki, she handed over her interface.

As Dad read, his already pale skin turned paler and his mildly interested expression became aghast. He murmured, "I had no idea..." His eyes leaden, he gave the screen back. "I see we have some talking to do."

26

Another nine years.

Wilder stared at the overhead. She'd turned on the light, but she couldn't get out of bed.

It would be another nine years before the *Sirocco* would arrive at her destination—assuming she didn't irretrievably break down on the way—and then what? What was there on Earth to look forward to? The Scythians would have already arrived. They had numerous ships, equipped and armed. What should have been a simple trip to gather living resources had turned into a last, desperate attempt to rescue humanity from domination and slavery.

It was hopeless.

Yet no one wanted to mention the fact. Most people, herself included, put on a mask of determination and optimism. Deep inside, they had to feel the same way as her. It was the great *Unmentionable*.

Each day she had to drag herself out of bed. Each day, the effort became harder. She worked in the Ark mostly, and her route led her past an airlock. Twice per active shift, once on her way to work and once on her return, she struggled with the temptation to step out of it.

And the bullying made everything so much worse. It had been going on for years. A snide remark just within her hearing here, a subtle push as she passed someone in a passageway there. Once, when she'd been sitting at a refectory table alone eating her dinner, a gob of spit had landed on her plate. She'd looked up to see Goslin's retreating back.

She'd told none of her friends what was going on. Not Cherry, Kes, Dragan, or Niall, though the latter was more of an acquaintance than a friend. She might have told Aubriot, who'd stuck up for her when the jump drive had malfunctioned, but what was the point? It would only make things worse. Her persecutors would find new, more cunning ways to hurt her, and Aubriot couldn't protect her around the clock. She could go to Captain Vessey, but the captain rarely left her cabin, spending most of her time drinking the ship's rotgut.

Her comm chirruped. She reached out and slipped it into her ear, forcing an upbeat note into her tone as she said, "Hi."

It was Cherry. "Glad you're awake. Are you on your way?"

Wilder checked the time and mentally cursed. She'd agreed to help with a harvest today. "I overslept, sorry. I'll be there as soon as I can."

"Great. See you soon."

She hopped out of bed, willing her limbs to move. After quickly changing from pajamas into her working clothes, she trotted to the Ark. "Which deck are you on?" she comm'd Cherry when she arrived.

"Four. Don't you remember? It's Fat Grains today."

Fat Grains. What a name. She'd forgotten who'd thought it up. Definitely not Kes. He would have given them a double-barreled Latin name no one understood. He probably had, in fact, and not bothered to tell anyone.

The common name was perfectly descriptive.

The plant had been discovered on a planet they'd visited

two and a half years ago, only the second planet on their journey that supported a diverse range of plant life. The first planet they'd visited, where so many lives had been tragically lost, had been the source of the majority of their crops, but it hadn't yielded a cereal grain. The addition of Fat Grains to their diet had been transforming. They could now eat bread of a sort, though it was unleavened and somewhat oily due to the fat in the seeds. But the readily obtained starch had seemed to boost everyone's energy and spirits—for a while, until the shroud of apathy and sense of just-hanging-on descended once more.

She exited the elevator.

An entire deck was devoted to the cultivation of Fat Grains.

A coppery-orange sea spread out before her. The plant used a red-hued chemical to gather energy from sunlight. As its seeds ripened and the plant began to die, the color intensified and deepened.

The sight was beautiful, she knew intellectually. But she couldn't feel it.

"Hey," Cherry called out. "Over here."

She was standing in a group of five. Dragan was here too, as well as Kes, Aubriot, and Miki. Cherry and Aubriot seemed to be getting along better these days after their massive falling out years ago. She guessed Cherry had learned how to ignore his arrogance and assholery. She had not.

"We waited for you," Cherry said as she approached.

"Sorry I'm late."

"Don't worry about it."

"Let's get started," said Aubriot tetchily, as if *he* didn't forgive her tardiness.

"Yeah, we haven't got all day," said Dragan dryly.

They did have all day, and the next, and the next. Fat Grains dried on the stalk and remained good for weeks.

Due to the fact the crop grew in a room only three meters high, with banks of lights hanging a half a meter below the overhead, there was no room to wield complex harvesting equipment even if they'd been able to build it. They were forced to cut and gather the stalks manually. She and Dragan had fashioned long, two-handled blades to scythe through the crop, and the person walking behind would scoop the cut stalks into a hopper.

As the two weakest harvesters, she and Miki would be the scoopers.

"Can you work with Aubriot and Dragan?" Cherry asked. The two men were a similar height, so it made sense they would be partners for the task.

"Actually," said Kes, "I'd prefer if Wilder worked with us, if it's all the same to you."

Lifting her eyebrows, Cherry replied, "Sure. It doesn't really matter."

Wilder was surprised Kes preferred to not work with his daughter too, but she was relieved she wouldn't have to spend time in Aubriot's company.

"I know," said Aubriot. "Let's make a competition of it. Whoever reaches the middle first—"

"Let's not," Cherry interrupted. "One, the blades are damned sharp and I don't want to lose my other arm or use up what's left of our medical supplies. Two, we should be focusing on doing a good job, not a fast one."

Aubriot curled his lip. "Whatever. Just trying to make things a bit more interesting."

"Thanks for your suggestion," Cherry replied sarcastically.

Maybe she hadn't forgiven him after all.

They set up at diagonally opposite corners of the room. Cherry's small stature implied she was weak, but her right arm was surprisingly strong, or perhaps not surprisingly considering she had to use it for everything.

The razor edge of the blade sliced the stalks as if moving through air. A fresh scent that always reminded Wilder of rust or blood rose up. She bent and cupped her hand around the fallen heads of grain before sweeping them into the wheeled hopper.

"I want to talk to you both about something," said Kes quietly from the other side of the row.

"Something to do with Miki I'm guessing," Cherry replied. "That's why you wanted Wilder to work with us."

"Is she okay?" asked Wilder. She loved Kes's daughters like sisters.

Kes answered, "She's fine. Too fine, in a sense. Stars, that girl's smart. She's found out about the Final Day Five."

Cherry halted. "How?"

"That's what I'd like to know," said Kes.

Wilder said, "But I thought everyone the girls spend time with knows they mustn't mention anything about the Five to them."

"They do." Kes moved forward. "Let's not stop. I don't want her to guess we're talking about her."

"How do you think she found out?" asked Cherry.

"How did any of us find out?" asked Kes bitterly. "Do you remember? I know I don't."

Cherry sighed. "It was a long time ago. You're right. I can't remember who told me. I recall you telling me about Garcia, what he said in the tent that night he disappeared. And then people began talking about how bad things always happened to the colony, that we could never seem to catch a break. The usual bellyaching."

"Was it Vessey who mentioned the Five?" asked Wilder. She seemed to remember the captain talking about apocalypse believers during one of her drunken rants.

"I don't think so," Cherry replied. "I haven't got any sense out of her in years. All I can remember is suddenly everyone was talking about them. Then discussions moved on to other things. But the FDF has always stuck in the back of my mind.

Every so often someone will mention them or slip them into a not-so-funny joke."

Wilder gave the hopper a shake to create room for more stalks. "Does it matter? Miki's fifteen, right? Maybe she's old enough to know about these things."

"Don't you think she has enough to contend with already?" Kes demanded. "Does she really need to worry about someone with a death wish blowing up the ship? She's just a kid."

"I was fifteen when I built my tree settlement and went with you to the Galactic Assembly."

"That was different! That was about living, not dying."

Kes appeared to be losing his temper, so she dropped it. He wasn't the same calm, kind man she'd known for so long. He was nearing the end of his tether, as they all were.

Another nine years.

How would they ever make it?

27

———————

Aubriot leaned his forehead against the shower stall as the hot water streamed over his shoulders and down his back. His muscles ached from the day's work, but not too badly. Others like that weakling, Kes, would be in worse shape. He smiled, recalling the punch he'd given him when Cherry had run off to his cabin. It was a few years ago, but the memory was fresh and he relished it.

He would have liked to punch him some more. It would have taken the edge off his anger and frustration, but Cherry had made him stop, threatening to give him the silent treatment forever. He'd done as she wanted yet she'd barely spoken to him for ages afterward.

So much for giving in. He should have carried on punching while he had the chance. It wasn't like he could hit Kes now for no reason.

She'd been unreasonable. Why couldn't she see that? She'd been in sick bay for weeks.

A man has needs.

Sure, it had been awkward and uncomfortable for everyone when she'd walked in on him and Maddox. He hadn't intended for that to happen. He did have a sense of decorum. It would have been better if she'd never found out. He'd planned on keeping it a secret. No knowledge, no harm.

Closing his eyes, he tipped his head back and gathered water in his mouth. After sloshing it around, he dropped his head forward and spat it out.

Women.

They were nothing but trouble. He and Cherry had had it good for a long time. Why did she have to go and spoil everything with her possessiveness? If she'd wanted to screw Kes, or...

Painful anger rose in his gut. He pushed away the thought of Cherry with someone else, turned off the water, and stepped out onto the mat.

The evening lay ahead. He dried himself off and put on pants and a shirt, the best he had. Everyone's clothes were wearing out. How long had it been since they'd run out of printer supplies? He couldn't remember. The printer probably no longer worked anyway. The engineers had scavenged all non-essential equipment for materials and parts.

Checking himself in the mirror, he wondered who might be interested in returning with him to his cabin tonight. Maddox? Goslin? Durbin? He'd bedded all the single women and several married ones too. Cherry had never slept with him again, and he'd never tried anything with Wilder. He had an intuition Kes would put a stop to it. She'd also made her dislike of him obvious.

Wilder was off limits, that was clear. She was out of bounds in the same way Cherry had been, emotionally, when she'd been in love with Ethan. Her feelings seemed to have changed over time. He'd had a sense he'd grown to mean more to her, but then...

He walked to the refectory where most people met at the beginning of the quiet shift. The atmosphere was already convivial by the time he arrived. Vessey was propped in a corner, already off her face. Goslin, Maddox, and Durbin were sitting together. That was a bad sign. Would he manage to separate one from the rest, like a lion singling out the weakest member of a herd? He had a sour taste in his mouth. He was growing tired of the hunt. Cherry, Kes, and Wilder were absent as always. The three had formed their own little happy family.

Dragan and Niall were here. He decided to join them. It would be good to be brought up to speed on the state of the ship.

He helped himself to a cup of ship-made alcohol from the jug and walked over. The two men acknowledged him with a nod as he sat down, though they didn't seem overjoyed to see him. *Never mind.* He'd never cared about being the flavor of the month.

"What is it tonight?" he asked, sniffing his drink.

"Purple Carrot Top brandy," Dragan replied. "Last year's. A fine vintage." He swirled the liquor in his cup before taking a sip and grimacing.

Niall snorted a laugh, but then said, "It might be nearly undrinkable, but can you imagine what this place would be like without booze? Personally, I thank the stars every day I was stranded on a lost ship with a bunch of biologists."

"Come on," said Dragan. "Are you trying to tell me you couldn't have made your own alcohol? It isn't hard. And who says we're lost?"

"Not me," said Aubriot. "We're on a direct heading. In my case, going straight home."

"Huh, home." Niall stared into the bottom of his glass, swirled the remains of his drink, and downed the dregs. "Not sure where that is anymore. By the time we reach the end of this voyage, I will have lived on this ship longer than I did on Concordia."

"And I'll be knocking on old age," Dragan commented.

Niall rose to his feet. "That's enough for me tonight."

"Leaving already?" said Aubriot. "The night's young yet." He'd been hoping to spend time with drinking buddies. Pulling women was losing its allure, and most of the men would have little to do with him. To be fair, it was understandable considering he'd screwed their girlfriends or wives. Neither Niall nor Dragan seemed to have any romantic interest in the women. Dragan had left a spouse behind on Concordia. What Niall's story was, he didn't know.

"Yeah, I'm done," Niall replied. "A man can only stomach so much hooch. And we have a long day ahead tomorrow."

"What are you doing?" Aubriot couldn't imagine any time-hungry tasks remained on the ship. Time was the one thing they had in plenty.

Dragan gave Niall a look, and the latter winced as if he'd said too much. Dragan leaned closer to Aubriot and said softly, "Keep it to yourself, but the man here had a brainwave about the jump drive. We're going to try something out, but we want to get the work done in a day. If we take longer, people will notice, and we don't want to get anyone's hopes up."

Aubriot got it. Morale was low and extremely fragile. It might only take one more disappointment to push certain people over the edge.

"Don't worry," he replied. "Won't say a thing. But what are the chances it'll work? Seems odd to think of something after all these years."

Niall shrugged. "Honestly? Virtually no chance. It's just something I noticed as I was re-reading the Fila's original engine plans for the millionth time."

Aubriot lifted his glass. "I'll toast to your success." Swallowing a mouthful of the liquor, he shuddered as the fiery sensation burned down his throat into his stomach. "*Shit.*"

The younger engineer was already up and making his way through the tables, somewhat unsteadily.

"Is Wilder in on it too?" Aubriot asked Dragan.

"Yeah, she—"

A shout of outrage broke into their conversation.

Aubriot looked toward the source. Niall was tumbling backward. Someone must have pushed him. The doc, Clarkson, was on his feet, hands clenched, face beetroot red and sweaty. All the cups in front of him were overturned and the table was awash with spilled alcohol. Niall must have stumbled into it. A minor offense, yet Clarkson was furious.

He reached for Niall, his other hand bunched into a fist, apparently about to haul him upright and hit him.

"Hey!" Dragan yelled. "Leave him alone!" He ran to Niall's aid.

The fist intended for the younger man swung around and connected with Dragan's jaw.

Aubriot shouted at Clarkson, "You! Put a lid on it."

Niall launched himself at Clarkson, and the two men went tumbling to the deck. Dragan was bent over shaking his head as if to clear his brain. Aubriot raced to the tussling fighters and tried to pull them apart.

Someone leapt on his back and pummeled his skull, screaming incoherently into his ear. He overbalanced fell backward, crushing the person beneath him. He felt the softness of a female figure but that was all he knew before someone else jumped on him.

He was in a melee of wrestling bodies. A blow landed on his ear. Pain exploded in his head. He punched and kicked, not even knowing who he was hitting. It could have been Niall and Dragan. It was impossible to tell. All he knew was he had to fight. He had to get to his feet or risk being crushed.

He took a punt to the eye. An elbow struck his nose. Hot blood coursed from his nostrils and down the back of his throat. He choked, coughed, and yelled, still fighting to get up, but the sheer weight of bodies pinned him down.

Somewhere in a remote corner of his mind, he saw the brawl from afar. He couldn't see himself, but he witnessed the battling mob, writhing like mating snakes. A decade of anger, deprivation, misery, and fear was erupting. Where it would lead, he couldn't guess.

28

C herry pressed Kes's door chime.
When the door slid open, Kes said, "You don't
need to do that. Just come right in. You're one of the
family."

"Aww, thanks." She was glad he didn't mind her coming
over so much. Aside from the farming, she had little to do, and
she loved spending time with the girls. As they'd grown older,
they'd become easier to handle and more interesting. "Miki and
Nina not home?"

"They wanted to help out in sick bay."

"They did? They're kinder than me."

"And me," said Kes. "I don't have time for those blockheads.
Let them suffer. It might make them think twice next time.
Bunch of animals."

Cherry was disgusted by the behavior of the people
involved in last night's fight too. "Do you know who took part?"
She sat at the desk.

"More than half the ship from what I can tell. I popped my
head around the sick bay door earlier. The place is full, but the
patients seem mostly walking wounded. Miki and Nina wanted

to play medic, so I let them. It'll keep them occupied for a while. I saw Aubriot in there."

"*That's* no surprise."

"And Dragan and Niall."

"That is. I can't imagine them in a drunken brawl. How did they look?"

"They weren't too badly off. They were on their way out, saying they had something to do."

"Wilder wasn't there, I hope?"

"Of course not. You know she doesn't join in the drinking sessions. She told me this morning she's busy today. I suppose she must be working with Niall and Dragan. Would you like some tea?"

It wasn't Concordian tea. They'd run out of that within months. But the foliage of one of the crop plants was aromatic and made an acceptable substitute.

Without waiting for an answer, he began a brew, inserting an element into a heatproof container and adding two spoon-fuls of dried leaves. While waiting for the water to boil, he sat next to Cherry.

"I'm glad we have a little time alone. I want to thank you for all your help with the girls over the years. It isn't easy being a single dad. You've been my savior on more than one occasion."

"You don't need to thank me. It's been a pleasure. And Wilder's helped too. I can't take all the credit. She was better than me with Miki and Nina when they were younger."

"You've both been tremendous," said Kes. "I couldn't have wished for better aunties. Izzy would have been relieved to know the girls had two amazing female role models in their lives."

The sound of bubbling water came from the container. He got up, turned off the element, and poured two cups of tea.

"You must miss her," said Cherry, accepting her cup.

"Yes, even now."

Cherry gazed into the rising steam. Kes had never asked her about his wife's last moments and she'd never offered to tell him, except to pass on Isobel's message of love. "I'm sorry if this is insensitive, but I think you were lucky to have the time you did."

"I know, and it isn't insensitive. I only wish I'd appreciated her more at the time, but there's no point in living with regrets. She gave me Miki and Nina, and for that I'm forever thankful."

Cherry took a sip of tea, and a comfortable pause in their chat developed. She enjoyed these quiet moments with friends best of anything she could do on the ship. They made life bearable. What would she have done if Kes and Wilder hadn't come along on the mission?

She looked up at Kes and found his gaze resting on her.

They held eye contact while seconds ticked past.

Slowly, he leaned forward. She remained still, not calling a halt to what was about to happen.

He kissed her, his hands resting on her shoulders.

Her pulse quickened. Kes had been a friend so long. She'd never consciously thought of him like this, and yet he was kissing her exactly as somehow she'd known he would.

He drew away and asked huskily, "Should I lock the door?"

She nodded.

SHE LAY NEXT TO HIM, shoulder to shoulder on the narrow bed.

Her passion spent, the cold reality of what had happened was hitting, hard.

Kes seemed to feel the same. He was focused on the overhead, not speaking.

Compelled to break the silence, she said, "That was...good."

"Yes," he replied dully.

She quietly added, "But..."

He turned and gazed at her earnestly. "But a-a mistake, right?"

Relief hit her like a wave. "*Big* mistake."

"I'm so glad you feel the same. I got carried away and—"

"So did I. I don't know what came over me."

Kes turned onto his back again. "I do. We're only human. Evolution drives us to procreate."

"Is that all it was? We need closeness as well. Intimacy."

"Yes, that too."

"Besides, I think I'm passed procreating now."

Kes's eyes snapped wide. "Stars, I hope so!" He sucked in a breath. "I mean, if you were to...I mean, it wouldn't be..." He faltered to silence.

"Don't worry. I really doubt anything will come of it. This voyage is sending us all crazy, right? If we aren't beating each other up we're falling into bed with the nearest warm body." This time, it was she who gasped at the implication of what she'd just said.

"It's okay," said Kes. "I know I'm not just a warm body to you." He wrapped an arm around her. "You know, I'm surprised there haven't been any pregnancies on the ship. I don't have to concern myself with contraceptives, but we must have run out of them a long time ago."

"There have been pregnancies." Cherry wasn't especially close to any other women except Wilder, but gossip was about the only interesting thing to talk about. "People try their best to avoid them but the doctors have had to deal with some accidents."

"I'm glad no one has been tempted to bring new life into this hellhole. I bet Aubriot has been responsible for a few of the accidents. You're well rid of him. You deserve better."

"I know. You don't need to tell me. But Aubriot hasn't fathered any babies. I know that for a fact. He's infertile."

"He is?" Kes's tone was shocked. "His gene editors really

screwed up. Did his parents ever find out? They would have sued the company into bankruptcy."

"It wasn't a mistake exactly. It's a side effect of..." Cherry hesitated. Did she have any right to be telling others Aubriot's secrets?

She recalled seeing him and Maddox together.

Screw him.

"The genetic engineering his parents arranged when they conceived him was ground-breaking and illegal. It was supposed to give him extreme longevity. It seems to have worked, but the downside was it made him sterile."

"Damn," Kes breathed. "That makes sense. Now I think about it, he hasn't aged a day since we left Earth. It's like he reached his late thirties and then just stopped. I don't know why I didn't notice. I must have been used to him looking like a male model and didn't think anymore of it. Poor Aubriot."

"Poor Aubriot?"

"Doomed to being an utter arsehole for all eternity."

Cherry chuckled.

They cuddled until she said, "We'd better get dressed before the girls come back."

29

"I'm against it," said Vessey.

Shadowed bags hung under the captain's eyes and she looked old, but she appeared sober for once. How old was she? She'd been middle-aged when they'd set out and she seemed to have aged even more than the decade they had been traveling. Aubriot had stepped back from taking a leading role once the personnel's survival was secure, leaving the tedious everyday running of the ship to the captain.

Kes didn't envy Vessey. She hadn't done a terrible job, but neither had she been the type of leader to inspire the crew or maintain morale. She'd been barely adequate, listening to specialists in their fields and following their advice. She reminded him a lot of Ethan's daughter, Meredith, who had ended up committing suicide. At least Vessey didn't have the pressure of being measured against the greatest Leader in the colony's history.

"Me too," said Niall.

All gazes turned to him.

"Huh?" said Wilder. "The fix was your idea!"

"That doesn't mean I trust it. In fact, if anyone has the final say on whether we try again, it should be me."

Vessey coughed. "We all remember very well what happened the last time we tried to jump. As I understand it, the result could have been much worse. And, actually, as captain, I have the final say."

Aubriot murmured something inaudible.

Everyone had to know what *that* was about. He was itching to be boss again.

Zapata said gently, "Perhaps this is one of the few things we should put to a vote. Considering what happened with the jump drive before, I mean. A second attempt could be putting everyone's lives at risk."

Kes was surprised to hear the pilot speak up. He'd kept mostly to himself ever since the jump drive malfunction. His only tasks aside from maintaining the *Sirocco* on her heading had been flying the shuttle on detours to star systems to harvest their suns' energy or visit a planet. He'd been laconic on those trips.

"It will be putting all our lives at risk," said Dragan. "No question."

"But continuing as we are, that's just as risky," Wilder protested. "If we don't do something, there's no guarantee we'll ever reach Earth. We're down to our last supplies of equipment and materials, and that's with eking out everything we have. I swear some systems are surviving on willpower alone. What if we lose the CO_2 scrubbers, or the water treatment bacteria die, or the Parvus's energy-harvesting system fails? You know what's worse than spending the next nine years traveling? Spending the rest of your life stranded in deep space."

"Nevertheless," said Vessey evenly, "these scenarios are hypothetical, whereas making another jump attempt will be a reality. We've survived so far, due to the resourcefulness, hard work, and positivity of everyone aboard. I'm not willing to put all our lives in jeopardy to avoid something that might not happen."

"Then you don't understand the situation," Wilder snapped, "and you have no imagination."

Kes studied her. She was under tremendous pressure like everyone else, but there was something additional underlying her words, something personal and emotional. She had an investment in the proposal to activate the jump drive she wasn't stating.

"Maybe Zapata's right," said Cherry. "Maybe we should have a shipwide vote on it."

"No," Vessey retorted heavily. "Out of the question. Are you forgetting what happened a couple of days ago? What if opinions are split down the middle? What do you think will be the result if a large minority don't get their way?"

It was a good point. Niall, Dragan, Aubriot bore the physical reminders of the brawl, if it could even be called that. After Miki and Nina had returned from helping out in sick bay, Kes had discovered he'd under-estimated the damage wreaked. There had been broken bones, deep lacerations, and dislocations. The least fortunate were still recovering.

Vessey's comment seemed to subdue Wilder at first, but then she blurted, "If we don't do it now, when the time comes we have no choice it could be too late. In an emergency situation we might not have a chance to get everyone into capsules. We can't keep a jump as a fallback option. It's insanity. And we're forgetting Concordia and Earth. We've forgotten the reasons for our mission. If the jump drive works, we might not be too late to save the colony and help Earth prepare for the Scythians' arrival. There might still be time to do both, but only if we act now."

"Wilder's right," said Cherry. "We've been focusing on saving our own lives. That was never the point. It doesn't matter if we stay alive long enough to reach Earth if we're too late to make a difference. Who cares if we bring back material to seed Concordia if the colony's dead? What makes our lives so important compared to all the ones we could save?"

A lead weight settled in Kes's chest. "Cherry, I..." He couldn't say it. His own life wasn't important. It hadn't been since Izzy had died, except that he hadn't wanted to leave his children orphans. But when he thought of Miki and Nina, his most basic instinct was to keep them alive at all costs.

Cherry looked at him, her eyes wet. "I'm sorry. You know how much I love the girls, but it's true."

Niall said, "Speaking as the person who suggested the fix, I say we—"

"I know what your problem is," said Wilder. "You don't want to take responsibility if the drive malfunctions again. Whether it means everyone dying or only being crushed by disappointment, you don't want that on your shoulders."

Vessey commented, "The disappointment from trying and failing is another thing I have to take into consideration. I don't need to explain how hard everyone's finding the situation psychologically. My own struggles are no secret." She glanced from face to face, reddening. "There are plenty of people who won't be able to take another setback. They're barely holding on as it is."

But Wilder didn't seem to have heard her. She rose to her feet and jabbed a finger at Niall. "Your problem is you'd rather live in an unhappy little bubble than step outside and risk *feeling* something. This ship is like your life. Cut off from everything that matters. You don't want to activate the jump drive because you don't *want* to get to Earth. You don't *want* to face up to what might be there, or what we might find on Concordia if we make it back. You're a coward!"

"Christ on a bike!" Aubriot exclaimed, also standing. "Sit down and shut up. This isn't a therapy session or couples counseling."

"No!" Wilder yelled. "*You* sit down." She marched over to him and put two hands on his chest and shoved him.

His jaw dropped and he sank into his seat.

"You're the last person to be telling me what to do," she went on. "*I'm* the one who invented the jump drive, and a-grav, and I'm the one who masterminded converting the Ark into growing rooms to keep every last person on this ship alive. What have you done except try to get into the pants of everyone with tits? Everyone knows you wanted to be captain. Everyone knows you want to run the show. But what kind of example have you set? What have *you* done to boost morale?"

Kes could only watch in admiration. Wilder was on a roll. It was good to see her knocking heads together and taking names. It was good to see her finally standing up for herself.

She turned to Vessey. "I hear what you're saying about divided opinions, but it isn't fair to keep the knowledge of the possible jump drive fix to ourselves. Every person on this ship has the right to decide whether they want to take the risk. We must take a vote, but only when Niall, Dragan, and I have explained everything as well as we can. Then everybody will be voting in full knowledge. It's the only way."

Dragan said, "I'm happy to do my share of explaining."

Niall gave Wilder a surly look before adding, "Okay. Me too."

"You already have my vote," said Cherry. "I'd hate to carry on living like this knowing I could be on Earth."

"Or dead," muttered Aubriot.

"If I'm dead I won't know it."

Kes sighed. "I suppose you have my vote too. I want Miki and Nina to live, but what kind of life is this? It's no life at all." He winced internally. His daughters were enduring almost exactly the same existence all the Gens had aboard the *Nova Fortuna*, except the generational colonists had enjoyed considerably more comfort. As one of the project's scientists, he'd condemned those thousands of nameless people to never walk on soil, breathe fresh air, or feel the rain on their face.

Mere existence was not enough. He wanted his children to really *live*, if they were to live at all.

Wilder was true to her word. She spent the next days talking to the *Sirocco's* personnel, outlining Niall's fix and the possible outcomes if it failed. If anything, she over-explained. Kes saw a couple of people tell her they didn't need to hear any more, that they didn't care. They were willing to take any chance to escape this purgatory, no matter how small.

Niall and Dragan did the same. Kes also witnessed a softening in Niall's demeanor toward Wilder, and he wondered if he'd been right about the young man all along.

After three days, the vote was taken.

When the results came in, they were unanimous.

Every single person had voted to attempt the jump.

30

As Wilder passed Niall in the jump room, he caught her hand. She halted, surprised at the friendly touch. "Can I talk to you outside?" he asked.

She followed him to a quiet section of passageway.

They'd been working on the jump capsules, repairing the broken casings and jammed emergency releases. Sadly, they didn't have to fix many. Several people who had begun the voyage were no longer alive. But the capsules that were to be used had to be completely up to scratch. They had no wiggle room when it came to safety.

As Niall paused, seeming to struggle for words, she frowned. "What is it?"

He'd been acting weird for days. He was usually quiet but lately he'd become almost silent, not even saying much to Dragan. Was he regretting suggesting the fix for the jump drive? If it didn't work, the failure would be a heavy load to bear. People were not forgiving about such things, as she knew too well.

He sucked in a deep breath. "I have an apology to make."

"You have? To me?"

This was new. She could probably count on the fingers of one hand the times she'd heard Niall say sorry about anything, least of all to her.

"Yes, of course to you," he replied irritably. "Unless there's someone else here?"

"Ugh, if you're going to be like that, I don't want to hear it."

"Wait, okay? Just wait and hear me out."

She leaned against the bulkhead, and folded her arms across her chest. "If this is about what I think it's about, it had better be good."

"You're not going to make this easy for me, are you?"

"Why should I?"

He sighed. "Fair point." His gaze focused on the deck, he continued, "What you said in the briefing room...It was true."

"Damn right it was." She paused. "Which part do you mean?"

"You're going to make me say it?"

"I swear, Niall, after everything you've put me through for the last twelve years—"

"All right!" he exclaimed, lifting his hands. "Okay, I get it. I've been an asshole."

"And then some."

He tipped back his head and turned his gaze upward.

He was looking everywhere except at her.

In a strangled tone he said, "You're right. I was—am—a coward. I don't want to attempt the jump. I saw how people blamed you, and I didn't want that to happen to me. When I thought of the fix, I was excited. You know, in that way you feel when you think of a solution and it's just perfect? When everything slots together in your head and you can't understand how you didn't see it before?"

She nodded. This was the level at which they really understood each other. There were no words to adequately describe the feeling he was alluding to, but, between them, no words were needed.

"And then when we did the work and managed to complete it, I was riding on a high. I could have solved the problem that had dogged us for a decade. I could have found the solution that would allow us to escape this living hell. But, after, I had time to really think about the implications. What if I was wrong? What if my 'fix' ends up killing everyone?"

She replied, "Like Cherry said, no one will be alive to care about it. Anyone surviving on Concordia must already think we died, and the people on Earth don't know we exist. So it cancels out. It doesn't matter. Unless you're bothered about what people here are thinking in their last few seconds of life. That would be pretty dumb."

"Thanks. If I ever need a boost, I know where to come."

"What do you want from me?" she asked. "A pat on the head? A cuddle? You want me to kiss it better? Is that it?"

"Gee, you're a hard woman."

She shrugged. He was wrong. She wasn't hard. She was only hard toward him. "Life made me this way. Is your apology done? Can we go back to work now?"

"I haven't finished."

His face twisted in discomfort. She was simmering with anger and felt no sympathy. She likened his expression to being badly constipated and stifled a laugh. Her ire faded, leaving only fatigue and anxiety over the coming jump attempt. "Just get it over with. Tell me."

His eyes finally met hers, and she saw the pain behind them. She reached out and touched his shoulder, compassion welling up.

"I need to apologize to you, too," he said, "personally. When the Scythian Plague was over, everything had changed. Our old lives were gone forever. I was only a kid and I'd been forced to grow up fast. I think that did something to me. I don't know what, but it was like I was scared to be happy. I couldn't allow it in case it was taken away from me again. I couldn't relax, couldn't enjoy myself. All the time, I felt like another disaster was around the corner and there was no point in taking pleasure in anything. I'm not sure if I'm making any sense."

"I understand," she said. "And you were right, about the next disaster looming, I mean."

"I took it out on you. I don't even know why. But you became my target. Just seeing you around brought out the worst in me. I should have left you alone, stayed out of your way, but building the *Sirocco* was the best thing I could do with the skill set I have."

"Dragan and I couldn't have done it without you."

"And you...you were a saint. I don't know how you've put up with me for so long."

"Some days, I don't know either."

He sighed. "I'm not good with words. I'd rather work with an engine any day than try to explain myself."

"You've done a pretty good job." She held out her arms.

As they hugged, he said, "I thought I didn't deserve a cuddle."

"You don't, but you're getting one anyway." Moments passed, and then she said, "You know what? Jamie Bond is a stupid name."

"So is Deadly After Midnight."

"True."

When they parted, he asked, "Now that's over, are *you* okay?"

"What do you mean?"

"Lately you've been...I don't know...preoccupied."

She gave him a tight smile. "It's nothing important. I'm looking forward to getting to Earth. Aren't you?"

"You say it like it's a given. I'm glad I got my apology out of the way. I'd hate to die knowing I haven't set things right between us."

"That's what I love about you. You're such an optimist."

31

Cherry lowered herself into her capsule. The last time she'd done this she'd been trapped in the awful gel that was supposed to protect them from the effects of the jump.

If they did jump.

Wilder and the other engineers did seem confident about their fix, but they'd been confident last time. She guessed they knew what they were doing.

She'd made sure to hug Wilder, Kes, and the girls and tell them she loved them. Similar potentially 'forever' goodbyes were taking place around the chamber. Tension thickened the atmosphere like the gel about to pump into her capsule. She'd caught Aubriot watching her as the goodbyes were going on. She'd quickly averted her gaze. He'd made his bed—with Maddox and most of the women on the ship—so he could lie in it.

She was aging much faster than him anyway. He would have moved on to younger prey soon enough, whether or not she'd spent a couple of weeks in sick bay.

Pretending the ache in her chest didn't exist, she closed her capsule's lid and mentally sought pleasant thoughts to occupy her while ensconced in the gel. Her mind immediately flew to her dalliance with Kes. She smiled and blushed. What a pair of middle-aged fools they'd been. She was glad he was on the same page as her regarding his feelings. He meant a lot to her, just not like that.

What a pity. He was a good man, but it was not to be. She seemed destined to be attracted only to unobtainable or unsuitable men, while he was in love with a ghost.

The last few capsule lids were closing. Once Vessey gave the command, the nozzles supplying the gel would open, the capsules would fill, and the *Sirocco* would jump—hopefully.

Try as she might to stay calm, her heart would not obey. Memories of the last attempt rushed into her head. The choking and fear were vivid. She sucked in air through her mask, staring out, the scene distorted by the transparent lid. Were others feeling the same? Any minute, she expected someone to leap from their capsule, screaming and crying. It wouldn't have surprised her. The pressure they were all under, had been under for years, was immense.

Soft clicking sounds came from every side of her capsule. The nozzles were opening. She braced herself, preparing to be swamped by the horrible, tepid gel.

She waited.

Nothing happened.

She raised her head and peered into other capsules. Confused looks were passing between the occupants.

Reclining her head again, she continued to wait.

Had something gone wrong?

Were they about to jump without the benefit of the gel as protection?

She looked out again.

A capsule was opening. Wilder stepped out and walked over to Vessey. A moment later, the captain's voice came over the comm: "Sorry, everyone. There's been a delay due to a problem with the gel emitters. You can exit your capsules but don't stray too far for now. As soon as I have an update, I'll let you know."

Angry chatter quickly filled the room as people climbed out again. Cherry looked for Wilder but she'd already left. Dragan and Niall were inspecting the capsules, telling annoyed enquirers to leave them alone and let them work.

Cherry went to find Wilder, expecting she was avoiding being accosted once more as a scapegoat. The passageway was empty. Wherever she'd gone, she'd gone there fast.

She comm'd her. "Where are you? Are you okay?"

"Yeah, I'm okay," the younger woman replied, her tone flat with what sounded like disappointment.

"Don't worry," Cherry said. "If it's only a problem with the nozzles, I'm sure it can be fixed."

"That isn't the problem. It's something else. Something I suspected as soon as the gel failed to appear."

"What is it?"

"Come to the gel tank and I'll show you."

Cherry didn't know where it was. She had to ask Wilder for directions. When she arrived, she couldn't see the problem. She'd expected there might be a leak similar to the one that had flooded the Ark. But instead Wilder pointed at a section of the tank wall. On closer inspection, Cherry saw a hairline crack running from the base to the top of the unit.

"I checked inside," Wilder said resignedly. "It's empty. There's nothing left except a thick, tacky residue. The original jump malfunction must have caused the crack, and the water content of the gel evaporated through it over the years. There's nothing to fill the capsules."

∾

"WE'RE SO CLOSE," said Aubriot. "Too close to back out now."

"Absolutely not," Vessey argued. "As I said before, we have a perfectly viable alternative. A much safer alternative, which is to continue as we are."

"We've been over this," Wilder groaned, her head in her hands. "The chances we'll survive until we reach Earth aren't as good as you think. We have huge obstacles in our way, probably some we haven't even thought of yet."

"My duty is to protect the lives of the people on this ship," Vessey replied, her voice growing louder, "and that means not subjecting them to risks. *Real* and *present* risks, like jumping without the protection of the gel, not hypothetical what-might-happens."

"That's about the stupidest thing I've ever heard!" Wilder exclaimed, leaping to her feet. "Just because there's a danger here and now, it doesn't mean a worse one isn't around the corner. You have to weigh up *all* possibilities. The gel was only ever a safeguard. The jump drive was specifically modified from the Fila's version to account for our differences in our anatomy and physiology. It's designed to be safe for humans."

"Was the drive ever tested without the subject encased in gel?" Vessey asked.

"No, but that was only because we didn't have time and we could only use people for the experiments. If we'd had animal subjects and a few more months..."

"Wilder's right," said Niall. "The gel was precautionary only, exerting a body-wide pressure to counteract the stresses of the jump. I'm not a biologist, but I expect the worst we'll see if we jump without it are burst capillaries, maybe some bad headaches, that kind of thing."

Vessey pursed her lips. "I suppose we could do the same as before. If you explain to everyone—"

"The result's gonna be the same," said Aubriot. "Everyone wants this. Everyone will want to take the risk. Our people are mostly scientists. They're smart. If they have questions they can ask the engineers, but I guarantee they'll do whatever they can for a chance to end to this nightmare."

The captain closed her eyes and murmured, "I've tried. I've done my best. It wasn't enough. I wasn't good enough. But I tried." She opened her eyes. "Go ahead. Do what you want."

They had come for her during the quiet shift after the big fight in the refectory, which Wilder hadn't even been aware of at the time. When the fight fizzled out, these brawlers had come to find her. Goslin, Marcus, Durbin, and Ryan. She didn't know any of them well. She only ever mixed with the people she trusted: Cherry, Kes, his daughters, Dragan, and Niall. Though Niall had expressed his dislike for her endlessly over the years, she'd known he would never hurt her.

Unlike the rest of them.

Goslin and Durbin were botanists, Marcus was one of Aubriot's muscle men, and she wasn't sure what Ryan did. All she knew was Ryan's partner, Trish, had died on the first plant-hunting expedition.

When her door chime had sounded, she hadn't suspected anything. No one she didn't know very well had ever been to her cabin before. No one had approached her on her home territory, so to speak. In her cabin, she'd assumed she was safe.

As soon as she opened her door, she knew her mistake.

They were clearly drunk. Goslin held onto the frame for

support. Marcus leered, his expression lopsided and pupils dilated. Ryan and Durbin were flushed and sweaty and looped arms around each other's shoulders like twisted versions of fairy tale characters. All four bore bruises and scratches.

"Glad to find you home," Goslin slurred. "C'n we come in?"

She stepped back. "No, I..."

Marcus caught the edge of the closing door and the four 'visitors' surged through the gap.

The door closed.

Four additional bodies had quickly filled the small cabin. The air seemed to turn thick with their exhalations, though of course that was impossible in such a short space of time.

"Wh-what do you want?" Wilder asked, eyeing the exit. It was impossible for her to reach it without pushing through the group.

"Simple," said Goslin, her eyes narrowing. "We want justice." The woman leaned in until her face was only centimeters from Wilder's, who could smell the alcohol on her breath. "We want to put things right."

"Yeah," Durbin chimed in, "after what you did to us."

"I didn't do anything to you," said Wilder. "I don't know what you're talking about." She edged to one side. Her ear comm was on her bedside table.

Goslin placed a heavy hand on her upper arm and pushed her back to her original position.

"Where're you going?" Marcus asked. "The night..." he gestured expansively "...is young."

Ryan and Durbin giggled. Goslin wasn't amused. She leaned even closer until all Wilder could see was her face with its open pores and bloodshot, crazed eyes. "Y' know exactly what we're talking about. You're the one who made that faulty drive. You're the one who told us it was okay. You're the one who got us in this mess. And now you're going to pay."

"That isn't true," Wilder protested. "I wasn't the only person who built the drive, and you chose to come on this voyage of your own free will. Do you think if I knew it was faulty I would have given the go ahead? I'm here too! I'm stuck here the same as you. Do you think this was all planned?"

"She didn't say it was planned," said Ryan. "She's only saying you're an idiot."

"Right," Wilder retorted. "The idiot who converted the Ark so you could all eat. I'm *that* idiot, am I?" Despite her clear danger, the senselessness of Goslin and the others' thinking frustrated her beyond belief. How could they be so stupid? They weren't fools—a fact that had probably kept her safe until now. Deep down, they knew they weren't being logical, that their hatred of her came solely from a need to blame someone for their predicament. It was the alcohol talking, and whatever these people did to her tonight they would probably feel remorseful for in the morning. But that wouldn't save her now.

Her appeal to their rationality seemed to have made a small impact. She could almost see the cogs of Goslin's mind whirring as she tried to think up a suitable response.

"Doesn't matter," said Durbin. "Doesn't matter what you did after. Y' can't make up for landing us here in the firs' place."

"S' right," Marcus agreed. "There's no taking that back."

"Well then," said Wilder, her pitch rising tremulously, "is hurting me going to get you to Earth? What difference is it going to make?"

"Nothing's gonna get us to Earth," Goslin said sadly. "Too late. Never gonna reach it now."

Wilder's ears pricked up. Was Goslin one of the rumored Final Day Five? Were her companions too? If so, who was the fifth member?

"It's about balance," Goslin went on. "Justice. Why should you be allowed to get away with what you've done?"

"I haven't done—" Wilder gurgled.

Goslin's hand had fastened around her throat. "Shut y' stupid mouth."

"That's it," Marcus said gleefully. "Let's get her to the airlock!"

He bent down and grabbed her around the waist. Ryan grasped her knees. Before she knew it, she was being carried out of her cabin.

A hand—she wasn't sure whose—was clamped so tightly over her face she could barely breathe, let alone cry out for help. She fought violently, her muffled screams loud in her ears, but her skinny frame was no match for the strength of four people, even drunk.

The lights overhead passed by, bright panels alternating with dark where they'd removed them to use in the growing rooms.

She knew the way to the airlock well. In the early days, there had been times she'd been tempted to take that route for a final time, like everyone else on the ship, no doubt. The end would be painful but it would be brief compared to the everlasting death of the voyage. But she hadn't taken that path. She'd turned away, trying her best to find small pleasures in day-to-day life, focusing on the present, not thinking of what the future held. She'd gotten by, and now these drunken morons were about to make all her efforts pointless.

Rage consumed her. She writhed like a mad thing. Opening her mouth, she bit down hard on the fingers that slid into it. A single scream got out, cut off immediately as the hand fastened down again. This time, its grip was so tight she really could not breathe at all. Her chest bucked as her lungs struggled for air.

Blackness closed in. The last thing she heard was laughter.

When she woke up, she was on her side on the deck. Confused, she stared at the smooth tiles. Someone was cursing. It was a male voice, and the person sounded drunk.

She gasped, remembering what had just happened. She

must have passed out, and they'd put her down when they reached the airlock. She couldn't see her captors. They had to be behind her, at the hatch, and they were cursing because…

Of course! They couldn't get it open.

After the suicides during the first year of the mission, airlock security had been upgraded. The systems required the biodata of two people before they would open: the captain's and one other high-ranking member of the ship's personnel. It had been so long she'd forgotten, and so had Goslin, Marcus, and their friends.

Huh, it won't be so easy to get rid of me and get your 'justice'. I only have to…

Slowly, she turned onto her front and moved her hands and knees under her body.

"She's getting away!"

Wilder leapt to her feet and ran. Fingertips snatched at her jersey, but she pulled away. She might not have much muscle compared to most people, but her lightness made her faster than most too, especially compared to these lumbering drunks.

Their thudding footsteps echoed behind her. A gasp of effort sounded. Hands closed around her knees. Her legs dragged from underneath her, she slammed into the deck.

She looked back. It was Goslin. The woman was grinning maniacally at her success. The other three were coming up fast.

Wilder bent her knee and drove her heel into Goslin's face. At the thud of impact, the woman shouted in pain and her grip broke. In an instant, Wilder was on her feet again and running. Had she broken Goslin's nose? Hopefully.

She swerved around a corner. Another long passageway lay ahead. When she looked back again, Goslin was nowhere to be seen and she'd put distance between her and her pursuers. They would never catch her now.

She didn't return to her cabin. She'd found a place to sleep in the Ark, on a pile of dry Fat Grain stalks.

It had been like the days at Sidhe, when she'd slept in out-of-the-way places to avoid going home to her fake parents. As her heart rate and breathing slowed, tiredness had overcome her.

What would happen tomorrow? Would Goslin and the other attackers even remember what they'd done? Probably not. They'd all been very drunk. But one thing was clear, things were reaching fever pitch. She wasn't safe anymore. What was worse, she couldn't tell anyone about it. What could the few friends she had realistically do to protect her? She couldn't live under lock and key for the next nine years. It was bad enough to be trapped on the *Sirocco*.

She really hoped Niall's proposed fix for the jump drive worked.

33

S ettling into her capsule, Miki peeked at Nina and saw her sister peeking at her. Miki smiled and gave her a little wave. Nina was a pretty nice sister, though she could be a pain in the ass sometimes.

This capsule was way bigger than the one she'd used in the first jump. She could see it from here. It looked so tiny, but Nina's old one looked tinier. They must have been specially made for them. She hadn't known that at the time. She remembered that first jump. It had been exciting to go on a big adventure. The gel covering her face hadn't been much fun, but that part was soon over.

This time there wouldn't be any gel, which was great.

What was taking so long?

She lifted her head again to look around the room. Dad wasn't in his capsule yet and neither was Cherry. They were chatting.

She guessed it didn't really matter when they jumped. They'd been aboard the *Sirocco* ten years. Another few minutes wouldn't make any difference. But it was annoying to wait.

There was that big man, Aubriot. She didn't like him, but he ignored her, so that was fine. He was in his capsule now. Who else? Captain Vessey was getting into hers, and the pilot, Zapata. As soon as the jump was over, he would have to go to the bridge to fly the ship the rest of the way to Earth.

Earth.

What would it be like? She'd seen pics and vids, but it wasn't the same as actually being there. She'd been on the surface of two planets and spent her early childhood on Concordia, so she wasn't a complete newbie, but she still found it hard to imagine. It was weird to think she was going back to the place Dad had been born centuries ago. Dad was *really, really* old. She giggled as she recalled teasing him about it.

"I want to run again," said a voice.

The engineers had arrived. It was Dragan, the older one, who had spoken.

"Actually run," he went on, "for kilometers."

"You already do that on the treadmill," said the other guy, Niall.

"It isn't the same."

Wilder was with them. Wilder was about her favorite person ever. She loved Dad, but Wilder was more fun. Wilder knew how to make things interesting. *She* would never have set an assignment on the ship's personnel.

Miki sighed and rolled her eyes. She hoped the days of boring schoolwork were over. On Earth, there would be too much else to do. She also hoped the adults would calm down. They'd been getting crazier and crazier. That fight they'd had! Some of the patients in sick bay had been badly hurt. Even now, days later, they wore arm slings and casts. She'd had no idea people who were supposed to be friends could inflict so much damage on each other. *Nina* was more mature than some of them.

What's taking so long?

All the capsule lids were closed now except one. Wilder was

at the control panel. She would start the countdown and get into place before the jump activated.

Miki caught her eye. Wilder gave her a quick smile and a thumbs up before climbing into her capsule. The lid swung closed, and Miki lost sight of her as she lay down.

She listened to the decreasing numbers. They had a whole thirty seconds to wait.

Dad had explained there was a small risk in doing it without gel but it should be fine. She believed him. He would never put her or Nina in danger if he could help it.

Twenty seconds to go.

She hummed a tune, her latest favorite song. She'd found it last week on an old file deep in the ship's database.

Come into my arms, baby
And I'll never let you go
I'll take you all the way
All the way to Arrival Day

All the way to Arrival Day. *Arrival Day*! She hadn't thought about what the words meant until now. The song had to be ancient, written around the time of the arrival of the *Nova Fortuna*.

How cool was that? Here she was singing a song about—

"Five."

"Four."

"Three."

"Two."

Earth, here I come!

"One."

She braced for...something. Would a shudder pass through the ship like last time? Would the jump drive make a noise?

No movement or sound came.

Would the Scythians attack them when they arrived? Dad had said it was unlikely they would have reached Earth before them, but not impossible.

She waited expectantly, listening and looking for a signal it was okay to leave her capsule. Craning her neck, she saw puzzled faces exchanging looks.

What had happened?

Wilder's capsule opened. She climbed out and crossed to the control panel. Her voice came over Miki's comm. "Please remain where you are, everyone. I'm checking our status. I'll update you as soon as I can."

She must have comm'd Niall and Dragan separately. Their capsules opened too. The three engineers left the room.

Nina's head was up and she was looking at her. Miki pulled a funny face, making her sister laugh. They mimed and gesticulated at each other to ease the boredom. By the time Wilder returned, Miki was breathless with laughter and her stomach muscles ached.

Wilder opened a general comm again. In a quiet voice, she said, "I'm very sorry to report the jump attempt failed."

Instantly, capsule lids flew open. Shouting and wailing echoed around the room.

Wilder was saying something else, something about the engineering team and the problem, but the noise drowned her words. Figures were moving toward her. Aubriot climbed from his capsule, and so did Cherry. The large man waded through the crowd, heading for Wilder.

Dad's voice came over the comm. "Stay where you are, girls. Don't get out until I say so, and try not to look."

34

A heaviness had settled over the ship worse than any Kes had known in the decade-long voyage. The nightly drinking sessions had ended. When people weren't working they mostly kept to their cabins, coming out only to collect food. In the passageways, no one made eye contact, keeping their heads down and their gazes focused on the deck. The place was eerily quiet. No sound of conversation was to be heard, no strains of music or vid audio tracks leaked from cabins or communal rooms, only the far-distant thrum of the engine as it carried them steadily and faithfully across abyssal space.

He tried to pretend to Miki and Nina that everything was okay, but they'd grown too big to fool. Too big and too smart. Initially, they'd been disappointed the ship hadn't reached Earth, but life on the *Sirocco* was normality to them. They'd accepted that things would go on as always and they'd bounced back from their disappointment with youthful resilience. Yet they were sensitive girls. They picked up on the despair and melancholy. It began to affect them, firstly as concern for the other passengers, and then the mood invaded them. The spark left their eyes and their bickering and banter stopped. They spent their time together quietly, helping each other and showing consideration for each other's feelings. It was then he knew something was seriously wrong.

He was also deeply concerned about Wilder. Now more than ever, she was under threat of an attack from a disgruntled crew member looking for someone to blame. If it hadn't been for Aubriot defending her, she might have been seriously hurt in the jump room when the most recent attempt failed.

Wilder was acting as though nothing was wrong, that she wasn't in danger. He couldn't let the situation continue. If something happened to her he would never forgive himself.

Cherry was first to arrive. She sat next to him. "Thanks for doing this. I should have done it myself days ago but I was preoccupied with work in the Ark."

"No problem. I was thinking I should have done it a long time go too. Thank the stars nothing's happened yet."

"Nothing we know of."

He looked at her quizzically.

"Wilder's a solitary and private person. She also loves us and wants to protect us. She wouldn't want us to worry about her. If something has happened already, she might not tell us."

"Hm, you're right. I didn't think of that."

Aubriot entered the briefing room. His gaze slid across Cherry as if she didn't exist. Then he gave Kes a nod before sitting opposite them.

It had been with great reluctance Kes had invited him. The less he had to do with Aubriot the better, but he couldn't deny the man would be useful for what he had planned.

Niall and Dragan appeared.

"Wilder not here yet?" asked Niall.

Kes replied, "The time I gave her is ten minutes from now. I wanted to discuss our approach before she arrives. I think we can all agree she isn't going to like any kind of intervention into how she lives her life."

Niall snorted a laugh. "No kidding."

Kes went on, "But I think we can also agree something needs to be done."

"Absolutely," said Dragan.

They quickly hashed out a plan. It wasn't hard. Just simple, rational precautions to keep Wilder safe.

"The stupid thing is," Niall said when they'd finished, "the jump drive fix was *my* idea, not hers. That's common knowledge. I don't understand why everyone seems to have it in for her."

"Simple," Aubriot retorted. "She's a born victim."

"Do you *have* to be so mean all the time?" Cherry asked.

"Just saying it how it is," he replied. He said to Niall, "You and Dragan socialize, have a drink with the rest. You're one of the crowd."

"Not intentionally," said Dragan.

"Intentionally or not, that's what you do." He turned to Cherry. "You're disabled so people feel sorry for you."

She spluttered, "I am *not*—"

"And Kes has kids," he continued, ignoring her, "making him a bit of a father figure. He's older than most too."

"Thanks," Kes muttered.

"Wilder's an oddball. Doesn't fit in. And physically she's no threat. The worst she could do is poke you in the eye with one of her bony elbows. If anyone on this ship is going to get picked on, it's her. That's obvious."

"Well, thanks for pointing all that out," said Kes. "I just remembered I invited Vessey. It looks like she's a no-show."

Wilder stepped into the room.

Five pairs of eyes turned to her as an awkward silence fell.

She halted. "Sooo...you've been talking about me. Nice."

"Please come and sit down," said Kes.

From the look on her face, he had a feeling that if it hadn't been he who had invited her and if they didn't have their long friendship, she would have turned right around and left. As it was, she moved slowly and warily as she took a seat.

"I'm going to be completely honest," he said. "We have been talking about you, and this meeting isn't about the running of the ship. I lied when I told you that because I had a feeling you wouldn't come if you knew the real reason."

"The real reason is me," said Wilder heavily. "*Great*."

Niall said, "We're only looking out for you."

"And what if I don't want you to look out for me? Do I get a say in this?"

"Christ," Aubriot said, "you haven't even heard any suggestions before shooting us down. Remind me to never do you any more favors."

"I didn't ask you to—"

"That's it!" Aubriot exclaimed. "I'm out." He rose to his feet.

"Sit down," said Cherry. "We've put Wilder on the spot and she's upset."

To Kes's surprise, Aubriot did as Cherry requested, though his lips moved as he murmured something under his breath. Kes caught the words, "*Ungrateful bitch*."

Cherry leaned over the table and put her hand on Wilder's. "Please listen to us. I can't stand the thought of you getting hurt. After what happened in the jump room, you can't deny you're in danger."

Wilder' face bore no expression but she didn't move. Her gaze flicked from person to person around the table. "I'm not staying in my cabin. I can't live like that."

"No one's saying you must," said Kes.

"And I don't want someone acting as my guard, trailing after me wherever I go."

"That isn't what we had in mind."

Her shoulders lifted and fell, and some of her tension

seemed to leave her. "Tell me your ideas and I'll see what I think."

"Good," said Kes. "Thanks for listening at least."

He outlined their plan. They would arrange their sleep schedules so someone would always be awake and contactable in an emergency. Cameras were to be placed over her door. She was to carry an alert button around her neck. The list went on.

After some quibbling, she agreed to everything they proposed in the end. Kes was relieved his long-time friend would be safe.

35

The alert button dangled from Wilder's neck as she leaned through the open maintenance hatch, clunking against a water pipe. She shone a flashlight around the interior. No drips were visible at the pipe joints and the areas beneath them were dry. Ever since the flood, she'd carried out regular visual inspections of the plumbing that supplied the growing beds, refusing to trust the sensors again. Everything seemed in order.

As she leaned back, the button caught between two pipes and tugged at her neck.

Softly cursing, she put down the flashlight to free it.

It was then they grabbed her.

Hands seized her arms, waist, and legs, lifting her bodily off the deck and dragging her backward. But the alert button remained at an angle, stuck between the pipes. She was trapped by the lanyard, her head inside the bulkhead cavity.

She yelled.

Trying to wrench a hand free to press the alarm, she writhed and fought.

A finger roughly pushed into her ear, flicking out her comm.

"Something's round her neck," someone said.

Another hand appeared. There was a soft *snick*, and the tightness around her neck disappeared. They'd cut the lanyard.

They pulled her out.

It was the same four who had attacked her in her cabin: Goslin, Marcus, Ryan, and Durbin. They'd snuck up on her quietly while she was distracted.

The other time had been no mistake. Drunk as they'd been, they'd known exactly what they were doing. They'd remembered, and this time they were stone cold sober.

She gathered a breath to scream for help. Goslin shoved balled-up cloth into her mouth. Marcus fastened a gag.

They'd come prepared.

This time, she was going to die.

They picked her up, lifting her to the horizontal so each could wrap their arms around her and prevent her from struggling. Still, she continued to fight and resist, summoning every ounce of strength she had to break free.

They carried her from the growing room and through the silent Ark. It was the quiet shift. She'd come here now purposefully in order to avoid encountering other people. It was hard being the most hated person on the ship. They must have been watching her movements, perhaps following her from her cabin, waiting for a moment like this, when she was at her most alone and vulnerable.

They didn't want to make any more mistakes.

Goslin was trying to slip something over her head one-handed, but Wilder was squirming too much, turning and jerking her head and shoulders. Whatever that thing was, she didn't want it on her.

"Wait until we get there," said Marcus. "It'll be easier."

Goslin heeded his advice. The pressure of her arm around Wilder's shoulders strengthened.

Where were they taking her? What had Goslin been trying to do?

"When we do it, that's the end, right?" asked Durbin.

"The beginning of the end," Marcus corrected. "This will be the trigger."

The 'trigger' was her death, no doubt.

"I can't wait for it all to be over," said Ryan. "We've been punished enough."

They had to be the apocalypse believers. They thought by killing her they were hastening the Final Day for humankind.

"What'll happen?" Durbin asked. "Will it be fast?"

"It doesn't matter," Goslin replied. "Fast or slow. As long as it's finished at last."

You're a bunch of morons!

Didn't they understand what they were saying? How could they be so deluded? Had the pressure and isolation turned them psychotic?

They put her down in a passageway not any different from the rest. She sat on the deck, knees drawn up, as the four stood around her. There was no sense in trying to run. They would be on her in a second.

What were they going to do?

Goslin fished in a bag she'd slung over her shoulder and brought out a rope.

For a moment, Wilder was confused. Were they going to tie her up? What was the point? It was four against one and they had her surrounded. They were also not inebriated like last time.

The end of the rope swung free.

A noose.

Her gut contracted. Her heart threatened to force its way out of her chest.

Dread oozing from every pore, she lifted her gaze upward.

This section of passageway hadn't been properly finished. Where there should have been overhead tiles were structural beams.

The Final Day believers had planned everything to the last detail, including the exact spot they would hang her.

A sense of crazed hysteria filled her. She almost giggled.

Why hanging? Why not strangle her, here and now?

Why not cut her throat?

Did hanging her have some kind of ritual significance? These people were out of their minds. They'd moved on from simply spacing her. Their insanity had become more elaborate.

Goslin moved to lift the rope over her head.

Wilder had a brief vision of herself hanging by her neck, gagged, eyes popping and face filling with blood as she slowly strangled.

NO.

She hadn't endured all the torments all her life, worked so hard for all she'd achieved, to die like this—at the hands of deranged clowns.

She fell to her side and, feet together, kicked Ryan's knees.

They bent backward at the impact and he screamed as he toppled to the deck. Durbin dropped beside him, wailing in distress. Goslin gasped. Marcus snatched the noose from her and reached out with it, trying to slip it over Wilder's neck. Wilder also reached out, upward, grabbed Marcus's head and dug her thumbs into his eyes with all the strength she had. Blood and gore erupted from the sockets.

Inhuman shrieks issued from his throat as he blindly clutched at his face, fingers scrambling to remove her thumbs.

"What..." Goslin breathed, her features pale and painted with horror. "What are you...?"

Wilder felled her with a punch and then took off. When Goslin and Durbin overcame their shock, they could still easily overpower her, and now their impulse to hurt her would be even stronger.

She only had to reach the *Sirocco*. If she could just alert one of her friends to the danger she was in, she would be safe. She couldn't risk going to anyone else. She didn't know who to trust and who might side with Goslin, especially if she spun them a story about what had happened.

She sped down the passageway, thanking the stars she was on Deck One. Goslin was already on her tail and so was Durbin, judging by the sound of the pursuing footsteps. She ripped off her gag and wrenched the sodden cloth from her mouth before throwing both down.

She turned a corner, turned another. There it was!

Racing across the bridge, she calculated which of her friends' cabins was closest. One of them was only a minute away. She risked a glance over her shoulder. Goslin's face was now a picture of fury. Durbin looked anguished as she labored beside her, gasping and panting.

One minute.

She was over the bridge.

She swerved to the left and then immediately right, hoping to confuse her pursuers. But Goslin guessed correctly. She was gaining. No alcohol slowed her down this time. She seemed determined not only to get her 'justice' for the predicament they were all in, but also to enact revenge for what Wilder had done to her pals.

A second right turn, and then a left.

How many times had she walked these passageways in the last ten years? Thousands. Tens of thousands. She could have gone anywhere in the ship blindfolded.

"Bitch!" Goslin yelled. "You're done. It's over."

She was only meters away, but Wilder was only meters from sanctuary.

Goslin leapt for her as she had the time before, wrapping

her arms around Wilder's knees. Wilder fell and Goslin fell with her, gripping her legs tightly.

It didn't matter.

She'd made it.

Wilder stretched out an arm and thumped Dragan's cabin door. He had to be in. It was the middle of the quiet shift. If he wasn't, she would scream and holler. Other friends were nearby. Someone would hear and come to her rescue.

The door opened.

Dragan stood in the frame in his pajama bottoms. His mouth fell open as he took in the scene.

"Wilder! Come inside."

Goslin released her hold, no doubt mortified that she'd been caught trying to commit murder.

Wilder clambered to her feet. Never more relieved in her life, she stepped into the cabin.

The door closed.

"Thanks," she said, her chest heaving. "You saved my life. It was the Final Day Five. They were going to..." Her words petered out as she took in the cabin's interior.

She'd never been here before, never had reason to come here.

Against one wall, a bank of figures rose from the deck to the overhead, lining slim shelves. Tiny men, women, and creatures in strange poses or fighting in combat. Each model had been intricately painted. What were they made from? She couldn't guess.

She turned on her heel.

More shelves, filled with figures, occupying every wall. Dragan's bed was a mattress on the floor.

Nothing else was in the room.

He was watching her.

"I had no idea you were so into..." She faltered. "What are these...?" She wasn't sure how to describe them.

"People. Just people, and some animals."

"Just people? But there are so many of them. I guess I'm surprised you never talked about your hobby."

His eyelids lowered. "Famous people, from history." He stepped to a shelf and picked up a figure of a man. "Alexander the Great." Putting it down, he picked up another. "Cleopatra." He picked a third figure from a shelf. "Charlemagne." He faced her. "They're all here. Every person of significance who ever lived. Well, maybe not *everyone*. Some will have been forgotten or didn't make it into the data files for another reason."

Uneasiness began to take root in Wilder's stomach. The amount of time and effort Dragan must have put into creating the figures bordered on obsessional. And she didn't recall him ever mentioning an interest in history.

"All the important names in human civilization," said Dragan. "The first Concordian Leader, Ethan, is here somewhere. You and Niall and I have a place too."

"We do?" She would have been flattered if she hadn't suddenly become very afraid.

"History begins here," he said, pointing to a low corner, "and here," he added, swinging around to point to a corner next to the overhead, "is the end."

The End.

The end of human civilization.

Shit.

Dragan was the fifth member of the Final Day Five.

He crossed the cabin and opened the door.

Goslin and Durbin were waiting.

36

"Help! Help me."

Aubriot squinted groggily as he tried to focus. The chirrup of his ear comm had dragged him from a deep slumber.

"What?"

He hadn't caught the announcement of the caller's name.

"Who is this?"

"M-Marcus. It's Marcus. I can't see. I think she...God, I can't see anything! My eyes! My eyes."

Another man's groans sounded faintly in the background.

"You can't see?" Aubriot echoed. "Has there been another fight? Comm sick bay. I'm not a medic." He angrily cut the comm, took out the ear device, and put it on the nightstand. After punching his pillow into shape, taking out on it some of his annoyance at being woken up, he tried to go back to sleep.

Why had the man comm'd *him* for help? Sure, he was the one who'd invited Marcus to come on the voyage, reasoning they would need some muscle as well as brains. Who knew what they might find on Earth? And, sure, he'd been useful on the plant-hunting trip, even though he'd managed to nearly kill himself by walking into quicksand, but it wasn't like they were close. Why should *he* be the person Marcus contacted when he was in trouble? Why not go straight to professionals who could handle a medical emergency?

Aubriot turned onto his back and opened his eyes.

Maybe Marcus was too out of it to know what he was doing. He *had* sounded like he was in a lot of pain.

Muttering "*Fuck it*" he re-inserted the ear comm. "Where are you?"

"Ark," Marcus mumbled. "In the Ark."

Aubriot comm'd sick bay, waking the medic on duty. "Someone's had an accident in the Ark. Name's Marcus. And someone else might be hurt too." He listened to the reply. "No, I don't know where exactly." After listening again, he asked, "How the hell would I know what's wrong with him? Why don't you go and find out? Isn't that your job?"

When the medic mercifully stopped asking stupid questions and left him alone, Aubriot lay on his back and stared into the middle distance, silently debating with himself. Half a minute later, he cursed aloud and climbed out of bed. After quickly pulling on clothes and boots, he went to find Marcus.

He found him before the medic, coming upon what almost looked like a murder scene. Bloody smears coated the bulkheads, hand prints and long finger trails from where Marcus had stumbled about, apparently wandering from one side of the passageway to the other. His face was out of a horror flick. Dark holes were all that remained of his eyes, along with the red-stained material hanging from them and coating his cheeks.

Aubriot was no stranger to swearing, but words to express his reaction to the scene didn't exist.

Marcus was on his knees, moving his head from side to side as he sightlessly scanned his surroundings, hands outstretched. The other man Aubriot had heard lay on his side, his legs at strange angles. He recognized Ryan. The second man seemed to have passed out with pain.

"Holy shit!"

The medic had arrived.

"About time," Aubriot snapped. "I comm'd you five minutes ago."

IGNORING HIM, she went straight to work. "Help's here," she told Marcus. "Please stay calm and remain still while I check on your friend." She knelt next to Ryan and felt his wrist while watching his chest.

Deeply curious about what had caused injuries of this magnitude, Aubriot approached Marcus and bent down. "What happened?" he asked. "Were you two fighting?"

"Wilder," he gasped. "Wilder, the bitch. What do my eyes look like? Are they bad? Will I see again?"

"Wilder?" Aubriot straightened up.

Wilder did this?!

He took another look at the scene. Why would Wilder attack two fully grown men? Had she lost her mind?

Then he noticed the rope. Dropped carelessly on the deck, it lay in loose coils, one end shaped into a noose.

Cold fear gripped him.

He opened a comm. "Kes, someone's tried to kill Wilder. See if you can comm her, but I'm guessing if she was contactable she would have called for help. I'm going to try to find her." He returned his attention to Marcus. "Where is she? Where's Wilder?"

"I don't kn—"

Aubriot's slap threw him into the bulkhead.

"Hey!" the medic yelled. "What the hell are you doing?"

"He tried to kill Wilder. He's a would-be murderer. A maniac."

"He's my patient and he's probably delusional. Leave him alone." She got on her comm, probably requesting help.

Aubriot thrust his face into Marcus's. "Tell me where she is."

"I really don't know." The man's tone was full of pain. "She ran off."

"Is she alone? Were there more of you?"

"Goslin and Durbin went after her. But you don't understand. The end is coming. Wilder has to go first for the end to begin."

Leaving Marcus rambling, Aubriot sped away.

HE MET up with Kes in the *Sirocco*'s briefing room. He hadn't been able to find Wilder and neither had Kes. Before they had a chance to speak, Cherry arrived.

"No sign of her?" Kes asked.

Her eyes full of tears, Cherry shook her head.

They'd decided not to put out a shipwide comm, not knowing who was a friend and who was an enemy. The last thing they wanted to do was to let others know Wilder was alone and vulnerable.

"Niall and Dragan can't have found her either," said Aubriot, "or we would have heard from them."

"Niall anyway," said Kes. "I couldn't raise Dragan."

"You couldn't raise him? Why not?"

"I don't know. Maybe he was drinking last night and he's out of it."

"He should be bloody well looking like the rest of us."

Cherry said, "It's odd he didn't wake up to his comm alert. That's pretty loud."

"It *is* strange," Kes softly agreed.

Niall ran in. After a brief scan of the room he turned his anguished face to them. "No luck?"

There was no need to give the obvious reply.

"Shit. I really hoped one of you had brought her here."

"Do you know what's happened to Dragan?" Aubriot asked.

"Isn't he searching like the rest of us?"

"No, he isn't answering his comm."

"He isn't? Why not?"

"That's what we're hoping you'll tell us," Aubriot replied through his teeth.

Niall ran a hand through his hair. "Dragan's been behaving oddly for a while, but he likes Wilder. He'd want to help her."

"What do you mean he's been behaving oddly?"

Shrugging, Niall replied, "It's hard to explain, but you know if you're friends with someone for years you can tell when they're a little...off?"

Aubriot was already on his way out of the briefing room.

"Where are you going?" Cherry called after him.

"Dragan's cabin."

37

No one answered the chime. Something was happening inside. Aubriot could hear muffled shouts and the thumps of heavy things hitting the deck and walls. As Kes and Cherry came running up, Niall following at their rear, Aubriot said, "She's in there. Has to be. How can we get in? Can any of you override the lock?"

Panting, Kes replied, "Only Vessey can do that."

"Comm her then," said Aubriot. He hammered on the door. "Wilder?! Are you in there? Dragan, you hurt a hair on her head and I'll fucking kill you!"

"Yeah," Niall commented sardonically, "that's going to make him open up." He stepped to the door. "Dragan? It's Niall. Is Wilder with you?"

A particularly heavy *thunk* reverberated, accompanied by a yell of pain.

Aubriot couldn't make out if it was a male or female voice. He pushed Niall away and leaned close to the crack. "Open the door! Vessey's on her way, so it's opening soon whether you like it or not. If Wilder's hurt, someone's going to pay. You better hope it isn't me who gets hands on you first."

"Get out of the way," Niall commanded. "Let me speak to him."

Aubriot stepped back. "Did anyone comm Vessey?"

Cherry replied, "She said she'll be here in two minutes."

A lot could happen in a couple of minutes. Aubriot found himself inexplicably anxious about what they would find when the captain opened the door. Why did he care? He didn't give a shit about the geeky girl.

Yet the thought of her dying stirred something in him. Pity? Sadness?

They would all suffer for her loss. She was smart. They needed her.

That had to be it.

Where the hell was Vessey?

Niall had continued to try to get an answer from Dragan, talking through the door, but without success.

The noises from the cabin abruptly stopped.

"Dragan?" Niall repeated. "What's happening? Are you okay? Is Wilder there with you?"

"Whatever was going on," said Kes, "it appears to be over, for better or worse."

Aubriot said, "If he's hurt her, I'll—"

"Where are Goslin and Durbin?" interrupted Cherry. "Do we know what happened to them after they left Marcus and Ryan?"

"I've comm'd them several times," replied Kes. "No answer from either of them."

"I'd bet a lot of money they're in there too," said Aubriot. "Marcus, Ryan, Goslin, Durbin, and Dragan. That makes five. The Final Day Five."

"Not Dragan," Niall objected. "He's no apocalypse believer. He's an engineer."

"This trip has changed people," said Cherry. "People have done crazy, stupid things, things they wouldn't normally do."

Aubriot looked at her but she didn't make eye contact.

She went on, "None of us can say what someone is or isn't capable of."

"I still say..." Niall protested, but he didn't finish his sentence. Vessey had appeared.

She jogged to reach them. "Can someone explain what's going on?"

"No time," said Aubriot. "Open the door."

"Opening doors without the cabin occupant's consent is a violation of priv—"

The door slid open.

Goslin's lifeless body slumped out. She sprawled on the deck, arms loose, mouth hanging open, face suffused red. Livid contusions ringed her neck.

She'd been strangled to death.

The cabin looked like a whirlwind had swept through it. Thousand of small figures littered the floor. Shattered shelves hung from the walls.

"What the f—"

"Wilder!" Cherry called in, leaning over Goslin's corpse. "Are you okay?"

There was another body. Female. Curled into a fetal position. Her head had been bashed in. Dark blood stained her black hair and pooled around her. The broken remains of a strangely shaped skull lay in the pool.

The dead woman wasn't Wilder.

Two people crouched in a corner.

Aubriot recognized Dragan, though only barely. It wasn't only the blood spattering his face that caused confusion, his expression was so full of horror it contorted his features.

Wilder had to be the person crouching behind him.

"I-I couldn't let them..." said Dragan as Cherry squatted down.

"It's okay." She reached out and touched Wilder's shoulder. "It's over. Goslin and Durbin are dead."

"What about Marcus," Wilder whispered, "and Ryan?"

The implication of her question hit Aubriot. It was obvious what must have happened but he'd been too preoccupied to put two and two together. "That was *you* who did that to them? Shit, I'm impressed. Never knew you had it in you."

Cherry turned and said, "For once, will you shut your big mouth?"

38

F or the second time in less than a week, Miki settled into her jump capsule seat. Maybe *this* attempt would work and they would actually go to Earth. She rolled her eyes. Grown-ups were so dumb. The fact they were in charge of everything was mind-blowing. She didn't know how some of them made it to adulthood, let alone did things like build starships and travel through interstellar space.

Dad hadn't told her half of what happened in the incident with Wilder, which had led to this third try of the jump drive, but she'd managed to piece the rest together by eavesdropping on gossip. She'd explained some of it to Nina, only the less gory parts. Nina was still only young and too sensitive. She didn't want to upset her.

The way Dad had explained it was there had been another fight, that some people had wanted to hurt Wilder. The people —he'd admitted when she pushed him on it they were the Final Day Five—had believed Wilder was to blame for the *Sirocco*'s predicament and she had to pay. They also believed they were on a final journey, the culmination of humanity's long path to destruction, retribution for squandering the gift of civilization. We didn't deserve to claw their way back to evolutionary success, and the universe was punishing us, thwarting each attempt to crawl out of the mire.

Given all the terrible events she'd learned about in history classes, it wasn't such a crazy idea.

What *was* crazy was the nutcases blaming Wilder for the current situation. Wilder was a nice, kind, smart person and would never hurt anyone if she could help it.

What Dad hadn't mentioned was the loonies wanted to *kill* her. Actually murder her. Just the thought of it made Miki choke up.

Thank the stars they hadn't succeeded.

From what else she could gather, Wilder might have died if it hadn't been for one of FDF, Dragan, changing his mind at the last minute and defending her. He'd killed one of Wilder's attackers with a skull he'd taken as a souvenir from a visit to a planet. They were friends, so it made sense he would want to protect her. It would have been hard for him to hurt Wilder, even if he did believe she needed to die for the final apocalypse to arrive.

She sighed and gave her head a little shake.

Grown ups were definitely weird. Yet she was nearly one herself. She would have to remember not to be stupid just because she was an adult.

The best thing was, Dragan had admitted he'd done something to stop the jump drive from working after the last fix. He'd thought if they made it to Earth, it would only be prolonging humankind's downfall. Everyone would suffer more. It was better to accept our fate and end things here and now.

I bet Wilder figured it out. She must have guessed what her friend had done when she knew about his messed-up thinking.

When they got to Earth she would ask her.

If they got to Earth.

Surely this time they would?

Everyone had been so depressed after the last failure, if the same thing were to happen again, living on the ship would be a real downer. And the more she'd thought about it, the more interested she was in seeing Earth.

The final few people were arriving. There was a big man with bandages over his eyes and another man on crutches. They had to be helped into their capsules. Two women were missing, but she knew where *they* were. There had been a double funeral for Goslin and Durbin—another thing Dad had tried to keep a secret.

No one else had to get into their capsule except Niall. He was going to start the countdown sequence this time, probably because Wilder had been getting way too much negative attention. Did she have a plan for what to do if the attempt failed again? Miki hoped so. It must be so hard to have nearly everybody aboard hating you. They *had* to get to Earth. Then all their problems would be over. They would have some new things to eat and plenty of water. And it would be great to see the animals she'd read about in children's books.

And birds!

She'd never seen a bird. On Concordia, only insects, shuttles, and helis flew. It would be amazing to see an animal flying.

The countdown had begun. She crossed her fingers.

Please, please, let it work this time. Please!

The computer's voice droned on, stating the decreasing numbers.

Would it make a difference that they didn't have the gel to protect them?

WILDER SHUT her eyes as the countdown droned on. The past twelve hours was a haze of pain, fear, sorrow, and elation.

She'd come so close to dying. When she'd realized Dragan was one of the Final Day Five, she really thought she'd had it. Trapped in his cabin with Goslin and Durbin at the door, she could never have escaped. Three against one? She hadn't stood a chance.

And Dragan had come so close to doing it. She'd seen the intention in his eyes. He'd been hardening his resolve, forcing himself to go through with it. But in the end, something had stopped him. Had it been a dose of sanity suddenly hitting him? Or maybe he just couldn't bring himself to hurt a friend.

The events that followed were a blur she didn't want to make clear. They'd fought Goslin and Durbin together, the two women attacking like maniacs, expending every last gram of strength and venom to fulfill their mad quest. She couldn't remember who had killed them and she didn't want to. All she knew was that one minute she was in a violent storm of hitting, kicking, punching, and the next she and Dragan were in a corner, alone with two dead bodies.

Her body ached but her mind hurt more. She longed for this journey to be over, to reach Earth.

If only they could reach Earth.

Reality shifted.

Her sense of her position in space had disappeared. Opening her eyes, she saw her view fold and then stretch. A piercing sound assaulted her ears and pressure clamped down, threatening to burst her eardrums.

Then it was over.

The jump drive had worked. It had damn well worked. Niall had been right.

But that didn't mean they'd reached their destination. The drive had worked before and sent them to an entirely different place. They might not be at Earth but perhaps so far away they could never reach it before dying in space. Perhaps they were in another galaxy.

Niall and she had agreed she wouldn't be the one to check their new coordinates, not after what happened before. If they'd messed up again, this time he would take the flack. He was growing braver every day. Just a few hours ago he'd told her he loved her, that he'd loved her since she was Deadly After Midnight and he didn't even know how old she was or what she looked like.

Her capsule lid opened.

Niall was already out and walking to the console.

All around the room, lids were opening and people were sitting up. No one seemed to be hurt, thank the stars. Miki waved at her. She waved back.

Now all gazes were on Niall. Not a sound could be heard, not a whisper or breath.

His head was down as he consulted the screen.

He looked up, and his facial muscles worked as he tried to control his expression. He couldn't control himself any longer. He broke into a huge smile.

"We're in the Sol System. We made it. We finally made it."

39

"At least it's still green," Aubriot commented.

Cherry watched the holo of a blue and green globe slowly revolving in mid-air on the bridge, half its surface in darkness. The land masses moving into the light of its star were indeed mostly green.

Earth. Humanity's home, but not *her* home. Concordia was several jumps away, only two weeks' distant, providing the jump drive didn't malfunction again. It was a hard fact to believe after the long years of the outward journey.

"What did you expect?" asked Wilder.

"Don't know exactly," Aubriot replied. "When I left the place was a mess. Could have been a global nuclear war since, or climate change could have turned the lands to desert."

"I thought the Natural Movement had taken over most political systems," Wilder countered. "Wasn't that what the scientists who built the Guardians said in their vid? That's what you said, Kes, right?"

Kes gave a nod.

"So nuclear weapons would have been banned."

Aubriot replied, "You never knew what was coming next

with those freaks. They could have done anything." He leaned closer to the globe, as if looking for something in particular. Whatever it was, he didn't mention it, only repeating. "Could have done anything."

"Well, we're here now," said Cherry. "What's the plan? Kes? You're head of the science team."

"The plan hasn't changed as far as I'm concerned. I have my list of items to collect and I have a fairly good idea of where to find them. I'll have to rejig the various team roles as we've sadly lost so many people."

Cherry asked, "Is there any point? We must be too late to save Concordia." When they'd visited the Galactic Assembly, traveling at near light speed, decades passed on her home planet. The journey to Earth had taken years. How much time had passed at home while they'd been gone?

"I haven't given up hope," said Kes. "Life is a persistent phenomenon. It endures, even when all odds are stacked against it. I haven't carried out a thorough survey of Concordia, but on Earth living organisms were found in the most unlikely places, from bodies of water sealed off for millennia to the upper reaches of the stratosphere. Micro-organisms had even been found on orbiting space stations and satellites. If we complete our mission and return I don't know what we'll find, but I doubt Concordia will be barren. Even if no one has survived, perhaps we can start again."

He gave a small cough and continued, "There used to be a seed vault on Earth, designed to last thousands of years. If the Natural Movement didn't destroy it, that would be a good place to begin looking for what we need."

Aubriot's upper lip lifted into a sneer. "I know the place you mean. That'll be long gone. It was the sort of place the loonies would target."

"I'm not so pessimistic," Kes replied. "As the Project neared completion, I noticed all mention of the vault had disappeared from the media, and when I searched for information on the net found nothing, not even in archived pages."

"Someone was thinking ahead," said Aubriot.

"I hope so."

"That's a good sign," Wilder commented. "Maybe the vault's still here. Do you remember where it was, Kes? I agree you should go there first."

"I know the rough location and I think I recall the external features. Most of it was buried in a hillside."

"We're forgetting something," Aubriot said. "Our little delay means the mission's changed. We don't only have to collect the seeding material, we have to protect Earth from the Scythians."

Vessey, who had been watching the globe in silence ever since it appeared, said, "We can't realistically do that. It took years to build the defenses to protect Concordia. Here, from what I can tell, the same infrastructure and technology no longer exists. How can we protect an entire planet from an advanced, hostile alien species with only what we have aboard the *Sirocco*?"

"I don't know the how," Aubriot retorted. "I only know the why. We have to face the fact that Concordia's probably screwed. From up here, Earth doesn't look much better. Look at the dark side of the globe. What do you see?"

"Nothing, of course," said Wilder. "It's night time."

"If there were cities you would see lights. When I lived here, the planet was lit up like a birthday cake at night. You could see all the metropolises, roadways, the lot. And look at the green parts. Where are the developed areas? Don't tell me everyone took to living underground. Are we picking up any transmissions? Radio? TV?"

There was a silence as his words sank in.

Wilder murmured, "Is anyone left, I wonder."

"Doesn't look like it," Aubriot replied harshly. "Which means the last remaining examples of human civilization in the universe are probably us. And," he added, "the Scythians know the two places we live. If we're going to survive—not as animals grubbing for food in the forest—but *really* survive, without losing everything we've achieved, we have to make our homes safe."

Cherry hated it when he talked sense. She couldn't help agreeing with him. "If a how exists, we won't know what it is until we get down there. Who's going to be in the first landing party?"

Vessey grimaced. "Everyone is itching to set foot on land, naturally, but I want to be cautious. Earth might be home to two of you but that was hundreds of years ago, and to everyone else it's unknown territory. We can't afford to lose any more personnel. I want to restrict the first landing team to five people only. When we have a better understanding of conditions, perhaps we can commit more people at a time to the many tasks."

"Five isn't a lot," said Aubriot. "It's better to have more in case things get hairy."

"The more people down there, the more we could lose. And we mustn't forget about the possibility of the Scythians turning up. If that happens, we'll need all hands on deck."

One of the first things they'd done after arriving from the jump had been to scan for other starships, but there had been no trace of any.

"It would be extremely bad luck," said Kes, "if the Scythians were to turn up at almost exactly the same time as us."

"Bad luck has dogged us ever since we left the Solar System," was Aubriot's bitter comment. Then he held up his hands and said, "Not that I'm saying there's anything supernatural about it."

He grinned and continued, "Getting back to the point, I want to be in the team that goes down first. Kes has to come too, since he wants to look for that vault. And Wilder should go so she can suss out what's what about planetary defense. That makes three. Who the other two are, I don't care. I don't think it matters too much."

"Seeing as I don't matter," said Cherry, "I'd like to go too."

Aubriot softly tutted.

"I'll let the Chief Scientific Officer decide on the fifth member of the team," Vessey said, "as beginning the seed material harvest will be the primary focus of the mission."

"Hm," said Kes, flushing slightly, "in that case, I'd like to take Maddox. She's the best surviving biologist we have. Providing her inclusion won't ruffle too many feathers, that is."

Aubriot shrugged. "Fine by me."

"Me too," Cherry said, trying to sound nonchalant.

"That's decided then," said Vessey. "There's no time like the present. Begin your preparations. I'd like to send you down within the hour."

"Uhh, Captain…" said Zapata. He'd been sitting at the pilot controls, silently monitoring the scan data while their discussion had been going on. "We've picked up a signal."

"We have? What kind of signal?"

"It's very simple. Just a single repeating tone, like an alert or warning."

A warning?

"Where's it coming from?"

"Right…" he did something on his console "here."

A light appeared on the holo. It pulsed, presumably in time with the signal the *Sirocco* was receiving.

"If I remember rightly," said Kes, "that's in the same area as the seed vault I was talking about. Perhaps it's a beacon, part of the original design to enable it to be found in the far distant future."

Vessey said, "I hope that's all it is."

40

Aubriot stepped from the shuttle. At first glance, Earth looked nothing like his dream. They'd landed in what used to be northern Europe. They were in the farthest northern reaches, on an island within the Arctic Circle. The place must have been sparsely populated even hundreds of years ago. It made sense the scientists had chosen it for the seed vault. At that time, the ground had probably been permanently frozen, which would have helped to preserve the seeds.

Things had changed.

Like most of the rest of the globe, the island was green. Not as lush and verdant as a jungle, but green nonetheless. The climate had already warmed significantly when he left Earth and the process had clearly continued. Here, the permafrost had melted, the sea level had risen, encroaching on the land, and vegetation had grown on what must have once been barren slopes.

The rotting metropolises or overgrown roadways of his dream were not to be seen, and there was no sign of people reduced to savagery. So far, it didn't appear his mind had conjured a premonition of what he would see when he arrived.

Perhaps it had been a vision of a period in the distant past. Yet he'd also seen Scythian ships descend. He dismissed the speculation. It must have been only a dream, sparked by the news that Wilder had figured out how to build the jump drive. None of it meant anything.

What did Kes think? The conditions on the island had to be bad news for seeds. He couldn't see the man's expression behind the visor of his EVA suit.

It would be hard to navigate the terrain suited up, but Kes had insisted they wore the protective clothing. According to the Guardians, a pandemic had ravaged the human population, sounding the final death knell for global civilization after the Natural Movement had severely weakened it. Kes feared coming into contact with local inhabitants. Even after all the years that had passed, the deadly virus could infect them. The current population would have a natural resistance to the disease, something Concordians lacked.

Kes had insisted they were armed too. Aubriot had no problem with that.

"Sure you want to check out the vault first?" he asked Kes over comm. "Not the signal origin?"

"I'm sure," came the man's terse reply. "That's what we're here for, to collect material to help Concordia."

It seemed a waste of time. Whatever Concordia's lack of biodiversity was going to do was done. But he was no botanist and it wouldn't hurt to let the others carry out their plan. After the disastrous voyage, people needed a hope to cling to. "All right, it's this way, yeah?"

"I think so. I'm working from memory, don't forget."

Kes had said the vault lay south of the island's airport, and Zapata discovered the airport's location on a very old educational program about Earth. Nothing remained of the structure. Woodland now grew in the spot. Zapata had struggled to find somewhere to land. In the end, he'd set down on a flat outcrop at the base of the hillside. Whatever road might have run from the airport to the vault was long gone. They would have to trek over the natural landscape.

"The external section of the vault is small," said Kes as they set off. "A set of double doors at the end of the entrance tunnel, which quickly sinks into the ground. But it's solid. Unless someone blew it up, it should still be there. We only have to find it."

They were climbing rising ground, thick with undergrowth and trees. Unable to see more than a few meters ahead, they had to use their HUDs to maintain a steady direction and avoid going around in circles.

"How does it feel to be home, Kes?" Cherry asked.

"I don't think it's hit me yet. I'm focusing on the job at hand. Ask me again later."

Aubriot noted she didn't ask how *he* felt. She hadn't said more than was necessary to him in five years. Her ability to hold a grudge was phenomenal.

"I can't believe this is really Earth," said Maddox. "It didn't seem real when I was growing up. It was just a place mentioned in history class, somewhere I'd never been and would never go to, yet it was supposed to be so important. It was almost mythical."

Wilder said, "I don't feel any connection at all."

"You don't?" Cherry asked.

"No, it's just another planet to me. What about you?"

Cherry didn't answer.

Aubriot spotted a set of boulders poking out of the ground. "I'll climb up there and take a look around."

The boots of his suit gripped the mossy surfaces well, and the boulders were riven with cracks, probably from the freezing and thawing of ice. He was soon standing atop the tallest one. A silvery ocean lay north of their position. He could also see the shuttle on its outcrop. He turned a hundred and eighty degrees and scanned the trees mounting the steadily rising ground.

Something caught his eye. Activating the zoom on his visor, he closed in on the anomaly in the low canopy. A line of gray concrete broke the repetitive green. "I think I see it." He fixed the position on his HUD and climbed down.

"This way," he said, pushing through ferns and bracken.

The team of five formed a straggling line, Aubriot at its head.

"Slow down," Kes warned. "We don't know if anyone else is around."

But Aubriot had seen no signs of people. They hadn't come across any tracks in the wood, not even animal trails, and he hadn't seen any rooftops or other signs of habitation in his inspection of the landscape.

After a couple of minutes, Maddox cried out, "I found something."

She was some distance back down the slope. He hadn't realized he'd been going so fast. When he reached her she was pointing upward and the others were clustered around her, also looking up. A rusted metal mesh about a meter square hung from a tree trunk, partially embedded into the fork of a branch.

"I wonder what it is," said Cherry.

"It's definitely something from before the fall of civilization," said Kes. "It was made in a factory."

"How did it get up there?" Maddox asked. "Who put it there, and why?"

"I don't think anyone put it there," Kes replied. "My guess is the tree grew through it, and as the tree grew taller, it lifted the metal up. Whatever it is, it used to be on the ground."

"Hmpf," said Aubriot. "We're not far from the concrete I saw. Let's go. We're interested in the vault, not bits of old metal."

When they reached their destination, the explanation of the metal in the tree became clear. Two or three similar panels lay on the forest floor. It was hard to tell exactly how many because they were deeply corroded, bent, and broken, their edges jutting up from the groundcover. They were the remains of a steel walkway.

A rectangular concrete facade rose from the forest, divided into three sections. Uppermost was a glass panel, shattered. Below it was a mesh like the walkway remains, rusted and full of holes. Flies buzzed lazily through it. At ground level, double doors faced the explorers, one standing open, hanging from its hinges.

Kes said nothing but his shoulders sagged.

"Is there any point in going in?" Aubriot asked. The place was a joke. So much for preserving a cache of seeds to benefit all humankind.

"We should take a look around anyway," said Kes heavily. "We might find something worth collecting in the deepest regions. Seeds can remain viable for remarkable lengths of time. Even thousands of years. And they would have been stored well here. Some might have survived the warm temperatures."

They stepped into the dark interior. Their helmet lights activated, revealing a shadowy corridor sloping downward.

In the first rooms mold grew on the walls and their feet crunched on rat droppings wherever they walked. Cockroaches had taken up residence too, quickly scurrying into the darkness whenever a beam of light hit them. Broken shelves and empty foil seed packets, ripped open, were all that remained of the vault's carefully stored contents.

The place had been ransacked.

"People must have come here during the pandemic," said Kes. "Food supply chains would have broken down."

"Were they looking for food or seeds to grow their own crops?" Cherry asked.

"Who knows? Growing the seeds would make the most sense, but if they were starving..."

The packets had been labeled with Latin names. Only Kes and Maddox could read them. They lamented as they recognized plants that would have grown on Concordia but the packets were empty.

"We need to go deeper in," said Aubriot. "We might have more luck there."

They passed more ransacked rooms. The temperature reading on his HUD dropped as they walked deeper underground. Narrower corridors branched out from the main. Kes selected one based on the sign at its entrance. He went ahead, but after only a few steps he yelled and backed up, crashing into Cherry who was directly behind him.

Bones lay on the ground. A skull grinned up at them. A collapsed rib cage, a pelvis... Aubriot turned away. "Let's try somewhere else."

"No," said Kes. "Grain crops for temperate regions were stored in this section." He delicately stepped over the bones and continued down the corridor.

In this colder region of the vault, no moss grew though humidity was high. How deep were they?

Kes tried a door but it was locked.

"That's a good sign," said Cherry. "Maybe no one broke in."

Aubriot said, "Or maybe someone's in there and has locked the door."

Kes slammed his shoulder into it.

"Shouldn't you be a bit more cautious?" Aubriot asked.

"Shut up and give me a hand."

"All right. Keep your hair on. Stand back."

When Kes was out of the way, he kicked the door next to its lock. The mechanism tore away from the frame and the door flew open. He darted to the side, but nothing and no one emerged.

Kes leaned in, his helmet light illuminating the place. "Jackpot."

Kᴇs's ʙᴀɢ of seed packets felt satisfyingly heavy as he returned to the shuttle, though a long road ahead remained. He had no idea if the seeds would sprout, or if they would grow in Concordian soil depleted of micro-organisms, but the packets were sealed in their triple layers of foil and the temperature in their storage room had been almost freezing. It was as much as he could have reasonably hoped for, if not more.

The light was failing. It was autumn here and in this part of the world the days were only a few hours long. Zapata had turned on the shuttle lights to help them find it—perhaps unwisely. They still had no idea who lived here or how they might react to strangers.

Still, Kes was grateful. They pushed through the undergrowth, following roughly the same path they'd taken to reach the vault.

Inside the shuttle, every face was smiling when they removed their helmets. There was a sense of elation in the air. Finally, after all their trials and tribulations, things seemed to be going their way.

Zapata appeared. "Vessey doesn't want you to investigate where the signal's coming from."

"Huh?" said Wilder. "Why not?"

"Something about it being too dangerous. She said it could be a Scythian trap."

"I suppose it's a possibility," said Kes. "They might have arrived before us and set something up."

"Like a booby trap?" asked Cherry.

"Exactly. Designed to draw us in if we return home."

"It does sound like something they would do," she said.

"They can't breathe Earth's atmosphere any more than they can breathe Concordia's. They can't live here, but they want their revenge for us taking over their planet."

Aubriot interjected, "We don't have to do what Vessey says."

"But we should," said Kes. "She *is* the captain."

The disdainful curl of Aubriot's lip showed what he thought about that.

"We have plenty to keep us occupied at the vault," said Kes. "It'll take us all day tomorrow and probably the day after to explore it thoroughly. Then we need to collect samples of soil, water, and plants from other regions. We have lots of exploring to do yet. The signal can wait."

41

Cherry watched as the plains of North America receded into the distance. The seas of deep-rooted, tall grasses were nothing like she'd ever seen on Concordia. Kes had said the area hadn't been like that when he left Earth. Vast tracts of farmland had covered the place. But the land had reverted to an earlier state, as it had been before Europeans had colonized it. Large-headed, heavy animals roamed it, living off the grass. They wouldn't be taking any of *those* home, thank the stars. She couldn't imagine what their hooves would do to the soft, rubbery groundcover that covered most of Concordia's mainland.

Kes had talked about bringing back smaller animals and insects, like bees. These were striped, winged creatures with stings, though they were rarely dangerous. He said if Concordia had bees, they could grow a wider range of crops. Bees were needed to fertilize the flowers. He said they also produced a delicious, sweet substance called honey. He'd been vague about *how* they produced it, which wasn't like him. She guessed there might be something unsavory about the process and he didn't want to put her off.

They would need to find the right bees, however. Only a particular kind would do.

Harvesting the seeding material was going well. And horti-culturalists on the *Sirocco* had already germinated some seeds from the vault in a section of the Ark they were using for exper-iments. It was a wonderful reward after the trials of their journey.

For now, they only had to concentrate on finding the wild plants and samples Kes wanted. She had a box full of the prairie soil. There were some worms and other creatures as well as the invisible micro-organisms supposedly essential to establishing diversity of life on Concordia.

Next stop was somewhere on the west coast with a warmer, wetter climate.

There were Earth people about. Of that, they were certain. In their travels they'd seen evidence of agriculture and some small villages. Vessey hadn't wanted them to make contact just yet, mindful of the disease risk and the potential for conflict. Cherry understood, but she was curious to meet some true Earthers. Kes and Aubriot didn't count. They were from another time.

Kes had said they wouldn't be able to understand the locals anyway. These humans spoke many different languages, not the single one everyone spoke on Concordia, and their speech would have evolved into something neither he nor Aubriot would even recognize. Yet they were still people. Surely they would find a way to communicate?

"Penny for them?" said Kes, sitting down beside her.

"What?"

"Sorry. I was asking what you're thinking about."

"Oh, the usual. Everything and nothing. How about you? Are you happy Miki and Nina will be coming down to the surface on the next trip?"

He grimaced. "*They're* definitely happy about it. Me, not so much. I'm not convinced it's safe."

"We haven't had any problems so far."

"That doesn't mean we won't have any. I'd rather they didn't come down at all, but if I insist I'll never hear the end of it. They're the only ones who haven't been here yet."

"It's their heritage, the place their father is from. You can't blame them."

"I don't. I do understand. That doesn't mean I have to like it. How about you? How do you feel about Earth now you've had a look around?"

"Hm, I think I like it. It's beautiful."

"It looks much better than it did when I left. Humans nearly annihilating themselves has done wonders for the place."

"It still isn't home, though. Concordia is where I belong."

"That's understandable. You fought so hard for it. And," he added, tapping the lid of the box on her lap, "you're still fighting."

"I guess I am, but this beats going up against the Scythians."

They chatted for the remainder of the journey until Zapata announced, "Touch down in five," over the intercom. "Found a nice little spot for you guys near the foot of a mountain."

"Excellent," Kes said. "Sounds ideal for our last expedition of the day."

After landing, as Cherry donned her EVA suit for the nth time, she noticed it was beginning to smell. Could she clean it? She peered into the open front before she secured the seal. Was it even possible? She put on her helmet and descended the ramp with the team. Aubriot and Wilder were on the *Sirocco* working on ideas for Earth's defense. Maddox was here again. So far, she'd had the decency to stay quiet.

Steep mountain slopes rose to their left, the peak out of sight. In front lay a wooded valley, deep green and thickly forested.

"It rains so much on the west coast," Kes explained as they descended, "this qualifies as rainforest, though the tree species are different from what used to grow here. I would expect to see some of these in a subtropical climate. The plants in this place would do very well in southern Lyonesse. I want to take plenty of samples." He slowed his pace. "You go ahead."

He was waiting for Maddox to catch up so he could speak to her. He was always careful to keep the two of them apart when he could. Cherry continued down the slope, glancing back every so often. Kes and Maddox were deep in conversation. The final time she looked back, Maddox was walking down alone.

Cherry stopped. When Maddox reached her, she asked, "Where's Kes?"

"He spotted something he wanted to collect. He said he'd meet us at the bottom."

Doubtfully, Cherry scanned the vegetation up the slope. She couldn't see Kes at all. Maddox continued on, and after a few moments, Cherry followed her.

When they reached a creek running through the base of the valley, they began to collect their samples. As Cherry only knew about the plants she grew on her farm, her task was to collect a range of soil samples. She scooped dirt from the creek bank and placed it in a box before filling in the label. Then she straightened up and took another look up slope.

Kes still hadn't arrived.

Where was he?

In case she'd missed him she asked Maddox, "Have you seen Kes?"

"No," she replied irritably. "I told you, he's collecting something up there." She waved vaguely in the direction they'd come from.

Dissatisfied—if Kes was only collecting a plant he should be here by now—Cherry climbed the slope again. She tutted to herself. Why not comm him? She tried. Nothing. She tried again. The hush of the forest was her only reply.

She ran down to the others. "Kes is missing!"

They took some convincing, Maddox assuring her he was about somewhere and probably distracted, but after Cherry comm'd him several times over without receiving a response, they were finally persuaded.

As they searched for him. Cherry alerted Zapata.

"Stay as long as you like," he replied, "though don't forget to pop back to replenish you suits' oxygen. I'll wait, and I'll comm Vessey to let her know what's happening."

They searched and searched, far and wide through the valley and up the mountainside, but they found no trace of Kes. He'd vanished into thin air.

42

"I don't want to be the one to tell Miki and Nina their father's gone missing," said Wilder.

Cherry was comming her from the shuttle after the long search for Kes.

"You have to tell them something," said Cherry. "They must have guessed there's a problem. We should have been back hours ago."

Wilder sighed. "Okay, I'll do it. I guess it'll be better hearing it from me than a captain's announcement. What's happening? Are you leaving now?"

"I don't want to but I don't have a choice," Cherry replied. "Vessey wants us to return to the *Sirocco*. She's worried that if someone took Kes they might attack the rest of us now it's dark."

"She has a point."

"I know, but..." The comm went silent as Cherry paused. When she spoke again, her voice was charged with emotion. "I can't help feeling I'm giving up on him."

"Don't feel bad. He wouldn't want you to put yourself in

danger for his sake. You know that. Besides, you can carry on the search tomorrow."

"But that means he'll be here all night. What if he's fallen and he's lying somewhere, injured and unable to call for help? And I'm not so sure Vessey will agree to us coming back. You know how ultra cautious she is."

"Kes is vital to the mission. No one else has his depth of knowledge. She won't abandon him so easily."

"You say that, but he was telling me the other day we have almost everything we need. And all the information is available to the other scientists. They could finish the job without his help now, I think."

"Cherry, worrying about what might happen isn't going to help find Kes. Come back to the ship, and together we'll persuade Vessey to continue the search when it's daylight there. Aubriot will help too."

"Will he? I'm not so sure. He and Kes never really got along."

"Aubriot doesn't get along with anyone. Consulting with him on planetary defenses has been damned hard work, let me tell you. It always amazed me how you put up with him. But even he knows how important Kes is, and he can be forceful when he chooses. If all else fails, he'll bully Vessey into agreeing."

With a note of sadness, Cherry said, "I guess I'll see you soon."

Wilder set off to bring the bad news to Kes's daughters.

But before she reached their cabin, Vessey comm'd her. "I need you on the bridge, immediately."

Grateful for the opportunity to put off her dreaded task a little longer, she changed direction. When she arrived on the bridge, Aubriot and Niall were there too.

"You'll never believe this," said Niall.

"Believe what?" she asked wearily. The three of them looked far too cheerful considering Kes was missing.

"Play her the recording."

Vessey hit a button.

"*To the starship currently in orbit around Earth, greetings from the Global Advancement Association. We apologize for our silence. We assumed you were an enemy ship. We have been delighted to discover you are human, like us. We would like to suggest a meeting at a neutral site so we may discover more about each other. As a gesture of our goodwill, we will return your crew member, who was mistakenly taken captive in a region of...*" the voice stated a name Wilder didn't recognize "*...today.*"

"Holy shit," said Wilder. "When did we receive that?"

"A few minutes ago," replied Vessey. "I wanted to discuss our response before we send a formal reply."

"We're meeting with them, right?"

"Of course," said Niall. "We have to."

"I don't want to act hastily," said the captain. "The message was in English, but according to what I've heard, that should be impossible. I don't know who it was, but someone told me that language on Earth would have evolved beyond our recognition. Why is it we can understand the speaker?"

"Because," Wilder said, "because... I don't know." She desperately wanted the message to be genuine but Vessey was making sense.

"I don't know either," said Aubriot. "Doesn't mean anything fishy's going on."

"No," said the captain, "but we can't forget the fact we know the Scythians have their sights on Earth. It isn't a safe place for us."

"How could the Scythians have learned English?" asked Niall.

"They could have been scanning transmissions on Concordia for years," Vessey replied.

Wilder's initial elation was slowly fading but she refused to give up hope. "We have to meet this group. If there's the slightest chance we can get Kes back, we have to take it."

Vessey's brow furrowed. "You're right. I'll draft a reply and we'll meet them. But I want to urge the utmost caution."

43

They'd grabbed him so quickly, he hadn't had the presence of mind to comm for help. He'd been bending down, easing a small plant specimen out of the soil, when hands had seized him and thrown him on his back. All of a sudden, four faces stared down, long hair hanging. Fingers pawed at his EVA suit. Understanding what they intended, he struggled. He couldn't let them take his suit. He understood it must make him look strange and frightening, but—

Too late.

They'd figured it out. Deftly, they unfastened the suit and snapped his helmet seals open.

No, no, no!

They tore off his helmet and tossed it into the undergrowth.

As they saw his face their eyes widened. He tried to sit up, but they forced him down. A gag fastened over his mouth, and a bag descended over his head. His wrists and ankles were tied, and then someone pushed a shoulder into his stomach and lifted him up.

He was being carried away from his friends and safety. In less than a minute, modern-day humans had kidnapped him.

HE TRIED to figure out which way he was being taken but it was impossible. He'd been disoriented during the attack. All he could tell was he was being carried upward. The person carrying him grunted with effort and staggered. He didn't struggle, fearing he might fall a long way if dropped.

Then his captors seemed to be walking along level ground. He counted in his head. *One, one thousand. Two, one thousand. Three, one thousand...*

He was passed to someone else like a sack of rice. The march continued.

Thirty-eight one thousand. Thirty-nine one thousand...

They grew tired of carrying him. He was placed on his feet, his ankle bindings cut, and he was pulled forward, someone tugging him by his wrist ties. He continued counting, though he lost his place several times. He estimated approximately forty-five minutes later, the ground turned significantly downward and the air grew cooler and still.

Voices burst out, loud with surprise and excitement. The man holding his wrist ties said something, and then he was unceremoniously pushed to the ground. His landing wasn't as hard as he'd been expecting. He was lying on a soft surface that rustled beneath him as he tried to sit up.

Hands pushed his chest, forcing him down again.

Someone pulled the bag off his head.

Similar faces to the ones he'd seen before gazed down, their long hair obscured their features except for their dark, curious eyes.

"Please," he said, "can I sit up? Please untie me." Or rather, that was what he tried to say. His gag reduced his words to muffled nonsense. He lifted his bound wrists.

These people might not speak his language but communication should be possible. It would be easier with his hands free.

Nervous laughter was the only response.

He had a sense that, now they had him, they didn't know what to do with him. It wasn't every day a spaceman appeared in the neighborhood. A woman began investigating his EVA suit, pulling at the gap where it hung open. He had no idea what had happened to his helmet. She commented to a man and pushed the open suit over his shoulders. The man untied his wrists and ankles, but only to allow the others to remove the suit. As soon as he was wearing only his normal clothes, they tied him up again.

Their activity had allowed him to get a better view of his surroundings, glimpsed in gaps between his audience of fifteen or so adults and children. He was in a cave, but these people were not cavemen. Humanity hadn't sunk so low. Electric lights hung from wires across the ceiling, and the place was furnished with plain wooden furniture. In a corner a mother nursed twins, an infant at each breast. That was as much as he saw before he was pushed down again.

A hand reached out to touch his hair. The woman who had instigated removing his suit leaned close and peered into his eyes. He guessed his coloring was unusual in these parts. In different clothes—they wore simple, homespun stuff that looked colored with vegetable dyes—these people could have been Concordians. They were uniformly black-haired and olive-skinned.

He plucked at his gag. "Please, let me talk." He lifted his wrists. "Untie my hands."

Chatter followed as the group apparently discussed his

request. They came to an agreement. One of the men unfastened the gag.

"Thank you," Kes breathed. "Thank you." He lifted his wrists again. "Now my hands. Please."

The woman shook her head.

Kes held out a brief hope that the gesture didn't mean *No* in this part of the world but he was wrong. His wrists were not untied.

No matter. He could still do a lot to make a connection with these people. He had to make them understand he wasn't a threat. Feeling like a character from a man-meets-savage vid, he said, "I'm Kes." He touched his chest. "Kes."

Several onlookers murmured, "Kes."

"Yes." He nodded. "Kes." He motioned, two-handed, at the nearest people. "You? What are you called?"

In his peripheral vision, a kid, no more than four or five years old, lifted a familiar object.

"No!" He launched himself on the child.

Lacking the use of his hands and legs, all he could do was force the girl to the floor. She lay under his chest, wriggling and yelling. If she accidentally pressed the trigger on his sidearm, they were both dead. "My gun," he tried to explain. "It's—"

Pain exploded in his head as someone kicked him. Another kick landed on the side of his stomach. Hands roughly hauled him off the girl, who was now screaming. The woman who had removed his EVA suit slapped him with a vehemence that told him she was probably the girl's mother.

"You don't understand," he protested, nearly weeping. "She could kill herself or one of you." It wasn't only concern for the child that terrified him. If anyone in the group died he was sure his own death would soon follow.

The woman seemed to understand his agitation was centered around the weapon. She took it from her daughter's hands, causing louder screaming and some stamping of feet.

As she turned the gun over in her hands to examine it, Kes said, "Please, please be careful."

The woman repeated slowly, "Careful." She lifted up the weapon. "Careful?"

"No. It's a gun. Gun. It can hurt you." He performed a very bad mime of firing a weapon, being hit, gurgling, and falling down dead.

Her eyebrows lifting, she stared at the gun once more. She looked down the barrel.

"No!" Kes cried out, waving his tied wrists. "No. Please, put it down." He mimed placing something on the floor.

A man took the gun from the woman and put it down.

"Yes, that's it." Kes sagged with relief and closed his eyes.

A hand shook his shoulder. It was the woman. Her eyes questioning, she pointed at the gun and then drew a finger across her throat.

"Yes! It can kill you." He gargled and toppled over onto his side. "Dead. You see?"

The little girl was on her hands and knees making a not-so-subtle attempt to nab the gun. She sneezed.

"No," Kes said, sitting up. He spoke sternly using his best fatherly voice and waggled a finger at her. "It's dangerous. Leave it alone."

Chagrined, the child crept backward and tried to act innocent.

Her mother admonished her and picked up the gun.

Instinctively, Kes ducked, but this time she was holding the gun more carefully. As he straightened up, she said something to the group. They had a short discussion and seemed to come to an agreement. One of them untied his wrists.

He thanked them gratefully and rubbed his head where he'd been kicked. The woman took his hand, inviting him to stand.

Chatter was going on all around him. These simple folk

were unsurprisingly amazed by the man in weird clothing carrying around deadly devices. They didn't seem to intend him any harm, and they'd probably been frightened by the arrival of the shuttle and team of collectors. He hoped they understood he didn't intend them any harm either.

He held out an open hand, gesturing for his gun.

The woman looked at it and then raised her gaze to him warily.

"I won't hurt you. I promise."

After a moment's hesitation, she handed the weapon over.

He scanned the room, found a bare expanse of rock, aimed, and fired.

The shock that passed through the group told him they'd never seen a pulse weapon before.

Turning the gun around, he returned it to the woman grip first.

At the burst of fire, her daughter had leapt to her side and continued to cling on, arms wrapped around her mother's hips. The woman caressed her child's hair and turned and spoke to someone Kes hadn't noticed before, sitting in a corner.

The man was crouched over a low table on which sat something resembling a simple ham radio.

44

The figures approached on horseback, wading through plains grass so tall it obscured the horses' legs. To Wilder, it was like watching a fairy tale come to life. Horses figured in old stories of Earth but she'd never seen any real ones.

She peered at each rider in turn but she couldn't spot Kes.

Vessey, who remained aboard the *Sirocco*, had mandated they were not to stray more than thirty seconds' running distance of the shuttle. Zapata hadn't left the controls and was ready to take off at a moment's notice.

"Stop!" yelled Aubriot through his helmet comm. "Don't come any closer. Where's our companion?"

"He's on his way," a member of the Global Advancement Association replied. "He should be here soon. We didn't want to meet you where he was found. We preferred an open space, where we can all see each other."

Wilder recognized the voice from the message.

"How come you speak our language?" she called out.

The speaker replied, "If you let me come over there we can talk face-to-face like civilized human beings."

"All right," said Aubriot. "Just you." To Wilder and Cherry he said, "Draw your weapons."

The man climbed off his horse and began to walk closer but then he halted. "Please, put away your...guns." He appeared to struggle to remember the final word of his sentence.

"It's only a precaution," Aubriot replied. "We won't cause any problems if you don't."

"I'm unarmed," said the man. He lifted the flaps of his open coat and turned in a circle. "I know what your guns can do. You could kill me and my colleagues easily. Our intentions are entirely peaceful."

"I think he's telling the truth," Wilder told Aubriot quietly. "Look at them. They don't even have vehicles. Our technology is way superior to theirs."

"Appearances can be deceptive, but..." He said to the stranger, "We'll put our weapons away."

"I wish I knew where Kes is," Cherry remarked as she stowed her gun, "and what the hell's going on."

"You and me both," said Wilder.

The man approaching them was bearded and wore a wide-brimmed hat. When he drew close enough to converse at a normal volume, he said, "It would be good to see your faces."

"Not happening," Aubriot replied flatly. "Before we begin any negotiations, we want to see our man alive and well."

"I wasn't aware we had anything to negotiate, but please accept my assurances your companion is unharmed and will be here within a few minutes."

"Why is it you can speak English?" Wilder persisted.

"I'm a lifelong student of ancient languages, fortunately for my group. Many times I've been, er, teased about my studies. But everyone forgot their teasing when I could understand what the man from space was saying."

"You've spoken to Kes?" Cherry asked excitedly.

"I have. I'm not sure why you are so suspicious and doubtful. We are all human, it seems. We have no reason to be enemies, though we're very puzzled about where you're from."

"Maybe if you hadn't kidnapped one of our party," said Aubriot, "we might like you more."

"Ah, yes. That was an unfortunate mistake. The people who took your friend captive were scared of him, of all of you. You have to admit, you dress strangely, and your transportation is remarkable."

"But you know about starships," said Wilder, "or you wouldn't have sent your message."

"We do, through historical research and...well, that's another subject we should talk about in more depth when we know each other better."

Aubriot said, a threatening edge to his tone, "No one's getting to know anyone better until we see Kes."

"What's that?" Cherry asked.

Then Wilder heard it too. A high-pitched whine had started up.

"I believe that's your friend arriving."

The sound was coming from a region of the sky. A dot appeared. All present watched as it grew larger. Soon, Wilder could make out rotor blades.

"You have helis?!" she exclaimed.

"That isn't what we call them, but yes. We've had them for a few years but they're very expensive and difficult to manufacture. You're lucky our branch of the GAA had one on site."

The small craft approached. Like the Concordian helis, it was small, a two-seater. Both seats were filled. The heli touched down, sending undulating waves through the grass. he passenger door swung open.

"Kes!" Cherry yelled, running to him.

"Don't come near me," he shouted. "Get me an EVA suit! Throw me a suit."

45

The *Sirocco's* sick bay quarantine rooms were small but comfortable. They included a bed, interface, comms, restroom, and a small exchange and sterilization chamber set into the wall where the patient could receive meals and return the used receptacles. Medics and doctors passed through an air-sealed anteroom to take vitals and provide medical care as required.

Kes had been the one to insist on the installation of quarantine chambers, mindful of the pandemic that had put the final nail in the coffin of Earth civilization. Wilder hadn't thought they would be necessary for the ship's first mission. They would only be spending a short time on the planet, collecting what was needed to replenish life on Concordia. Who would be dumb enough to expose themselves to human viruses against which they had no natural protection?

Kes was in his room four days before he fell ill.

There was no telling if it was the disease that had wiped out most of Earth's population, a mutation, or another virus entirely. Something new could have crossed from animals to humans in the centuries since the departure of the Guardians' ship, the *Mistral*.

All anyone knew was on day four of Kes's quarantine, his temperature suddenly spiked, he lost his appetite, and he began to cough and sneeze.

"It might only be a cold," he reassured Wilder over comm as he lay in bed.

"What do you mean?" she asked, leaning her forehead on the transparent barrier separating them. "You aren't cold, you're hot."

"It's the name of a very common virus. It was everywhere when I lived on Earth. People caught colds two or three times a year, sometimes more in a bad season. For the Project, we kept it and all other viruses off the *Nova Fortuna*. The generational colonist candidates spent a month in isolation and were thoroughly screened before they could board."

"But didn't you have a vaccination for the cold virus, like you developed for Scythian Plague?"

"We had many vaccinations but not for that. It's only a mild illness, and there are so many varieties, it didn't make sense."

"So you won't get very ill?"

"If that's all I've got."

Miki and Nina came to visit him every day, often chatting for hours at a time. Wilder sometimes suggested they should leave and let their father rest, but he always argued against it, saying he wanted them to stay. They asked him what Earth was like and all about the people he met. He wouldn't allow them to go to the surface without him, so they remained frustrated in that regard. But they were good girls. They had to know he was frightened for their safety because they didn't push it.

They told him what they'd been doing when they weren't with him, which was helping out with cataloging and storing all the seeds and samples the teams had collected. Nina seemed to have a real flair for biology like her father. Miki didn't care for the subject much, preferring to focus on the mechanics of the storage systems. The growing rooms in the Ark had been re-converted to fulfill their original purpose. The Global Advancement Association had assured them they could supply all their dietary needs for the return journey to Concordia.

Cherry popped in frequently, when she could spare time from meetings with the GAA. She would give updates, new information, and progress, but in truth Wilder couldn't take much of it in. She was too focused on her friend.

On the fifth day, Kes's face and hands were flushed and Dr Clarkson looked worried as he peered into the room. Enclosed head to toe in protective gear and breathing external air through a long tube, he drew a privacy curtain around his patient's bed for a physical examination.

When, after a long time, he emerged and Wilder asked him how Kes was doing, he only replied, "Worse than yesterday, I'm afraid."

His voice slurring slightly, Kes asked for Miki and Nina. They came, and he told them he wanted to talk about their mother. He asked them if there was anything they wanted to know about her.

Wilder stepped away, overcome. Her eyes filling with tears, she quickly left sick bay. When she'd regained control somewhat, she returned.

Kes's daughters were listening intently as he talked about how he and Isobel had met. He described what his future wife had been wearing and the first words she'd said to him, which had been, *I know who you are, Earthman.* The girls giggled, and Wilder had to leave again. They didn't understand. They didn't know why their father was telling them the stories.

When they'd gone, Wilder returned and asked softly, "Isn't there anything to be done?"

"Hundreds of years ago, maybe. Before the Natural Movement destroyed health care, we had anti-virals, all kinds of things. But there was no need for them on Concordia and civilization here is too undeveloped. Clarkson is going to speak to the GAA but I don't hold out much hope. It's bad, Wilder. I can feel it."

"I can't believe there's nothing that can help you."

"Don't feel sorry for me. I've had an amazing life and I've known great love. There aren't many who can say that."

The sixth day, Kes spent mostly unconscious. His neck was swollen and his face was almost as red as his hair. When Clarkson came to check on him, he reported the GAA had no record of diseases with Kes's symptoms, and their standard of medical care seemed inferior to the *Sirocco's*. He spent only a short time with his patient before leaving without meeting Wilder's eye.

In a brief moment of lucidity, Kes whispered, "Hey."

She swallowed and smiled. "Hey."

"Whenever I wake up, you're always here."

"Of course I am."

"Don't you have anything better to do?"

"No, nothing."

After a pause, he said, "I'm glad. You know, I used to have a sister like you."

"I know. You've told me before."

"I have? I don't remember. I'm forgetting a lot lately."

"It's okay. I like it when you tell me."

His eyes closed and she thought he'd fallen asleep again, but then they popped open. He croaked, "I remembered something important. Tell Clarkson to take my blood. It'll contain antibodies...you understand?"

"I understand. I'll tell him."

Due to Kes's illness, they would be able to vaccinate everyone from Concordia against the virus.

On the seventh day, Dr Clarkson announced it was time for final goodbyes.

Wilder had tried to explain what was happening to Miki and Nina the previous evening, but they hadn't seemed to take in what she was saying. They arrived in sick bay looking shell-shocked. Cherry turned up at the same time. For some reason, Aubriot had come too, though little love was lost between the two men.

"Shit," Aubriot said as soon as he laid eyes on Kes. It was the first time he'd seen him since the meeting on the prairie. He folded his arms and leaned on the bulkhead, his head down.

Cherry put her open hand on the transparent barrier, her chest working, tears dripping from her cheeks.

"I want to see my Dad," Miki whispered to Wilder, her eyes pleading.

"He's right there, sweetheart. Say anything you want to him. He'll hear you." Wilder wasn't sure this was true but it would comfort the girl. Kes was lying on his side, facing them, his eyes only slits and his chest barely moving. He appeared to hover between life and death.

Miki said stubbornly, "I want to go in and *see* him. I want to-to-to hug him."

Nina was on her knees, staring at her father disbelievingly.

"You can't go in," Wilder replied gently. "It isn't safe."

"I want to see him!" Miki marched toward the anteroom.

"Miki, no!" Wilder grabbed her but she wrenched free.

She almost reached the anteroom before Aubriot caught her. She fought him like a wild thing, biting, scratching, kicking, screaming, "I want my Daddy! I want my Daddy!" over and over.

Nina held onto her knees and rocked, quietly keening.

"Give me a hand, can't you?" Aubriot asked angrily as he took another blow to the face from a flailing elbow. But Wilder didn't know how to help him.

Dr Clarkson ran in. When he saw what was happening, he locked the anteroom door.

"Miki," said Wilder, trying to catch one of her waving arms. "Miki, please try to calm down. Your father wouldn't want this. Please give him peace."

Her words made it through the girl's pain and panic. Miki's struggles eased. Aubriot released his hold on her and she collapsed. She crawled to the wall and said to Kes, "I love you, Daddy."

Just above the sounds of grief came his quiet reply, "I love you too, my darlings."

His eyes closed and he was gone.

46

K es's funeral took place three days later on the wide open plains of North America, attended by everyone who could be spared from the *Sirocco*. Wilder had cried so much she was hoarse and her eyes had puffed up. She didn't know how she would carry on without her friend.

As she stood at the graveside, Niall put an arm around her shoulders. He'd been trying to comfort her, but nothing he could do would ever fill that hole left by Kes's death. She could see in her mind's eye, clear as day, her friend's face looking up at her through leaf fronds the morning he'd come to her tree settlement. He'd brought her a bottle of sluglimpet repellent to spray on the tree trunks. Since then he'd been her greatest ally, supporter, and advocate. When she needed someone he'd always been there. What would she do now he was gone?

Vessey was giving a speech, listing all the contributions Kes had made to the Concordia Colony. All the captain needed to say was, without him, the colony would not have existed. Of all his achievements, his greatest had been saving everyone from certain destruction by the Scythian Plague.

"Do you think he ever imagined he would be buried on Earth?" Cherry asked quietly as Vessey droned on.

"I don't know. I don't think so. But I think he was happy to be home. And this is a nice place to be laid to rest." Wilder gazed over the grassland as it rippled in the wind.

"Was he from around here?"

"No, another country. I can't remember its name."

Kes had rarely spoken of his life on Earth. Wilder had the impression the subject was painful for him because it triggered memories of his sister and other loved ones he'd left behind.

"I'll miss him," murmured Cherry.

"Me too. Beyond words."

Miki and Nina were weeping but otherwise they were holding up well in the circumstances. It was the first time they'd been coaxed from their cabin since their father's passing. Hopefully, their youth would give them resilience and they would heal with time.

Save for the sound of the wind in the grass, all was silent.

Vessey's speech was over.

One of the ship's crew lifted a shovelful of soil and tossed it into the grave.

"Take as long as you want to pay your last respects," said the captain. "We'll return to the *Sirocco* when everyone is ready."

Miki took Nina's hand and led her away from the grave.

Wilder noticed a significant member of the ship's personnel was missing. "Where's Aubriot? He didn't come? I don't believe it. I know they didn't get along, but that's so disrespectful. Isn't he worried what people will think?"

"Aubriot doesn't care what anyone thinks," Cherry replied. "He was there when Kes died. He probably thinks that was enough."

"He *did* help with Miki."

"Yeah. That's the thing with him. He isn't kind, hell, he isn't even likable, but when he's needed, he's there."

"I suppose we have to give him that."

They walked through the grass. To try to distract herself from her sadness, Wilder asked, "What's been happening in the meetings with the GAA? I must have a lot to catch up on."

"You do. Where to start? The good news is that civilization is more developed here than we thought."

"I guessed it was when I saw they had helis."

"They have more than helis. Communication networks, electricity generation, schools, industries. The people who captured Kes were country folk, poor and uneducated, scraping for survival in the mountains. They weren't representative of typical Earthers."

Something didn't sound right. "Are you sure the GAA aren't trying to impress us? We've hardly seen any evidence of development. The only transmission we picked up was that repeating signal, remember? And who are the GAA anyway?"

"They're the central group coordinating worldwide technological development. They collect and study old data, books, anything they can find, and share it. And we didn't pick up any communications because their networks are underground. Old networks they've discovered and are repairing. They don't broadcast through the air if they can help it. We told them about the signal but they didn't know what it was. They weren't aware of it, and when we mentioned it they were concerned. They're going to find out where it's coming from and close it down."

"Why don't they want to use air transmission?"

Cherry took a breath before replying, "You remember the message they sent to the *Sirocco*? They said they thought we were an enemy ship."

It took her a moment to work it out. "Oh, no. This is the bad news."

"Yes. Sadly, yes."

"The Scythians got here before us."

"From the Earthers' description of their ships, it has to be them. They arrived a little over two years ago. Their ships are even faster than the Guardians' *Mistral*."

"But they left again? There's no sign of them."

"After destroying some burgeoning cities. According to all reports, their ships never landed. No actual Scythians were ever seen."

"Well, they can't breathe the air, so..." Wilder frowned. "I get it. The Earthers have gone to ground, like we did on Concordia."

"They have. We told them about the Scythian spiders and how they traced us by scent. That terrified them."

"They should be terrified. Dammit. We were beaten in the race to reach Earth despite Niall's fix for the jump drive."

"On the plus side," said Cherry, "we're here now. We made it. Things could have been a lot worse. We still have time to help the Earthers defend their planet. You were working with Aubriot on ideas about that. Did you get very far?"

"No, not far at all. And now what you've told me has made all our discussions irrelevant. I'll need to consult with the GAA and find out what tech they already have before we can figure things out."

"You should get started right away. We know from past experience the Scythians will be back. They won't be happy until they've destroyed Earth like they tried to destroy Concordia."

Right away?

Kes was only just buried. She needed time to mourn. And she wasn't even sure this was their fight. "Shouldn't we go home first? We've spent the last couple of weeks collecting everything we need to reseed our planet. Helping the Earthers prepare their defenses will take months, maybe years. What about *our* world?"

"I have to admit, the same thought occurred to me. But then

I thought what Kes would want, and..." Cherry's features twisted and her eyes filled with tears.

"Don't," said Wilder, finding herself suddenly weeping too. "I know. I know what you're saying. I'll think about it. It's too soon to make any decisions." The pain was too fresh.

A voice was calling faintly on the breeze. Wilder blinked as she noticed how far they'd walked from the shuttle.

Vessey was a small figure, waving. It had been her calling.

The captain's voice burst from Wilder's ear comm. "Back to the shuttle now! Everyone, back to the shuttle immediately."

"Huh?" Cherry's hand was on her ear. "What's the...oh, shit." She stared at a spot behind Wilder's left ear.

Wilder turned, and froze.

In the deep blue of the distant sky, a crescent-shaped space-craft was descending.

NEXT BOOK

The story of the Concordia Colony continues in:

REDEEMER

Sign up to my reader group for a free ecopy of *Night of Flames,* the prequel to Space Colony One, and for more free books, discounts on new releases, Review Crew invitations and other interesting stuff:

https://jjgreenauthor.com/free-books/

Printed in Great Britain
by Amazon

81122145R00151